Esther Campion is from Cork, Ireland and currently lives in north-west Tasmania. She attended North Presentation Convent in Cork and has degrees from University College Cork and the University of Aberdeen, Scotland. Esther and her Orcadian husband have lived in Ireland, Scotland, Norway and South Australia. They have a grown-up daughter in Adelaide and the two youngest at home in Tasmania with an over-indulged chocolate Labrador and two horses, which Esther firmly believes are living proof that dreams really can come true.

Esther Campion

Leaving Ocean Road

hachette
AUSTRALIA

hachette
AUSTRALIA

Published in Australia and New Zealand in 2017
by Hachette Australia
(an imprint of Hachette Australia Pty Limited)
Level 17, 207 Kent Street, Sydney NSW 2000
www.hachette.com.au

10 9 8 7 6 5 4 3 2 1

National Library of Australia
Cataloguing-in-Publication data

Campion, Esther, author.
Leaving Ocean Road/Esther Campion.

978 0 7336 3615 8 (paperback)

Irish – Australia – Fiction.
Family secrets – Fiction.
Widows – Fiction.
First loves – Fiction.

Cover design by Christabella Designs
Author photo courtesy of Michelle DuPont
Cover photographs courtesy of Trevillion and Shutterstock
Text design by Bookhouse, Sydney
Typeset in 12.1/18.6pt Sabon LT Pro
Printed and bound in Great Britain by Clays Ltd, St Ives plc

MIX
Paper from
responsible sources
FSC
www.fsc.org   FSC® C104740

To Ger Morgan,
for telling me, in no uncertain terms,
that I should write

Prologue

It was the kind of day that shouldn't be wasted. A glorious day full of sunshine and possibility. Far too good to be spent lying in bed.

Ellen ran through her mental checklist as she and Nick packed the boot of the Chrysler. Meat for the barbie, check. Enough potato salad to feed a small army, check. Drinks, check.

'Nick, would you go in there and get Louise moving?'

The laundry load would be finished. If she got that hung out, it would be dry by the time they got home. It was something she'd always loved about living in South Australia. Bone-dry straight-off-the-line washing.

Nick joined her at the Hill's Hoist, Paddy in tow as ever. He took a pair of her smart work pants from the basket.

'She'll be out in a minute.'

Ellen rolled her eyes.

'I spend the last two hours trying to get her out of bed and you ask her once . . .'

He gave her that cheeky smile that always annoyed her when she was stressed. It was only the annual Christmas lunch at the foreshore with her work colleagues, but she liked to be on time. She eyed him in despair as he pegged up the trousers by the legs.

'Holy God, how long do we have to live together for you to learn how to put up washing?'

He stood back with his hands on his hips and laughed as she unpegged the trousers and hung them up by the waistband.

'Oh no! I've married a girl with . . . how you say . . . ODC?'

'OCD,' she corrected, already on to the next item. God, he drove her mad, but she loved him.

'If it wasn't for my OCD, which I don't even have, this family would never get anywhere.'

He'd given up on the washing and stood watching her.

'What are you looking at?'

He smiled that smile again, his gorgeous brown eyes fixed on her.

'The beautiful Irish girl I fell in love with.'

She stopped and let out a deep sigh.

'Am I still that girl to you, Nick?'

He moved closer and slipped his hands around her waist.

'You will always be that girl to me.'

She let the pegs drop to the parched grass as he bent to kiss her. They might be twenty years older, but that kiss was as tender as their first.

'Get a room, you two.'

Louise skipped down the steps of the veranda, radiant as a sunbeam in her floppy hat and sunnies, transformed from the grumpy teenager Ellen had been trying to rouse for most of the morning. She finished the laundry as Nick went to help Louise find a space in the boot for her beach bag among the eskies and camping chairs.

'Can I drive?' Louise asked, already sticking one of her P plates to the windscreen.

Ellen looked at Nick. Their daughter would drive her round the twist not to mind drive the car. As ever, he knew what she was thinking but held out his palms and shrugged his big shoulders.

'We're late already,' Ellen started, 'if you'd been up when—' But Nick was holding out the keys to Louise who had climbed into the driver's seat.

She bent down and took Paddy's face in her hands.

'Mind the house, Pads,' she told the dog. 'And enjoy the peace without this lot.'

A gentle breeze was blowing through the gum trees as they hurtled down the gravel driveway.

'Not too much speed, Lou,' Nick cautioned.

'Okay, Dad.'

If Ellen had said that, her daughter would have gone off. In her head, she replayed the familiar script. *I'm eighteen. I have my Ps. Will you stop telling me what to do?* She looked out over the coastline with its changing palette of blues, greens and yellows, so familiar to her now.

'I could just drop you both off,' Louise suggested as they neared the town.

'It's a family event.' Ellen was emphatic. 'And we're a family.'

Louise looked to Nick for sympathy, but in his own calm way he backed her up.

'Your mum's right, Lou. All her workmates bring kids.' There was silence for a moment before he added, 'Big kids like you and me.'

'Okay,' Louise acquiesced, 'but you have to swim.'

He shook his head. 'I think I left my bathers—'

'I packed them for you,' Ellen interjected.

'Oh no!'

Louise shook her head of beautiful fair hair and laughed as only her dad could make her laugh. It was the sound that never failed to lighten Ellen's mood and soothe her soul.

Chapter One

Ellen stood at the edge of the paddock, still in pyjamas at four in the afternoon. Whoever was calling was not going to give up. She walked back to the house, Paddy shuffling at her heels.

'I've been ringing for the past hour. Did you get my message?'

Tracey could be as annoying as she was loyal.

'I was in the paddock, feeding Spots.' Ellen held the phone in place between her ear and shoulder as she dried the dishes from a breakfast she'd eaten at noon.

'Good on you,' said Tracey. 'That horse looked a bit skinny the last time I was around.'

'He's up to his knees in lush grass.' Ellen tried to mask her irritation.

Tracey laughed. 'How has your day been?'

'Great,' she lied. 'You must be busy yourself.'

'Flat out as usual.'

She waited for Tracey to elaborate, but there was none of the customary, dramatic retelling of everyday events in the world of the Popes.

'I'd better let you go.'

'I have news.' Tracey paused. 'You may be having a visitor.'

Ellen took the phone in her hand and held the plate and tea towel at her waist.

'Don't worry. I put him off,' said Tracey. 'Told him you'd be away for at least a week.'

'Who?' Her voice came out as a croak.

In the time it took Tracey to formulate her next sentence, Ellen had run through a myriad of possibilities: anyone from the taxman with one of those forms she'd ignored, to a census worker asking awkward questions.

'Some Irish bloke, said he knows you from way back.'

'Did you get a name? What did he look like?'

'If you give me a chance, I'll tell you.'

She pushed the phone back between her ear and shoulder and rubbed vigorously on the plate she'd already dried. It couldn't be an Irish taxman; she hadn't worked in Ireland in over twenty years.

'Gerry Canty, or was it Clancy?' With no sound from Ellen, Tracey continued. 'Tall bloke, well built, not fat, you know the type.'

The plate fell with a crash.

'What was that?'

'Nothing.' Ellen looked at the ceramic shards strewn across the worn lino. 'Where is he now? Has he left?'

'I'm not sure. Said he was visiting his son in Adelaide, that you'd be expecting him . . . something about a letter . . .'

She was thinking quickly now. She swallowed hard and straightened her shoulders. 'Tracey, ask at the post office for my mail. I'll phone and tell them I'm sick and can't collect it.'

'How long is it since you collected your post?'

'Too bloody long by the sound of things. Just do it, will you?'

'Keep your knickers on. I'll bring it round tomorrow.'

Ellen hung up and sat at the kitchen table, stunned.

—

Gerry Clancy pulled his rented four-by-four into the driveway of the Sunshine Motel. He could hardly believe he was in Australia. There'd been nothing but rain since he'd arrived in the country a fortnight earlier.

'Just the one night, Mr Clancy?' The woman behind the counter eyed him over her glasses.

'I'm not sure. I'm here to see a friend, but the lady at the petrol station seemed to think she might be away.'

The woman drew down the glasses and let them hang on a knitted sweater. 'Who is it you're here to see?'

'Ellen O'– I mean Ellen Con-stan-tinopoulos,' Gerry stuttered.

The woman smiled. 'Yes, I know Ellen. Irish, are you?'

'I'm from Cork, Ellen's hometown I suppose you'd say.'

'I didn't know Ellen was away . . .' She opened her mouth, but then replaced her glasses and got on with the booking. 'Stay as long as you like, Mr Clancy. It's a quiet time of year in South Australia. Enjoy it before we're overrun with summer visitors.'

Five minutes in town and the two people he'd spoken to knew Ellen. He thought to tell the woman about his son in Adelaide, but something told him the bush telegraph would be relaying enough information about him already.

—

The motel room was basic but clean and had an uninterrupted view of the beautiful foreshore. With only a short walk to the main street, Gerry went to sample the local cuisine in one of the nearby restaurants before partaking in a couple of Aussie beers in a hotel bar that reminded him of *Crocodile Dundee*. He'd managed to escape to the safety of his room before the brawling broke out, but not before being quizzed by the barman and regulars about his origins and travels. He'd even gleaned a little insight into Ellen's Australian life and that of her Greek husband.

'Tough break for the family,' said one of the locals. 'Good bloke, Nick. Not shy of a day's work.'

'Not shy of a drink either,' his mate chipped in, raising a chorus of garrulous laughter.

'Haven't seen Ellen in a while,' the barman said, looking thoughtful as he poured a schooner. 'Used to come in every Friday and collect him. Even took a drink herself now and then.'

It was hard to imagine Ellen in her early forties. Gerry had only seen her once since she'd emigrated, and that had been some years back; a quick embrace and offer of condolences at her mother's funeral. He sometimes ran into her brother and cousins in Cork and caught glimpses of her in them. It had seemed so final when she'd told him she was moving to Australia. He'd been tied to the family business by then, and she'd won a scholarship to do her final year at university in Sydney. Their summer romance had never had a chance once she'd made up her mind to leave the likes of him behind. Hindsight was a great thing, but if he'd had less pride and more balls, he could have followed her. By the time he'd thought about it, Jessica Sheehy had her sights set on him, and when he was asked to be best man and she bridesmaid at Pat Clohessy's wedding, well, that as they say, was that.

He took the bundle of letters from his suitcase and propped himself up on the bed with the pillows. He looked at each letter in turn, carefully keeping them in order. It was after her mother's funeral that she'd sent the first letter, said she wanted to keep in touch, to hear news from Ireland and how his life had turned out. Oh, he knew she had old friends in Cork who still phoned or emailed, or at least sent Christmas updates, but there was something in the tone of that first letter, the very fact that she'd wanted to be back in touch, which had made it impossible to ignore. They'd agreed early on that all communication be via snail mail. Her style was friendly. She loved to write, and he wasn't a big fan of computers. And so their relationship was relaunched like a salvaged shipwreck, a shadow of its former self but still in existence. She wrote mostly about Louise, updating him on her only child's achievements. She said her husband worked away a lot. He kept his letters light, preferring to bemoan the Irish weather and update her on family and friends in the exaggerated style that used to make her laugh.

Had she received his last instalment? Was it possible she didn't know he was here? Surely he'd put his mobile number in the letter. Maybe she'd tried to call but he'd left out some digits for the country code. Come to think of it, he'd had some odd looks when he mentioned she was out of town. Surely to God, she'd be glad to see him. He flicked through the envelopes with their exotic stamps of koalas and kooka-burras until he came across an early letter in which she'd drawn a rough map. It had a house, and a field with a horse in it, and an old-fashioned car in a driveway that led to a road. There was a signpost at the end of the road where she'd written *Port Lincoln*. He looked closer at the page. *Ocean Road*. Tomorrow, he would see if he could find it.

Ellen bent down and collected the pieces of crockery from the linoleum floor that was crying out for a mop. The cupboard doors looked like they could walk off their hinges. A smell from under the fridge reminded her of the resident mouse. Paddy whined about it now and then, but at thirteen he'd lost his taste for the chase, let alone the kill. She emptied the wreckage into the bin and went to the lounge room, picking up the remote before plonking herself down on the sofa. The ironing board stood beside the television she hardly switched off. It had been her intention at the end of summer to iron the lighter clothes and put them away. As the months went on, she'd watched plenty of mindless television but the clothes had only accumulated and formed an untidy pile on the worn leather armchair. In the early months Louise had come home regularly to help, but she was young. It wasn't fair to put so much on her daughter. Ellen had done her best to reassure her things were getting better, that she'd be able to cope.

The phone rang. Ellen checked the wall clock: six. It would be so easy to ignore it, but Louise would only worry if she didn't answer. She stood up, turned down the sound on the TV and took the phone from its cradle.

'Hello, darling. How was your day?'

'Good, Mum. How was yours?'

'Oh exhilarating, like all my other days.'

'I hate it when you're sarcastic.'

She heard the exasperation in her daughter's voice. 'Sorry. My day's been fine. You're not to worry.'

'Did you speak to anybody?'

'Just Tracey. And Spots and Paddy, if that counts.'

'How is Paddy?'

'Oh he manages.' She didn't want to over-egg the details of the ageing dog's decline. 'He's a trouper. Keeps me going.'

Part of Ellen wanted to tell Louise about Gerry Clancy, but it was too hard. Instead, she listened to what was happening in her daughter's life, grateful for the ten-minute insight into the trials and tribulations of a university student. There were assignments and student union events she always seemed to be organising. Nick would have been so proud. He would have done a much better job of this, asking the right questions, encouraging Louise to open up and say how she was really getting on, what those assignments and events actually involved.

'Okay, Mum. I'd better go. Talk to you tomorrow night.'

'Thanks, love.'

Ellen held the phone to her chest with both hands. This should have been the part where she handed Louise over to Nick and left them to talk as they always did, laughing at intervals, the sound making her smile. God, she wished Louise didn't have to call home every night to make sure she was holding it together. Weren't mothers supposed to worry about their daughters, not the other way around?

In Adelaide, Louise slipped her phone back into the pocket of her jeans and left the bathroom cubicle. The girl beside her at the washbasins smiled at her. A friendly smile, or an I-feel-sorry-for-you smile, she wasn't sure. Didn't other students phone their mothers every night? No, of course they didn't. They were too busy being uni students. 'Work hard, party harder,' they'd told her in orientation week. She undid her hair from its elastic tie and shook out her long light brown locks. Toby said he loved it. Yes, Toby the happy handsome uni student who didn't have to phone his mother every night and who was waiting out in the restaurant for her, oblivious.

The girl was gone. Louise leaned on the sink and took a good look at herself. What was that expression her mother had about being old before your time? Well, hadn't her life been fast-tracked months ago? No, she wasn't going to go there. Toby would be waiting. This was supposed to be a romantic dinner. She'd made the call. Her mother sounded fine. She'd call again tomorrow. Her parents had worked hard to send her here. The last thing they'd have wanted would be to burden her.

She gathered up her hair and retied it in a tight bun. 'You've got this,' she told herself.

⁓

Someone was pounding on the front door. Ellen threw back the duvet and swung her legs over the side of the sofa. As she stretched her arms over her head and forced her eyes to stay open, she felt her stomach tense. The knocking came again.

Oh, my God! It can't be Gerry.

Sunlight had just begun to brighten the room. She looked at the clock: six-thirty.

'You okay, Mrs C?'

She shook her head at the sound of the familiar voice, stood up and nudged the sleeping dog at her feet. Paddy groaned and opened one eye.

'Come on, boy. Let's see what Tyson wants.'

Paddy stretched and staggered after her to the hallway, managing a hoarse bark in protest at the disturbance.

She opened the front door to see her next-door neighbour's burly figure almost filling the doorframe.

'What do you think you're doing waking decent people at this hour of the morning?'

'I came to see if you was all right, Mrs C.' Tyson scratched his chest through a stained T-shirt. 'You don't look like you've been taking too good care of yourself this past while. I could come in and cook you up a nice breakfast.'

She could smell the alcohol on his breath. He meant well, but the last thing she needed was him coming in and feeling sorry for her. Anyway, he had enough problems of his own and she didn't have the energy for those either.

'Thanks, Tyson, but I was just getting up to go to town.' The white lie would get rid of him.

Paddy had thrown himself down beside her and lay with his eyes closed again.

'If you're sure, Mrs C.' Tyson moved his massive frame away from the door and slowly turned to go.

She grabbed an empty egg box from a shelf in the hallway, opened the screen door and handed it to him.

'Take a few eggs on your way home.'

'Well, thank you, Mrs C. I shall do that directly.'

As much as she could do without his appearance at odd hours, she couldn't ask for a better neighbour. He'd be the first to help in a crisis, just as he had when Nick . . . well, whenever there'd been any trouble.

She watched as Tyson swaggered down the steps and wandered off toward the chook pen. Curling back up on the sofa was tempting, but the sun gleamed through the windows and it had the makings of a nice day, one of the first in months after the miserable winter. Of course the day would have looked even brighter had the windows not been thick with dust, but before Ellen let herself be overwhelmed by the thought of all the work that needed to be done inside and out before any visitor could see the place, she vowed to take one step at a time and start with breakfast and a shower, like a normal person.

Goddamn it, Gerry Clancy, couldn't you have left well enough alone and stayed in Cork?

She went to the bedroom and scrambled through cupboards to find something clean to put on. After the shower, everything about her smelled of coconut and frangipani, but her bedroom smelled old and stale. She ignored the cobwebs hanging between walls and furniture, grabbed what she needed and got out of there as fast as she could.

Her best jeans she kept for going out slipped down at her hips. She forced herself back into the bedroom to find a belt. Track pants were so much easier; she'd spent the winter months rotating a couple of pairs of them and a few long-sleeved T-shirts, washing them by hand and throwing them over the makeshift line under the back veranda. The mirror she usually avoided caught her eye. She wanted to blame the coating of dust for the dullness in her pale Irish skin and the lacklustre green of her eyes. The shirt was crumpled, but a quick rub of the iron and it would be good as new.

It would take more than a little ironing to turn the house back to its former glory, but at least she was trying. If she kept it together, surely she could make it look to Gerry as though she were on top of things.

—

By the time Tracey arrived, Ellen felt she'd done a day's work. A massive network of cobwebs had had to be removed from the Hill's Hoist before she'd managed to hang out a load of washing, but it felt good to see freshly washed clothes and linen blowing in the light September breeze.

Tracey thundered up the driveway in her Ford Falcon, dust clouds dispersing behind her.

'How're ya goin'?' she called out.

Ellen was sitting on the veranda taking a well-earned coffee break and imagining the contents of the letter her friend had promised to bring. She watched as Tracey came up the steps, rifling in a vast handbag.

'Rosie at the post office said you never phoned, but she was okay with me taking them.' Tracey set the stack of mail on the wicker table and eyed the coffee mug. 'Okay if I grab myself one while you look at these?'

Ellen just wanted to rip open the letter with the Irish stamps that poked out between bills and useless catalogues, but Tracey might go opening her grimy fridge or witness the bombsite that was her living room, ironing board or no ironing board. She shot up from her chair.

'Have a seat. I'll bring one out.'

'Longlife?' Tracey's face was a grimace at the first sip of coffee.

'Yes. I just ran out.' Ellen fingered the pile of post.

'Oh, don't mind me.' Tracey grabbed a supermarket flyer. 'I'll see what's on special while you read your letter.'

Ellen could have lifted Tracey off her garden chair, placed her in her Ford, and set it on autopilot back to town, but Tracey was the one link with the town she had left.

> *Ellen,*
>
> *You won't believe it. I'm coming to Australia for a holiday. Kieran's in Adelaide since finishing the Leaving Cert. His friend is playing football for the Adelaide Crows (don't know if you know them) and he got Kieran some work through his contacts. Thought I'd take the short flight to your neck of the woods when I'm there. It will be great to see you after all these years. I'll sort myself out for accommodation. Should be arriving in Port Lincoln on . . .*

My God! Ellen scanned to the top of the page to find a date. The letter must have been lying in her post box for weeks.

'You all right, love?' Tracey asked.

With Gerry's letter in her lap, Ellen grabbed at the official-looking envelopes and tore them open. The red ink on overdue bills made her wince. When Nick was alive, she'd always paid her bills on time. She couldn't hold back the tears.

'Oh, darl, it can't be that bad,' Tracey soothed.

'Look at these.' She stifled the desire to scream. 'I'm a mess. My house is a mess, my husband is dead, my daughter's left home.' She gathered the papers in a bunch and slammed them on the table, a tremor rippling through her body. 'I can't even pay my bills, Tracey, and this blast from the past thinks he can just pop in . . .'

Tracey moved her chair closer and put an arm around her. Ellen let her head drop against her friend and sobbed into her flowery shirt.

'You've had a rough trot, darl, but it will get better.'

Ellen sat up and wiped her tear-soaked cheeks with a sleeve.

'How do you know it won't get worse?'

'Because I'm going to help you.'

Looking into Tracey's soft brown eyes, Ellen wondered where her small-town Australian friend got her self-assured notions. But it was true. Tracey was the one person who could help her.

'Might as well start now as I've got the day off.'

That was it. She'd let her guard down and it was payback. Tracey would be on a mission to whip house, garden, even her into shape.

'What are you doing?'

Tracey had taken her mobile phone out of a side pocket in her handbag and begun scrolling through the numbers.

'Can I book an appointment for a cut and colour tomorrow?'

Ellen made a grab for the phone, but Tracey made off around the veranda, confirming times.

'A little makeover is just what you need, darl,' she said, ending the call.

'Tracey, don't you get it?' She was shouting now. 'I can barely get out of bed. My life is a shambles, and you want me to go to the hairdresser's?'

Tracey looked resolute.

'Look, I know you're grieving for Nick and that Gerry Clancy is just an old friend, but if you saw him, you'd know you'd want to look your best.'

'What are you saying?'

'He's a good-looking bloke. I'm sure he'd rather see you healthy and fresh than looking like a dag . . .'

'But I *am* a dag. I don't mind being a dag, living in my daggy house on this daggy block . . .' She was crying again.

'Oh, Ellen, I'm only trying to help.' Tracey leaned back against the veranda and took a deep breath before speaking again. 'We've been friends a long time, Ellen. Remember when our girls were born?'

Ellen smiled at the memory of the first time she'd met Tracey, when their girls were born a day apart and they got chatting over the incubators.

'I was freaking out with worry,' said Tracey, 'but you explained what was happening and set my mind at ease.' She lifted a hand from the rail of the veranda, sending her bangles jangling. Ellen looked away with embarrassment. 'You were always the one helping me. You always knew what to do when the kids were sick or naughty, what to say to teachers at school meetings, what books to buy . . . When they were teenagers we couldn't wait to get them off our hands so we could have some fun.' She sighed and, leaning her head to one side, made Ellen look her in the eye. 'Well, girlfriend, when will the fun start if I let you die of depression?'

Ellen bit her lip and gazed out over the lawn, past the vast yellow swathes of canola and out to the sea beyond. She turned around and went to say something, but Tracey had gone into the house.

'O ... M ... G!'

Ellen stood in the hallway and watched her friend take in the scene.

Tracey threw her hands up in the air. 'Looks like I came by in the nick of time.' Before Ellen could respond, she was apologising. 'Sorry, didn't mean to mention Nick. Well you know what I meant . . .'

Ellen was fixed to the spot. She couldn't believe Tracey had marched in here uninvited and uncovered the extent of her sorry existence.

There was a loud bark from outside.

'What's Paddy barking at?' asked Tracey.

'Nothing, I'd say. He's as deaf as a post. I suppose he feels he has to bark at some—'

They both heard the car pull into the driveway.

Chapter Two

'Pretend I'm not here. Say you're feeding the cat.'

Ellen ducked down under the windowsill in the living room as Gerry Clancy closed the door of his rented four-wheel drive and took in his surroundings.

'Are you mad?' said Tracey. 'That man has only come all the way from Ireland to see you.'

'To see his son,' Ellen corrected, peering over the sill.

Gerry gave Tracey's car the once-over before turning his eyes on the house. 'Anybody home?'

Ellen went to duck down again, but had to scramble to her feet as Tracey grabbed her arm and shoved her toward the front door.

'I can't do this,' she hissed.

'You can and you will.'

There wasn't time to argue. Before she knew it, Ellen was standing on her veranda with Gerry Clancy on her front steps and her best friend blocking her retreat. She tried to assess her appearance without looking down. Had she put on the blue or the green shirt? Did she look too thin?

'Ellen! You're back. I wasn't sure if . . . I said I'd take a chance . . .'

She felt her body seize up. She wanted to burst out crying and tell him that this was a mistake; he should never have come. That she was a fraud, completely unworthy of his visit.

Tracey rescued them from the awkwardness. 'You must be Gerry. I met you at the roadhouse.' She thrust her hand out and shook his vigorously. 'I'm Tracey.'

Ellen took in the greying hair and the few wrinkles about the eyes that only seemed to add to Gerry's good looks. She must be getting old if that was attractive, she thought, as she forced her body to relax enough to greet him.

'Can't believe you're in Australia,' was all she could manage and before there could be any physical contact, she heard herself saying, 'I'll put the kettle on.'

Gerry was about to follow her inside when Tracey wedged all of her pint-sized frame between him and the screen door and gestured to the garden furniture.

'Have a seat, Gerry. Shame to be inside on such a beautiful day.'

He gave a resigned smile and did what he was told.

'I'll just give Ellen a hand,' said Tracey, scuttling into the house after her.

'I can't, Tracey.'

'Don't deny me my ten minutes of heaven listening to that accent,' Tracey pleaded.

'It's not funny. I'm nearly having a heart attack here and you're on cloud nine.'

Tracey ignored her and began spooning coffee into mugs. 'Does he take it black or will I give him the longlife?'

'How do I know how he takes it? I haven't had coffee with him in over two decades.'

'Isn't this the most exciting thing that's happened to us in years?'

'You're unbelievable,' said Ellen. 'You can have your moment of heaven, but don't let him see the inside of my house.'

Tracey rolled her eyes. 'Can I trust you to come back out when this is done if I go talk to him?'

'Go, and behave yourself or I'll tell Pete.'

Ellen said a silent prayer in desperation while the kettle boiled and then filled the coffee mugs. Carrying them on a tray, she carefully pulled open the screen door and stepped onto the veranda. Gerry stood up to help, but she reached the table before he could move any closer.

A bundle of mail stuck out of Tracey's handbag.

'I just put them in there out of the way,' said Tracey, following her glance.

The three of them sat in silence and sipped the hot drinks. Ellen could feel Tracey's disgust at the taste of the milk, but was grateful Gerry drank his unfazed.

'This is a grand place altogether,' he said, taking in the view out over the bay, apparently oblivious to the tension.

Ellen wondered if he knew about gardens, and hoped he didn't know a weed from a prize chrysanthemum. It hadn't come up in their letters, but she couldn't be sure. He was probably being polite, but all she could see was a block gone to the dogs.

Paddy appeared from behind the house and went to check out the four-wheel drive. He cocked his leg unsteadily against one of the tyres.

'What kind of a spotty mongrel is that?' Gerry asked.

Ellen found herself smiling at the unapologetic turn of phrase. This was the Gerry she remembered.

Tracey looked at him as though *he* were the mongrel.

'It's actually a thoroughbred blue heeler,' said Ellen before Tracey could speak. 'They're Australian cattle dogs, a proper breed, you know.'

Gerry looked unconvinced, but put his hand down to let the dog have a sniff as he hauled himself onto the veranda.

Paddy gave a low growl.

'Paddy, behave,' said Ellen. 'Gerry's a friend.'

'He misses his master,' said Tracey with unexpected melancholy.

'Oh, yes, I was very sorry to hear about—'

'That's okay, Gerry,' said Ellen. 'So tell me, how are they all in Cork?'

He looked relieved to have averted the awkward subject of Nick's death, and told them about his divorce, and how they'd had to fold the family business. There'd been mention of these events in his letters, but it seemed more real hearing them now. Bakeries had gone out of fashion, he said, and since his father wasn't ready to retire, they'd decided to invest what they had in the pub-restaurant trade instead and set his parents up for retirement on the profits. Ellen couldn't imagine the Clancys doing anything other than running their bakery.

'And how is Kieran getting on in Adelaide?' She'd be fine as long as he was the one doing the talking.

The mention of his son set him off on an enthusiastic account of how Kieran's friend had been drafted to play for an Adelaide football team. When he checked if they knew of the Adelaide Crows, Ellen thought Tracey might throttle him, but somehow Tracey managed to keep her passion for her favourite team to herself, and let him go on to tell them all about meeting Kieran in Melbourne and staying at a backpackers' before heading to Adelaide where his son had secured a job at the cafe in the Adelaide Oval.

'I'd love to have come out here to work when I was younger,' said Gerry. 'We met so many Irish backpackers – made me wish I was in my twenties again.'

Ellen caught his eye and he held her gaze just long enough for Tracey to notice.

'Since we've got so much to do today,' Tracey said, her big eyes boring into Ellen's, 'why don't you and Gerry arrange to meet up tomorrow, in town, after your appointment?'

Under the table, the weight of one of Tracey's wedges almost crushed the phalanges of Ellen's left foot.

'If that's okay with you, Gerry,' she began. 'It's just that we've got a bit of—'

'—renovating to do,' Tracey cut in.

'I'm not afraid to get my hands dirty if you want a hand,' he offered.

'No, this is . . . women's renovating,' said Tracey.

Ellen shrugged and gave Gerry a weak smile. Rude as she felt this was, she knew Tracey had bought her time to get her house in order.

As Gerry's car disappeared at the end of the driveway, Ellen touched the cheek he had kissed and thanked God she'd had a shower.

'Women's renovating?'

'He'd have been here all day if I hadn't butted in.'

'I thought you loved listening to him.'

'Yes, but he's a man and that means a big appetite. What were you going to do with him when he got hungry?'

'Good point, Tracey.' She pointed to her head. 'Up there for thinking, down there for dancing.'

'Come on, you mad Irishwoman. We've got a house to clean. Have you any bread that's not blue?'

'Yes, I made it myself just a couple of days ago,' said Ellen, proud of the fact. It made her feel less than completely helpless.

'Okay, we fuel up with French toast and then we hit the housework.'

That was it. Tracey set her bangles and earrings on the kitchen bench and, taking a hair tie from her wrist, drew her unruly curls into a ponytail before striding off to the lounge room. Ellen got on with the job of making lunch, trying to block out Tracey's exasperated sighs. The ironing board hadn't impressed. She took a few deep breaths and concentrated on frying the bread as Tracey stomped to the laundry, banging cupboard doors before returning to the lounge room armed with a laundry basket full of cloths and cleaning products. Ellen cringed as she caught a glimpse of Tracey pausing at the lounge room door, looking over-whelmed as to where to start. When she looked again, Tracey had loaded the laundry basket with the tower of clothes that had sat on the armchair, and balancing it with her chin, was propelling it upstairs.

'Just leave those on the landing,' Ellen called after her. The last thing she wanted was Tracey taking it upon herself to rearrange her wardrobe and inadvertently discovering Nick's ashes. It was hardly a fitting final resting place, but that was another job on the ever-increasing list of things that should be getting done but that she couldn't bear to think about.

Tracey did as she said and came into the kitchen.

'Tell you what, darl, how about we keep lunch warm in the oven and finish the lounge room?'

The only thing Ellen had consumed so far today was that one cup of coffee with Gerry, but Tracey was on a roll. Together they pushed back the heavy leather suite. Ellen winced at the dust rising in the sunlight. The timbers the furniture had hidden were their original colour, devoid of dog hair and the grime that was now evident over the rest of the floor space. But Tracey wasn't standing around dwelling on the drop in her friend's housekeeping standards. No, she was running hot water into a bucket in the laundry and summoning Ellen to find the mop and vacuum. They dusted and polished every surface before scrubbing the floor to a brilliant shine. Tracey didn't stand on ceremony either; pictures were taken down, sprayed and wiped to a gleam that took years off their subjects. Ellen knew she would have folded had the task of cleaning the photographs fallen to her. She'd hardly let herself look at them these past months, let alone touch them.

When they finally stopped for lunch on the veranda, Tracey checked her fitness wristband.

'Woohoo! An extra thousand steps and we're only getting started.'

Ellen stifled a yawn at the thought of it.

'We'll have the place in shipshape in no time,' said Tracey.

'We will,' Ellen agreed, forcing herself to share in her enthusiasm.

By the time Tracey left, Ellen was so tired from physical labour she didn't have the energy to feel depressed. Her friend had gone mad with the vacuum and the sofa was no longer an option for sleeping. The throw had been washed and hung on the line, leaving the soft leather exposed with all its war wounds from years of supporting jumping children and weighty adults. If a piece of furniture could talk, this one would tell of the highs and lows of the Constantinopoulos household, of making up after arguments and cross words, of great nights with friends from near and far, of a well-loved child and playmates watching DVDs. Ellen stroked the faded patches in the leather and looked around her decluttered living space. Like a face mask, they had peeled away the grimy layer and exposed the home's rejuvenated skin. But the emptiness prevailed. That awful gut-wrenching emptiness she'd faced every day for the last nine months. Nick wouldn't want her to grieve forever, but she didn't know whether her broken heart would ever mend.

Chapter Three

Ellen couldn't remember the last time she'd woken up in the bed she'd hated not sharing with Nick. It had the fresh smell of newly cut flowers, only because Tracey had insisted on changing the bedclothes, vacuuming the mattress and hanging the duvet over the veranda for several hours. It was a Norwegian thing, she'd said, something she'd learned from her grandmother. Where Ellen came from, hanging anything out in public view was considered the height of coarseness, but what could she do? Tracey was unstoppable.

Two showers, two days in a row – this was a record. Ellen tried not to think about going into town, sitting for hours in a salon full of people, having her head massaged by someone she hardly knew, and managed to be ready to go when Tracey arrived as promised.

'You right to do this?' she asked once Ellen had buckled her seat belt.

'Drive, before I change my mind.'

Now I know why people use hip flasks, Ellen thought as she pulled her handbag tight into her shoulder and looked both ways on Tasman Terrace. The road was clear. Tracey was already halfway across, but Ellen stood rooted to the spot, her tummy clenched like a fist. Tracey looked back and held out her hand. There were two choices. If she didn't catch up with Tracey and keep up with her friend's efforts to reengage her with normality, she'd be back to square one. Tracey beckoned as a car approached from the north end of the street. Ellen jumped off the pavement and they ran to the other side. Not taking any chances, Tracey linked arms with her and kept up a brisk pace until they were inside the door of the salon.

'I'll see you later. Enjoy the pampering.' With a wink and a smile, she was gone.

The male trainee slid about the salon floor in chequered canvas slip-ons. He came toward her with a nylon cape and, without as much as a 'by your leave', fastened it round the back of her neck and drew her hair out from under the collar.

'Come and take a seat,' he said, a hand stretched out in one direction, eyes looking absently in another.

She counted to fifty as he and the stylist tousled at her hair, drawing out strands as they talked through the technicalities of what they were about to do to her.

'We'll have you looking like a million bucks in no time,' the stylist told her reflection.

Ellen smiled back at her, hoping she could endure the process.

The arrangement was to meet Tracey and Gerry outside the post office at noon. Although pleased with the result of the past couple of hours, Ellen was relieved to be out in the fresh air with the gentle breeze ruffling her newly brightened locks. She'd asked the stylist to apply a little makeup when her hair was done. There was no doubt the whole experience had her looking better than she had in months. She could only hope it would be enough to hide the nervous wreck that lay beneath the façade.

'Well, who's the hottie before my eyes?' Tracey teased. 'Could it be my daggy best friend?' She ran her fingers through Ellen's hair.

Ellen wanted the ground to open and swallow her as she saw Gerry turn a shade of pink that couldn't be sunburn.

'Are you ladies ready for a spot of lunch? I'm starving,' he said.

'I'll leave you tourists to catch up,' said Tracey. 'I've got a roadhouse to run.'

Ellen wanted to grab her by the arm and insist she join them, but Tracey gave her a quick kiss on the cheek and took off down the street. Ellen could have sworn she'd seen tears in her eyes, but maybe it was just the wind.

'So where are you taking me?' Gerry asked.

'Do you mind if we grab a Subway and take it along the foreshore?'

She needed to steer this if she were to last away from her own four walls without going to pieces. It had been months since she'd left Ocean Road. After Nick's death, she'd come to rely on Tracey and Louise for company as well as transport on trips into the town. But with Tracey's dad not well and Louise busy in Adelaide, she would have had to come in on her own. It was a challenge she hadn't had the strength to face.

'Sounds perfect. My shout,' he said.

Her order in, she pointed him in the direction of Subway and nipped into the post office. Rosie looked surprised to see her when she got to the counter, but the long queue made for a minimum of conversation.

'Nice to see you out and about,' said Rosie, handing Ellen the bill receipts. She stuffed them in her handbag. Having them paid off felt almost as good as the haircut.

She took a seat at a picnic table beside the beach and watched Gerry make his way through the lunchtime crowd. She was grateful for the distance between them as she gathered her thoughts. Surely he'd only be here for a few days; she could manage a couple of daytrips to show him round, maybe cook him dinner one night, and then he'd be off home again.

He grinned at her from across the street as he came back with their lunch in a paper bag. There was something easy about him. In many ways he'd hardly changed. Of course, there were the pesky grey hairs that befell them all, but the stature was the same – tall, broad-shouldered, and he didn't look bad in a pair of shorts either. *Typical Irish, getting the shorts on when it was still cool by Australian standards.*

'You're looking gorgeous by the way,' he said, taking a seat beside her on the picnic bench.

'Tracey made me do it,' she said. 'Not that I'm ungrateful.'

'What is it with you two? Are you joined at the hip?'

She laughed. 'Tracey's a bit full on, but she's got a heart of gold. Only for her . . .' She wanted to say, 'I wouldn't be sitting here eating lunch with you', but let it go. He didn't need to know.

When the seagulls got too much, they took a walk along the footpath. A few people she hadn't seen in ages said hello, but they seemed to be taking more notice of Gerry than her. Tongues would wag in the small town, but she was beyond caring. It felt good to have company, to take a walk in the sunshine in a beautiful part of the world with a handsome man at her side. To think this used to be an ordinary occurrence when she had Nick. She drank in the moment.

Gerry told her about the new business and how different it was to the bakery. He mentioned how hard they worked, how having to cover the bar and restaurant made for long hours and crazy shifts.

'Tell me if I'm talking too much,' he said.

They were on the beach now. She bent down and took off her shoes.

'No, you're fine. It's great to hear your news. I still can't believe we're talking face to face after all the years of letter-writing.'

Gerry stopped and stood in front of her at the water's edge.

'Why did you suddenly decide to write to me?'

She couldn't move forward, trapped by the searching in his eyes.

'I told you,' she began, as her mind raced to find a way round the question she wished to God he hadn't asked. Why couldn't he just have gone on talking in his lovely Cork accent, familiar as an old armchair and smooth as the sand on her bare feet? 'I was curious, homesick maybe.' At least that part was true. His letters, with their echoes of Ireland, had been one of the few links she still had to her formative home.

'But you had lots of friends in Cork. Why me?'

'Is that why you came? To ask me why I wrote to you?' He moved away a little and shrugged.

'Sorry, Ellen. I didn't mean to upset you. I came because . . . because we're friends.'

'Good,' she said and walked on, watching her feet as they pushed into the wet sand. She knew exactly why she'd written to him. The problem was, she'd never actually managed to put it in any of her infrequent letters.

'Have you ever seen a whale?' she asked over her shoulder.

'And where would I have to go to see whales?'

'I'll take you tomorrow.' She pulled her sandals back on and headed up the beach. 'I've got to go and meet Tracey. She's giving me a lift home.'

—

He was about to say he could run her home, but something in her expression told him Ellen had had enough for today.

His phone rang.

'How're ya goin', Gerry?' Tracey's voice again. Ellen must have given her his number. Before he could answer, she was giving him orders.

'Tell Ellen I'm at the Tasman. You got any warm gear?'

'Yeah, I—'

'No worries, Pete'll sort you out. He'll pick you up at your hotel at three. Hope you like fishing.'

She rang off. He held out the phone and looked round for Ellen, who was making her way towards the road.

'Who's Pete?' he called after her.

'Tracey's other half,' she shouted back. 'Have fun.'

Ellen felt like a teenager when she flopped into the car beside Tracey. Her cheeks glowed and it felt good.

'You're looking pleased with yourself,' said Tracey as she drove out of town in her usual haste.

'Oh, it's just nice to talk to someone who speaks my language,' Ellen joked.

'So any rekindling of old flames?'

'Tracey, you're incorrigible.'

'I'm not sure if I know what that means, but I like the sound of it.'

'It means keep your nose out of my business because you've done enough meddling.'

'Is that what you call it? Meddling.' Tracey looked indignant. 'If it wasn't for my "meddling", you'd be stuck out on that block crying into your longlife milk.'

She glanced over at Ellen. They both knew she'd gone too far, but Ellen brushed it off.

'And I am eternally grateful,' she said, 'but I can't wait to get back into my house. I feel a bit like a tortoise that's lost its shell.'

'Okay, but you've got to promise me that all my "meddling" hasn't gone for nothing and you'll keep your chin up.'

'I'll do my best,' she smiled.

─

Once inside the house, Ellen went upstairs to make the bed she'd been in too much of a rush to make that morning. It was the little things that would keep her sane, she realised. The small routines she'd let go in the height of her grief. Only suddenly and in a fit of shame at the thought of Gerry Clancy seeing the state of the place had she been spurred into action. Maybe the timing of his visit hadn't been so bad. But it was just as well Tracey had intercepted him, or he might have found her in the grip of that weight of grief she'd been sinking under for months. Plumping up her pillows, an overwhelming desire to sleep made her slip under the duvet.

When she woke, it was nine o'clock at night. She couldn't believe she'd slept that long. Downstairs, she made herself some supper. Tracey had been kind enough to do a little shopping for her, and she laughed as she topped up her mug with fresh milk.

The answering machine flashed.

Louise!

She grabbed the phone and dialled her daughter's number.

'You okay, Mum? I was worried. I always ring at six.'

Ellen sensed the frustration in her tone.

'Oh sweetheart, I'm sorry. I was sleeping when you called and never heard a thing.'

'Have you had a bad day?'

'No, I've had a brilliant day. I've had my hair cut and coloured, I've had lunch with . . .'

She wasn't sure how to tell her about Gerry.

'With Tracey?'

'Yeah. It was great fun. But how are *you*?'

Louise filled her in on the day's events, but even though these conversations with her daughter were what kept her going, she was distracted by thoughts of Gerry. Louise was about to ring off when she finally mentioned him.

'An old friend from Ireland is in town for a few days.'

'Is she staying with us?'

'No, it's a man and he's at a hotel in town. Tracey's helped me organise the place, so I'll be able to invite him for dinner if that's what you're thinking.'

'Did you do my room? I was thinking of coming home this weekend.'

'Is everything all right?'

'Yeah. Just need a break from the city.'

'That would be perfect,' said Ellen, crossing herself and asking God and every saint in heaven why Louise had to pick this weekend to feel like a trip home.

Chapter Four

Louise stared at her laptop, hands resting on a knee drawn up to her chest as she sat at the desk in the student dormitory. A shoulder of her dark cropped cardigan fell down one arm, exposing a singlet strap, black against her pale skin. Her bird's nest of hair was held together with a dark elastic tie. Exams weren't far away and a weighty aquaculture assignment was due tomorrow. She scratched a spot on her scalp with a pen, not sure if she even understood the question.

In a former life, she might have Skyped home and asked her dad for help. He'd always loved relating her study to the real world, especially the world of fishing. It had been around this time last year, nearing the end of Year 12, when she'd begun to doubt her chances of a university place and had been fit to throw in the towel. Her dad had sat her down and gently reminded her of how far she'd come and how close she was to the finish line. Together they'd formulated a study plan and promised to talk every day, whether he was home or away, to keep her on track.

Despite her mother's university education, well-paid job and love of books, Louise had always preferred her dad's help with homework. It wasn't that her mother was less willing or able, but her dad didn't push. He relished the opportunity to learn alongside her, happy to pore over her textbooks together or tap her suggestions into the search engine on their home computer, his callused fingers connecting heavily with keys and those deep brown eyes scanning the screen.

He was a handsome man. In fact, she'd often wished she looked like him, with thick curly dark hair she'd grow to her waist. She would have liked some of his height too, but no, she got the Irish genes, fair and freckled.

She could have done with some of her mother's pushing now. 'Study hard', 'Get your uni score', 'No, you can't go out this weekend'; it had driven her mad at the time, but she'd gladly swap it now for having to keep tabs on the woman who used to make most of the decisions in the Constantinopoulos' household. She wanted to cry out to the ether and demand her parents back, exactly how they were. If it hadn't been for her dad's big dreams for her, she might have put the whole uni thing on hold. Those first weeks were tough, but on her mother's advice, she'd gone to one of the student counsellors, a mature caring woman who was happy to see her whenever she needed to talk. It had been a huge help, but she wished her mother was better at taking her own advice. She might even be driving and back at work by now if she'd sought help too.

There was a knock on the door.

'Come in,' she said, stifling the urge to sob.

'Anybody home?'

Toby Scott let himself in.

'I tried calling you . . .'

'I know. I was on the phone to Mum.' She moved the mouse, absently looking over the computer screen.

He perched himself on the edge of the desk and stretched out his long legs.

'You homesick?'

'No.' She glared at him.

'Must be short of cash then,' he laughed. 'That's usually when I call Mum and Dad.'

She raised a feeble smile, but didn't answer.

Leaning back, he inclined his head and looked her in the eye.

'Everything okay on the home front?'

'It's fine, Toby. I'm just busy.'

She frowned at the screen, shutting down that conversation. She'd already told him about her dad's accident, the facts at least, if not the ongoing effects.

'There's a bunch of us going to the Den later. You wanna come?'

She eyed her boyfriend of three weeks and wondered what had possessed him to go out with her in the first place. He was a popular boy, too popular; perfect pectorals, awesome smile, sun-bleached hair, all balanced by brains and a fun-loving personality. He'd told her she was pretty and she'd believed him. They'd been out every night since.

He dropped down to his knees beside her, encircling her in his arms, his face right there, ready to kiss her, but she pushed his shoulder and turned back to the computer.

'I've got assignments coming out my ears. There's an essay due tomorrow I haven't even started.'

His lips moved in again. He'd come all showered, clean-shaven, expectant.

She put a firm hand on the chest of his laundry-fresh polo shirt and turned away.

'At the rate I'm going, I'll be pulling an all-nighter.'

He drew back a fraction. 'Have we time for a quickie before I go out?'

Louise bristled. Is this what it came down to? A quick shag before going out with his mates? No thank you.

'I'll ignore that question.' She tried to sound assertive. 'And I'm going home for the weekend, so you won't see me until next week.'

He looked crestfallen.

'What about tomorrow night?'

'I'll be busy – packing and stuff.'

There was silence between them. As he stood up to his full height, Toby took her hand in his.

'We can take it a bit slower if you like, Lou.'

God, why did he have to call her that? It was what everyone close called her.

'See you next week, Toby.'

He bent down, returned her hand to her lap, and kissed her awkwardly on the cheek. She was already typing into the search engine when he let himself out.

She wished she could have leaned on her mother, told her about Toby and asked her advice, but that shoulder was no longer an option for crying on. How ironic; her mother, who she'd always seen as strong and independent, was a mess without her father. She needed to be the strong one now, or she too would unravel.

If only Jennifer hadn't taken a gap year! Her best friend would have had Toby Scott sussed and helped her work out if this was the real deal or if she was only setting herself up for further heartache. Sure, she'd made friends in the city, but first-year uni friends were like a football team of rookies, still at the trust-building stage. She would need to take care of herself. Getting her degree in marine biology was her dream. She wasn't about to let her father down, and if that meant disappointing the best-looking boy in her year, she'd just have to wear it. Going home mightn't make her pass her exams, but she needed to feel that special connection she felt with her dad every time she'd gone home to Ocean Road. Besides, her mother could probably do with help entertaining her visitor.

Chapter Five

When Ellen couldn't sleep, she went to the shed. She'd tried reading but it was no use. She was wide awake, her mind like a cinema screen, playing out the events of the day, of the past and speculative events of what might become of her in the future. She wondered if the movies in her mind would have a happy ending, or if she would wallow in the guilt and sorrow of grief and loss for the rest of her life.

The key felt cold as she took it from the hook by the back door and stepped out onto the veranda. Paddy twitched in his sleep and let out a yelp, eyes firmly closed. Perhaps he too dreamed of his past, of his youth. Nick had brought him home from a neighbouring farm as an eight-week-old pup and presented him to Louise on her sixth birthday. She'd lavished him with love and they'd become inseparable, Paddy following her to the paddock when she later acquired Spots and accompanying them on the rides they took through the scrub. He was the perfect companion for an only child, and Ellen thanked God for Nick's kindness. Louise had talked about taking Paddy to Adelaide when she was bigger, but by the time she reached eighteen and moving had become a reality, she knew he belonged on the block with her parents.

Baby Lou in the big city! Ellen rubbed her arms against the cool night and hoped her daughter was really doing as well as their short phone calls would have her believe. She'd been a pretty good kid. Not as prone to the dramas some of her friends' children got caught up in. She and Nick had had such a beautiful relationship. Hardly a cross word. The downside of course was that she'd had to be bad cop when any discipline was needed, but it was mostly small stuff like reminding her to pitch in with chores or telling her off when she went out with friends and forgot to let her know where she was or when she'd be home. At least that had been the case until she'd turned sixteen, when boys and parties became an issue. Ellen remembered doing a lot of shouting and grounding. Louise would storm off, slamming her bedroom door, but their fights didn't last long. Nick usually intervened with his calm wisdom. Sometimes Ellen suspected Louise stored up her problems for when Nick came home from business trips or weeks at sea on his fishing boat. Still, between them they'd managed to get her to eighteen and on to university. Life couldn't be plain sailing in Adelaide, but Louise had managed to get through most of her first year without complaint. At least not to her mother.

In those six or so weeks after Nick died, Ellen had been the strong one. She'd talk about Nick and his dreams for them all and somehow, Louise had found the determination to keep those dreams alive. Ellen hadn't meant to fall to pieces, but once Louise was settled in Adelaide and she found herself alone, it had all proven too much to just carry on. The regular trips to see her girl in the city hadn't transpired, and when Louise had come home in the holidays, she'd had so much to pack in; helping out at home, studying and seeing her friends. Ellen wished she could have been a better support and not been so caught up in her own pain that she'd almost cut her daughter adrift. This weekend would be an opportunity to make amends. She'd make a bigger effort to talk things out.

Moonlight fell on the Chrysler as Ellen pulled open the sliding door of the shed and stepped inside. She gave a sigh as she looked over the white and turquoise vintage car that had been Nick's pride and joy. He'd called it their Sunday car. Other men bought pleasure boats and camper trailers, but Nick wasn't interested in any of that. He said he had enough with boats at work, and he never could understand the Australian obsession with camping. Ellen didn't mind. She didn't care much for boats, and a road trip around the state when Louise was young had been enough to turn her off camping for life. She'd even sold her runabout and used the Chrysler for getting in and out of town. Somehow it had eased the long stretches of not having him around, and she was happy for him to be in the driving seat once he was home and wanted a change from his trusty ute.

She let her hand run over the chrome trim of the roof and down onto the bonnet, touching cool metal but feeling Nick's warm presence.

'You loved this old jalopy,' she said aloud. 'Remember the Sunday drives to Tumby and Coffins, Louise sitting in the back like a princess, and you proud at the wheel like a millionaire?'

The wind ruffled her hair, and she pulled her fleece tight around her. She gripped the handle of the driver's door and, before negative thoughts could take over, climbed into the driver's seat. Did it still smell of Nick or was she imagining it? The creamy leather supported her frame. It was like being in his arms again: safe, cared for, happy, not unhinged and fearful as she'd become without him. From the outside looking in, one would have been forgiven for thinking she'd worn the trousers in their marriage. Sure, she'd been the one keeping them all on track, but she couldn't have done it without him. He'd been her rock. There were photos, mementoes, and of course the urn of ashes she'd placed in the wardrobe, but Nick's presence felt more real in this car than in any of those things. Sitting inside it was the one way she had left to connect with her dead husband. Tracey had said she should go for counselling, but she hadn't. This had been her therapy, the place where she came to remember the good life she'd had before that terrible night. The place where she tried to convince herself that she'd drive again in time.

—

Behind her tight-shut eyes, the tragedy unfolded again as it had done every day since that fateful night in January. They'd had a special family Christmas, pulling out all the stops, acutely aware of Louise's imminent departure. She'd finished Year 12, been accepted into Flinders University and was busy planning the big move, packing in as many social events as humanly possible. The house had been heaving with teenage bodies. Nick and Ellen kept running into parents they hadn't seen in years or hardly knew, such was the collective sense of caring, every one of them eager to be on hand before their grown-up children went out into the world.

'We're losing our Baby Lou,' he'd said. 'It won't be the same.'

Ellen had been less sentimental at the time. She knew Louise was ready, and after eighteen years of mothering, she was too.

'She'll be home with dirty washing before you know it,' she'd told him. 'The Chrysler will be able to find Adelaide on its own with all the trips you'll be doing back and forth.'

He'd been driving home late in his work ute after dropping off some of Louise's friends. Ellen had gone crook at their daughter earlier in the day, saying she was demented from sleepovers and feeding people. Ever the mediator, Nick had offered to drive the carless ones home. Without as much as a goodnight, Ellen and Louise went to bed. She remembered waking with a start, not having meant to doze off. Her book hit the floor with a thump. She checked her mobile phone. Three hours had gone by and there were no messages. When she rang Nick, there was no response. She woke Louise and, as calmly as possible, asked her to ring her friends. They'd been delivered safely home.

'Stay here in case he rings,' she told her. 'I'll get Tyson to drive me into town. Dad might be broken down. Knowing him, he's trying to fix it himself.' She remembered kissing Louise's soft hair.

Tyson came to the door in his boxers, shoving his arms through an old T-shirt. Ellen noticed his toned triceps and chastised herself for thinking about such a thing at a time like this.

'That you, Mrs C?'

'Tyson, can you drive me into town? I think Nick must have broken down. I can't get him on his mobile.' Then to quell the rising panic in her voice, she added, 'Mustn't be charged.'

Tyson didn't hesitate. He slipped on the sandals he wore in all weathers and jumped in his battered old Holden. They sped down the dirt track that led to the road, but Tyson braked suddenly when they rounded the first corner. The ute was crashed against a sturdy mallee tree, Nick slumped over the wheel. His head had gone through the windscreen. There was blood, glass, and bits of ute spread out over the road. Ellen let out a primal scream.

'No, no . . .' She bolted from Tyson's car, pulled open the driver's door and began clutching at Nick's lifeless body.

'Do something, Tyson,' she pleaded.

Tyson was rooted to the spot, a metre from her. She curved her arms about Nick's body, wanting desperately to give him life.

'Hit a roo, Mrs C.'

She looked around and saw Tyson point to a shape in the darkness. It was a kangaroo, as dead as she knew Nick was.

—

The police car and ambulance roared up Ocean Road, drowning out the incongruous night sounds of crickets and possums scratching in the undergrowth. Ellen remembered wanting it all to be a terrible nightmare and to wake up beside a handsome sleeping Nick, his olive skin unbruised, his curls unbloodied. She'd even felt a flash of sympathy for the paramedic who'd confirmed him dead, but the overriding thought was how to tell Louise. God knows what she'd have done if she hadn't had Tyson by her side. He'd been the one to call triple zero, he'd answered the police officers' and paramedics' questions and when they were assured there was nothing more to be done, Tyson had taken her home.

With hands shaking, she'd turned the handle on Louise's bedroom door and paused before padding across the carpet, wishing she could let her sleep as she'd done countless times when she'd gone in to check her as a child. Dropping to her knees beside the bed, she'd touched Louise's shoulder hesitantly. Louise stirred and, opening her sleepy eyes, she looked at Ellen.

'Is Dad okay?'

Tyson had been there for them when the wailing and screaming were over, and only sobbing was left. When he finally went back to his own house, the women climbed into Ellen's bed, and held each other, eventually dropping off to the mournful sound of their neighbour's didgeridoo.

Chapter Six

Gerry turned off the highway and followed the uphill curve of Ocean Road. Vibrant yellow fields of canola lined both sides, punctuated by clumps of a purple flower he didn't recognise. He wanted to take a picture, but not as much as he wanted to see Ellen again. He put his foot down. He could get a photo later. In his mind, he framed the shot, Ellen in the foreground, her slender body leaning against a fence post, arms hanging loosely at her sides, like someone at ease with themselves, yet unaware of their beauty. Her light hair would billow gently in the breeze, like yesterday when she walked toward him at the post office. She had the same enigmatic smile that had always unnerved him. Seeing her again after all these years was like meeting an identical twin, so much the same but somehow distinctly different.

Ellen was sitting on the veranda when he pulled into the driveway. She stood up, gave Paddy a scratch behind the ear and walked toward the car. She'd slung a backpack over one shoulder and gathered her freshly washed fleece jacket into the crook of her arm.

'I made us some morning tea,' she said, setting the backpack on the floor of the jeep beside the olive loafers that matched her trousers.

'Looking very safari,' said Gerry as he put the car into drive and turned it round.

She registered the tone that had driven her mad when they were younger – a mixture of mockery and admiration. She didn't respond, but imagined he could feel the heat radiating from the broad grin spreading to her blushing cheeks.

'That dog of yours okay?'

'What do you mean?'

'Oh, he just seemed less interested in eating me today.'

It was true. Instead of the angry reception he'd given Gerry yesterday, today he'd just lain at her side looking disinterested. She didn't need reminding that he was getting old. She shook her head and smiled, determined to keep this light. 'Probably knows you're harmless.'

'Okay if we stop for a photo?' Gerry was already pulling in at the viewing point.

'Sure.' She got out of the car, a little surprised to be stopping so soon. She'd rather have headed straight to Sleaford to see the whales, but she reminded herself he was a tourist and she should have expected the camera to be pulled out, especially here in such a beautiful part of the world. She wandered over to the fence and looked out over the sloping farmland to where Boston Island rested like a leviathan in the bay. It was indeed a beautiful place, her home of twenty years. There'd been times in the early days, especially in the harsh dry summers, when she'd wondered if she would ever get used to the place. So different from Ireland with that reliable rain people made a pastime of complaining about. But good people, like anywhere, made them feel welcome and helped weave them in to the fabric of the community. She couldn't imagine living anywhere else.

'Can you just turn around there, Ellen?'

She turned, half dreaming, and saw Gerry aiming the camera at her. Too late to protest, she smiled at him and let herself be immortalised among his holiday mementoes.

'Perfect,' he said, looking pleased at the camera.

'Yes, it is a perfect spot, isn't it.' She was back in the car before he could say anything else.

Port Lincoln was quiet as they drove through town. She wasn't up to doing the whole tour guide bit, so apart from giving directions at turn-offs, they sat in companionable silence for the thirty or so kilometre trip. Driving along Proper Bay Road that skirted the coastline, she could see Gerry was taking it all in: the racecourse, the fish farms, the clutch of houses at Tulka before the turn-off to the national park. She quietly marvelled again at how lucky they were to live in a place with national parks on their doorstep, where dense bush and open plains merged with small coves and endless lengths of white beaches, some calm and inviting, others forbidding with surf crashing over hazardous reefs.

'Some byways you've got here,' said Gerry as they hurtled along the unsealed stretch of road to Sleaford. 'Hope the hire car crowd don't mind me bringing this back covered in desert dust.'

'It's hardly desert, ya eejit,' said Ellen, letting her guard down for the first time since he'd arrived. She saw the twinkle in his eye. They drove on toward the ocean, wheels grinding over potholes, bush spreading out on either side.

'Holy mackerel, you weren't joking about whales.'

Gerry was almost out of the car before he'd turned off the engine. She gathered up her backpack, pulled on her fleece and watched him stride toward the cliff edge, his unzipped jacket flapping against a crisp striped shirt. His hair looked almost fluffy in the wind. She had an urge to touch it.

'This is amazing!' He pulled the camera out of his pocket and focused on a huge southern right whale swimming slowly through the waves no more than twenty metres from the foot of the cliff.

'There's another one . . . with a calf.'

She pointed to a female drifting just under the surface with what looked like a giant jelly milk bottle attached to her belly. Gerry was enthralled. He'd been quiet this morning but now he was positively speechless, his camera making more noise than himself. This had been an annual event with her little family. Each winter the tourist office reported sightings, and tourists and locals alike would arrive to admire the awesome animals coming from the Southern Ocean, year after year, to give birth in the warmer waters of the Great Australian Bight. It felt surreal to be standing here with Gerry Clancy, sharing this special place with its wind-sculpted sand dunes, whales nursing their young, and surf crashing against the yellow limestone bluff winding its way west along the coast.

'They must have known you were coming,' she told him as a pod of about eight moved closer to shore, spray spurting from blow holes and dark flukes rising out of the water and disappearing again in what looked like a rehearsal for a fabulous aquatic performance. Despite the animals' amazing beauty, her eyes were drawn to the treacherous waves crashing tens of metres below, reminding her of how far out of her comfort zone she'd pushed herself. But she couldn't dwell on that now. She needed to keep it together.

'We can sit back and enjoy the show if you like.' She sat down on a rocky ledge a little way back from the edge and began to unpack the flask and cups.

Gerry could hardly take his eyes off the scene and stumbled as he came to sit beside her.

'Sorry,' he said, reaching for her shoulder to steady himself. The strong grip of his hand surprised her as she grabbed for his elbow to help him.

'Careful how you go there, Gerryo.'

'Those whales have me mesmerised,' he said, his face flushed as much with embarrassment as wind chill. She distracted herself with morning tea, taking a couple of scones from a plastic box and cutting them in half on the lid.

Gerry settled beside her on the ledge. She handed him a serviette.

'Cream and jam?'

'Oh, yes please.'

They sat in silence as she took two small sealed pots from the bag and spread a generous dollop of whipped cream onto each scone half, followed by a teaspoon of homemade kiwi jam. Out of the corner of her eye she saw the curious frown across Gerry's forehead.

'Haven't you ever had kiwi jam?'

'Kiwi jam? For a minute there I thought it might be frog spawn.'

'Cheek!' She nudged his arm. He shook his head and took a bite.

'Mm ... If I'd known about this, I could have done a sideline and the bakery might still be afloat.' He licked the cream off his top lip and devoured the rest. 'Any more where that came from?'

'High praise coming from a pro.' She handed him the box and let him help himself, relieved that her efforts at home baking had passed the test she'd been dreading since six that morning when excitement and apprehension had driven her to the kitchen in a frenzy. She didn't need to tell him the scones were from a Country Women's Association packet mix, and that the jam had been given to her months ago by a colleague who'd come to ask when she would return to work. There was a time when she'd been known for her culinary skills, but these days it was enough to manage the basics.

She filled two camping mugs from the coffee thermos. Scrabbling around in the bag, she realised she'd forgotten to pack sugar.

'Just milk okay? I forgot the sugar.'

'Don't take the stuff,' said Gerry. 'Sure, aren't I sweet enough?'

Ellen wanted to tell him he was very sweet and hadn't lost an ounce of his charm, but that might take them back to a time she'd kept locked away in the treasure trove of her memory. She thought to broach the subject of the letters, but he was captivated by the scene. They packed up and headed along the cliffs, Gerry getting plenty of shots of the spectacular scenery. When they eventually got back to the car, she longed for the comfort of her four walls and asked him to drive her home.

It intrigued Gerry that Ellen didn't seem to work or have commitments, but there was a barrier between them that he daren't cross for fear of upsetting the balance of a relationship he was beginning to renew. Just when he thought she was how he remembered her, she seemed to freeze him out, renege on the warm welcome he'd hoped to receive and he'd perhaps naively expected her to give. Her brother Aidan had told him about the accident. He could only imagine what it was like to lose someone so tragically. His own divorce had come with its particular trauma, but what Ellen had gone through was so much worse.

As they drove back towards town, the mystery of what she must be going through nagged at him. There were so many questions he wanted to ask; like why had his last letter been sitting on her veranda only two days ago? *God, she's beautiful*, he thought, wanting to reach out to her right then, but there was something untouchable about her.

'I need to fill up at Tracey's place,' he told her as they neared the roadhouse.

Ellen left him to put petrol in the jeep and wandered inside. A young couple sat in the dining area, transfixed by the antics of their toddler sitting in a high chair. Country music hummed in the background and the warm smell of pies and pasties wafted from the counter cabinets. There was an ease to walking in, and although she told herself it was because Tracey and Pete were there, she knew it had a lot to do with Gerry too.

'G'day, matey,' said Pete. He'd always made her feel like she was about twelve when he said that. 'Tracey, love, Ellen's here,' he called over his shoulder toward the kitchen.

'I want to pay for that petrol when it comes up, Pete. Just let me grab a few things.' She went around the small shop, gathering what she needed, and landed her basket on the counter as Gerry walked in the door.

'I'm getting this,' she said, putting up her hand to stop any protest.

'Any chance of an ice cream?'

'You cheeky thing! You're supposed to have a standing-up argument with me, insisting that you pay.'

'Ah, Pete, what are we to do?' said Gerry. 'One minute the women want to modernise ya, the next they want all that chivalry stuff.'

'It's not easy, mate,' said Pete. 'Over twenty years of marriage and my wife still remains a mystery to me.'

'I'll tell her that,' laughed Ellen.

'G'day folks. What did I miss?'

Tracey came in wearing an apron over a bright printed top and cropped jeans. Despite the busy physical work, she was adorned with bangles and a heavy beaded necklace, her thick head of curls unruly as usual. Ellen couldn't help but smile.

'So what have you young ones been up to?' Tracey asked.

'Ellen's had me out whale watching at ... is it Sleaford Bay?' said Gerry.

'Did you see some?' asked Pete.

'There must have been eight or ten of them,' said Gerry. 'A baby as well. It was awesome.'

'You should take some of that fish we caught yesterday and cook yourselves a nice tea,' said Pete.

Ellen didn't want to sound ungrateful, but the thought of making dinner for Gerry daunted her. Before she could say anything, Tracey had her by the arm and was leading her out to the back area.

'I put some in the fridge. They're gutted and ready to go.'

'Tracey, I'm not sure if I can—'

Tracey interrupted her. 'I don't know if it's the fresh air at Sleaford or the effect of our friend here, but you haven't looked this good since . . . well, since last year.' Her eyes bored into Ellen's now. 'Whatever it is, you have to grab it and hold on.'

Ellen wasn't sure what it was either, but she had to admit she did feel a lot better than she had in a long time. The only thing she was certain of right now was that Tracey was a stalwart. She hugged her tight. 'You're the best, Trace.'

'Now, about those nannygai . . .' Tracey put the back of her hand to her eye to stem the flow of mascara before finding a bag for the fish.

A change of subject was needed if the pair of them weren't to dissolve in tears in front of Gerry.

'Louise is coming home for the weekend,' said Ellen, backing away slightly at the smell as Tracey transferred the fish from a plastic container.

'I heard. Jennifer had a text from her.'

'How's the romance going?' The intricacies of their daughters' lives were a regular topic of conversation. Ellen knew Tracey wasn't happy about Jennifer's decision to defer her university place and take a gap year with the ulterior motive of spending time with a boyfriend who had no aspirations to move to the city.

'If the time she spends at home is anything to go by, I'm sure the relationship is going fine. We hardly see her.' Tracey knotted the bag tightly.

'It must be love.'

'What about Louise? Any romance there?'

'Not that I know of, but I don't think she'd tell me if there was. She'd have told Nick.'

Tracey linked Ellen's arm as they returned to the shop. 'As long as she comes home, that's what matters.'

'Maybe catch you for a pint if you get a chance, Pete,' Gerry was saying.

'Nice one. I'll give you a call.'

'Have a good night,' said Tracey.

Ellen hoped the common Aussie expression didn't give Gerry the wrong idea.

Chapter Seven

Gerry hesitated at the doorway before following Ellen into the house. From the outside it looked homely. The duck pond stone and bullnose veranda of the original part was 1900s, according to Ellen, but he especially liked the two-storey extension they'd added in keeping with the traditional style and materials. A small balcony overlooked the bay and surrounding farmland. He imagined what it must be like waking up to that view, leaning on the wooden rails, looking out to sea.

In the kitchen he took in the bright lemony tones and generous table with six straight-backed chairs and thought the house must be lonely for her now.

'Go and make yourself at home,' she told him, gesturing in the direction of the living room. 'I'll get us a cuppa when I'm done.'

The living room smelled of Ellen, but its contents served only to remind him of how much he didn't know about her, all the years they'd spent apart, and the different paths they'd chosen. Photographs, dotted about on walls and furniture, showed him the unfamiliar characters of her story. The story of a child growing up told through a series of school portraits and happy family shots. A tall good-looking man with a broad smile held a newborn baby in one picture and showed off a huge tuna in another. There was a striking photo of Ellen poring over a book, soft lighting falling on the contours of her face. He could almost see Nick taking the shot and realised, not without a twinge of jealousy, that she'd been truly loved. Above the fireplace, the happy couple stood beside a vintage car Gerry thought might be a Chrysler. He thought of his own photos, and the home he'd shared with Jessica and the children. How quickly the house he'd enjoyed, and prided himself in maintaining, had become out of bounds.

For all its size, the room had a cosy feel with feminine touches, like the hand-knitted throw folded at one end of the sofa, and the occasional tables with small stained-glass lampshades. Gerry browsed the bookcases that lined one wall, taking in the neatly arranged sections, from massive encyclopaedias to well-worn children's books. The cookery collection impressed him. There were Greek cookbooks, in Greek of course, together with volumes by all the popular TV chefs. He could hardly believe his eyes when he saw a signed copy of a book from the Cafe Paradiso in Cork. That was an old haunt where he and Ellen would sometimes go with friends for a bit of posh nosh.

'How'd you come by this,' he asked, taking the book to the kitchen.

Ellen closed the fridge door and smiled as she turned to look. 'Aidan sent it one Christmas. He's been very good to us over the years. Always remembers our birthdays.'

Gerry sometimes ran in to Ellen's brother, usually in a pub somewhere. He'd always revelled in hearing news of her from Aidan. It only dawned on him now how much they must miss each other.

'He's been out a couple of times, hasn't he?'

'Yeah, when Louise was about eight, and then for the funeral.' She turned away again and focused on the contents of a cupboard as she continued talking. 'That meant a lot to me, having someone from my family here.'

'What about your family in Sydney?'

'That's a long story.'

He wondered if it was a story she wanted to share with him.

'I'm on holiday, remember? I've got all the time in the world.'

For a moment, he thought she might open up to him, but she stood straight and lobbed a bag of potatoes into his arms.

'If you're staying for dinner, you'd better make yourself useful.' She was back in control, the barriers firmly in place. 'You can cut the chips. I like mine chunky.'

'Yes, ma'am,' said Gerry. He mightn't be getting any stories just now, but he was staying for dinner, and he had a cunning plan that included a couple of bottles of chardonnay Pete had insisted he take at the roadhouse.

Ellen set about filleting the fish and making a batter. She still couldn't quite believe Gerry Clancy was standing at her kitchen sink peeling spuds, shirt sleeves rolled up around his elbows, all laidback in his jeans and socks. She suppressed a wave of anxiety. *This is an old friend*, she reminded herself. *You could do with the company. Relax.*

'Thirsty work, this.' Gerry gathered the potato peelings in plate-like hands and deftly deposited them in the bin.

'I was supposed to be making you coffee. Sorry.'

'I fancy a glass of that chardonnay actually. Will you join me?'

Ellen couldn't remember the last time she'd had a social drink. There'd been times, months ago, when she'd overdone it on the bottle of ouzo Nick kept for special occasions. She'd hated the loss of control. But a glass of wine wouldn't hurt.

'Haven't used these in a while,' she said, wiping the dust off a couple of generous wineglasses. 'It's no fun drinking on your own.'

Gerry fetched one of the bottles from the fridge. 'Sounds like the voice of experience.' He took the glasses from her hands and poured them both a drink.

'We should make a toast,' said Ellen, letting his comment go and hoping not to betray her nervousness.

'To old friends,' said Gerry, raising his glass and moving closer to her.

'To old friends.' She sipped her drink without looking at him, afraid to confront the possibility in his eyes. She glanced round at the food preparations. 'Let's get this show on the road.'

She filled a saucepan with oil and put it on to heat, then mixed egg and breadcrumbs in a large bowl and set Gerry to work dipping the fish in the batter.

'If my old man could see us now,' he said.

'He'd be cracking the whip, that's for sure. He drove you boys pretty hard if I remember.'

'He certainly taught us to earn our money,' said Gerry. 'It was sad to see the business go, but we'd grafted in that place since our teens. Up at all hours when everyone else was in the Land of Nod. No let-up at weekends either once shops started opening on a Sunday. Even the day I got married, Dad was in there at two in the morning, firing up ovens and writing out instructions for the staff. If he'd had a mobile phone, he'd have been on to them every five minutes to make sure they were on top of it.'

'I really liked your dad,' said Ellen.

'And he liked you. Told me I missed my chance when you moved away.' She blushed, but Gerry didn't turn from his task. 'Said to make sure to say he was asking for you, by the way.'

She put the chips in the pan. 'Seems like only yesterday I worked with you all.'

'It was a summer to remember all right.'

When she glanced over, his face was serious as he carefully coated the last fish fillet with the same care he might have taken to ice a wedding cake.

It had been Ellen's mother who'd secured her the job at Clancy's Bakery the summer she'd finished her third year at university. Maureen O'Shea had been a regular customer, not to mention a pillar of society as the housekeeper in the parish presbytery. When Mr Clancy told her that one of his office staff was due to have a baby and he needed someone reliable to cover for the summer, Mrs O'Shea – never backwards in coming forwards – suggested her daughter as the perfect candidate for the job. Mr Clancy agreed without requiring as much as a reference. There was no need as his own Gerry had been in the same grade in high school as Ellen, and he knew exactly who she was.

Her mother had been adamant about Ellen saving up her own money for Australia, but it was no hardship; she'd loved working at Clancy's. Coming into work in the mornings was like walking into food heaven, with the smell of fresh bread and cream cakes enveloping her from the minute she opened the front door. Most of her time was spent in a small office off to one side of the main shop counter. In there, with the door open, she sometimes felt more like she was in her grandmother's house in West Cork than at work.

The big old farmhouse in the lush countryside could have been a bakery for all the cooking and baking that went on to feed the visiting relatives and the steady stream of callers that sat around smoking and having cups of tea and conversations that lasted for hours, always slipping the children a few coins and marvelling at how much they'd grown since their visit the previous summer. The house was a zoo compared to the quiet and strict home her mother presided over in Cork, and although coming back to the city after the summer holidays brought with it some sense of relief, Ellen always looked forward to going again by the time the next year came around.

Gerry had gone straight into the family business after leaving school. He worked in the cavernous kitchen at the back of the building, but that didn't stop him making a habit of wandering into the office on the pretence of clarifying an order. He'd say his father couldn't understand Ellen's writing, or that a particular customer didn't normally order a dozen soda bread and could she check the order and get back to him. Then he'd stick his head round the door at the end of his shift and say something like, 'Are you sure you'll cope under that mountain of work?', or 'I know it'll be hard for you, but try to survive without me.'

Her cheeks burned when he appeared at the door, or worse still, when she was trying to concentrate on a phone call to a customer or supplier and suddenly realised he'd been standing there for ages watching her, leaning against the doorframe, hands in pockets, his long white apron tied at the middle and neat hat cocked like a navy cadet's.

'I'll have to have a word with your father,' she'd tell him. But there was never any need to go to Gerry Clancy Senior as his voice would bellow out over the entire bakery, shop front and all.

'Gerry, I'm not paying you to fraternise with the summer staff. Get your behind in here and bake, or it isn't wages you'll be getting.' Yes, Mr Clancy could be a tough taskmaster, but Ellen knew he had a soft spot for her when he'd appear behind Gerry, voice booming, and give a quick wink meant only for her benefit.

She remembered the day Gerry asked her out. They'd fancied each other in secondary school, but had never gotten further than a few dates. This time there were none of the scripted lines he'd used when they were younger. He just appeared at the door of the office one day at the end of her shift, all changed from his work gear into a new pair of 501s and a leather jacket. 'Hungry?' he said. He'd already booked a table at a favourite Chinese restaurant. She had to admire his courage. If she'd said no, he'd have been mortified having to cancel. As they waited for their meal, she could tell he was nervous. There was less of the flippant banter, like he was more intent on impressing her than before. She could still feel the warmth of his hand as they'd crossed Patrick's Bridge that night. It was to be the beginning of the most romantic summer of her life.

'You want to go and put some music on while I fry up these fish?' she asked.

'Any preferences?' he asked, washing his hands and pulling a tea towel off the oven door to dry them.

'Surprise me.'

Minutes later, her frown of concentration disappeared as she turned to look at him and burst out laughing. With

Michael Jackson playing in the background, Gerry was trying to moonwalk backwards, sending a chair crashing into the one beside it.

'Keep watching the YouTube videos,' she told him as she flipped the fish in the pan.

'I was a demon on the dance floor in my day, as you should know,' he said, picking up the chair.

'It's your table-laying skills I want to see, not your terrible MJ impersonation. Cutlery's in the drawer over there.'

'God be with the days when we used our fingers to eat fish and chips.'

Ellen lifted the basket from the oil and tossed the chips into a ceramic bowl lined with kitchen paper.

'You'd even deny me the grease off my chips,' he said as he watched the paper absorb the hot oil.

'Grab a couple of plates from that cupboard and stop whingeing. It's bad enough giving you fish and chips without giving you a heart attack into the bargain. After you've come all this way, I should have prepared haute cuisine.'

She looked at him to check he understood the reference.

'Nothing wrong with a few *pommes frites*,' he said, raising an eyebrow. 'I've had a couple of holidays in France, you know, not to mention having seen every episode of *'Allo 'Allo!*.

Ellen felt a little ashamed. Education had always been a sticking point between them. She'd been a swot in secondary school, always getting good grades. Gerry was an able enough student, but he'd been in a hurry to join 'the real world' as he called it. He used to tease her about being brainy and boast about never having to open a book once the Leaving Certificate was behind him. In hindsight, she'd taken it all too seriously. When she got her wish and went on to university, she still lived at home and the school gang kept in touch, but she was torn between them and her new friends.

There were always sparks when she and Gerry met on one of the gang's nights out. Friends would see them on the dance floor and the rumour would no sooner have spread that they were an item again, than they'd be at loggerheads, usually over some flippant comment Gerry made about her college friends and their brains. She called the tingling sensation she got whenever they met the 'five-minute fling'. Her heart would pound, her cheeks catch fire, but five minutes into the conversation and she was over him. Until that last summer when she decided to give him a chance. That summer in Clancy's Bakery, when Ellen realised her school boyfriend had turned into a hardworking, down-to-earth young man. But by then her one-way ticket to Australia was booked and paid for, her aunt in Sydney had agreed to support her, and she was as good as on the plane. Besides, if she'd had any second thoughts about taking up her scholarship, he'd quashed them the night before she left.

—

'We should be having salad with this,' Ellen fussed.

'Would you stop it? 'Tis far from salad we were reared.' Gerry reached behind her to replace the tea towel on the oven door. He'd expected her to move, but she stood there rooted to the spot.

'I'm afraid I've let the veggie patch go to rack and ruin.'

Gerry thought he saw her eyes glisten. *Keep it light, Gerryo.* 'Does ketchup count?'

Ellen blinked as if coming out of a trance. 'You haven't changed a bit, have you?'

She grabbed the ketchup from the fridge and set it on the table. Gerry dished the food onto two large dinner plates and set them down at one corner of the table. He held out a chair for her and was rewarded with a smile.

'Ho– ho– hot. God, that fish is on fire,' he said after his first mouthful.

Ellen jumped up to get him a glass of water, but he took a gulp of his wine and quickly recovered. 'This is great,' he said, getting stuck into his meal.

'There's plenty more when you've got through that lot,' she told him. 'I can't have you going home to Cork and telling them I nearly starved you.'

'Oh there's no fear of that. I'm a growing boy, as Harry Flynn would say. Remember him and the doorsteps for sandwiches he used to bring to school?'

<hr/>

Gerry had her in stitches with memories from their schooldays. People she'd long forgotten appeared in her mind as clear as though she were back in the classroom at Madden's Secondary.

'Didn't your aunt teach History?'

'Auntie Betty, aunt in-law really, Mrs Keane to you.'

'She hated me.'

'She did not,' Ellen laughed, but now she remembered, Gerry had done a fair bit of messing in History.

If it hadn't been for Auntie Betty, she might never have ended up in Australia. Her mother had never had a kind word to say for the woman who'd scuppered Granny Keane's plans for her youngest son to enter the priesthood. Uncle Frank and Auntie Betty had inspired her, even if her mother had seen it as 'giving her notions'. Apart from her brother, Auntie Betty had been the only relative to visit when Louise was small.

'I swear that woman had it in for me,' Gerry was saying. 'She used to make me do extra History homework in detention.'

'I'm sure she was only trying to help. If you'd done the work to start with, you wouldn't have been in detention.'

'Do you remember when she got pissed at the grads?'

That was it. He was off on a roll about the night of their graduation ball, recalling funny incidents as if it were yesterday. She pushed her plate away, unable to take another morsel for the laughing.

'Those were the days,' said Gerry.

She watched as he cleared the dishes, then filled the sink with warm water and squirted in washing-up liquid. She'd never let Nick do the dishes. He'd worked so hard to build his business, Ellen didn't think it fair to deny Louise a moment of her dad's precious time at home. She drank her wine now and rested an elbow on the back of her chair, not sure if it was the alcohol or Gerry's easiness that made her revel in the moment.

'Holy God,' said Gerry, looking out the window. 'Whose is the spotty horse?'

'Gerry, you're such a city boy. That is an Appaloosa, and it belongs to Louise.'

'Do you ride it yourself?' he asked.

'I haven't ridden in a long time.' There were a lot of things she hadn't done in a long time, none of which she wished to share with Gerry. 'Louise is the rider of the family.' The reference to her diminished family almost derailed her, but she deflected attention to Gerry's children. 'Yours were into piano and Gaelic football, weren't they?'

Gerry finished the dishes and leaned against the workbench.

'Stephanie's still at the music. Herself and a few school friends even formed a band.'

'How cool! You and Jessica must be so proud.'

'Well "we" were, but now that there's no "we" . . .' he shrugged. 'Kieran's lucky he got out of it. He's his own man. I'm not so sure about Steph. She's all tough on the outside, but there's a softer side to her she doesn't let you see very often.'

As much as she felt for him, Ellen didn't want him to be maudlin.

'Do you have any pictures?'

He pulled his phone from his jeans pocket and found one to show her. The leggy teenager stood posing for the camera, her long dark hair framing a heavily made-up face that made her look older than her sixteen years. Her slender arms clutched a collection of shopping bags.

'She's a beautiful girl,' said Ellen. She was about to say 'so like her mother', but stopped short of paying Jessica Sheehy the compliment. 'Likes her shopping by the looks,' she laughed, but Gerry gave a defeated sigh.

'Sometimes I think, in her eyes, I'm only as good as my bank balance.' He shook his head.

'I'm sure you mean a lot more to her than that.'

Ellen had never met Gerry's children, but Jessica Sheehy had been a year below them in school. She was a beautiful-looking girl and came from a wealthy family, but Ellen had never felt she had much in common with her. When news of their marriage had reached Australia, she'd been shocked. But then she'd had no right to be critical under the circumstances.

They took their wineglasses and moved into the lounge room where Gerry was drawn to the photographs again. 'Nice wheels. Was it Nick's car?'

'Yes. I've still got it. Take a look if you like. It's in the shed at the side of the house.' She set down her glass. 'I'll just give Louise a quick ring and follow you out.'

Chapter Eight

Louise and Maxine were stalking Toby Scott's Facebook page where *Thanks for a great night* had been posted by a skinny second-year from the Arts faculty. Their heated speculation as to what exactly the girl meant was interrupted by Louise's Beatles ringtone.

'Hi Mum, I was just about to phone you,' she lied, not wanting her mother to think she'd forgotten.

'Good timing,' said Ellen. 'All set to fly home tomorrow?'

'Yes, can't wait. Just need to get an assignment in first thing, then a few cruisy classes, and I'm off for the weekend.'

'Was work okay about giving you time off?'

'Yeah, no dramas there.'

Louise hadn't had to take a part-time job when she went to university, but her father had said it would give her great life experience. 'As long as it doesn't get in the way of your studies,' he'd cautioned. When he died, her mother assured her that there was enough money to get her through, but

Louise had made up her mind. Once she'd begun to find her way around campus and had worked out her timetable, she took the bus to Glenelg and asked her father's friend to give her a job in his Greek restaurant. All the staff were, in one way or another, related. Stavros and his wife, Kristina, treated her like family too. Although she suspected some of what sounded like heated arguments in the kitchen were the result of her mixing up orders or terrible pronunciation of food names, they showed her nothing but patience and soon she had their menu down pat, even if her Greek was a work in progress.

'Will I book a taxi for you?' her mother asked.

'Jennifer's offered to come get me.'

It was a given that her mother wouldn't be driving. She could offer to take her for a practice again this weekend as she had on every visit since her dad's death, but it probably wouldn't do any good. There was an excuse every time; she was too tired, the roads were wet, holiday traffic, she'd drive next time. Despite masses of encouragement and attempts at persuasion, her mother could never muster the strength to just do it. No, she'd have to do the driving herself and help with shopping for enough tinned and frozen food to last her mother until the next visit.

She rejoined Maxine who was already well into a round of text messages to friends for eyewitness accounts of what had happened at the Den last night. The cyber smoke signals had reached Toby.

It wasn't what you think, he texted.

What's that? Louise texted back.

She's a friend of a friend. We were just in a group. Had a few drinks.

Spare me, she replied.

By the time she'd finished her assignment and packed her small suitcase, Louise had concluded from the constant stream of cyber messaging that Toby Scott had indeed cheated on her. In her mind, she replayed their conversation from the evening before. Okay, so she'd been a bit off, but she'd told him she'd see him next week. It wasn't exactly grounds for going out and hooking up with the first girl he met. Right now she hated herself. How the heck was she supposed to keep all the balls in the air? Couldn't Toby Scott have kept his hormones in check for once and let her be annoyed or sad or whatever she was. Falling onto her bed, she pulled a pillow around her face and sobbed. Sometimes it seemed impossible to be the girl who'd known exactly where she was going before she'd lost her dad. She wished her plane was leaving tonight.

~

Gerry pulled his hood up against the fresh spring gust and dug his hands in his pockets as he walked toward the shed, feeling somewhat in awe of Ellen's property with its sizeable paddock and views over countryside and sea beyond. He'd considered building a house out of town early on in his marriage, but Jessica, firmly ensconced in suburban bliss, had shot the idea down in flames. It was something he'd thought about again after the divorce and the demise of the bakery, but like his father and brother he'd ploughed his money into the pub instead.

In the twilight he could see a single neighbouring house with a garden resembling a scrap heap. A banger of a car was parked in the overgrown driveway, and there were bits of corrugated iron and plastic remnants scattered about. Who lived in such stark contrast to Ellen's beautiful home? Was it safe for her to be living so far out of town with shady neighbours? He had to concede she'd lived here for years, with a husband who worked away for weeks at a time.

The Chrysler took up one side of the shed. Gerry was no expert but he walked around the car like one would a museum exhibit, admiring its quality and design. The steel wheels with their whitewalls and chrome caps took him to Hollywood. The 50s tailpins and two-tone paintwork charmed him and he imagined Ellen in a figure-hugging fifties outfit, complete with chiffon headscarf and sunglasses, behind the steering wheel. He looked in the driver's window and was checking out the vinyl dashboard and cream leather upholstery when someone grabbed him from behind. Before his body could even react, he was whirled around and pinned to the side of the car.

'What the—' he started, but before he could duck, a large fist connected with his jaw. It came to him that if the punch didn't knock him out, the smell of alcohol might. He managed to push his assailant off and was getting ready to block the next punch when Ellen appeared.

'Jesus, Mary and Holy Saint Joseph, what's going on here?' she shouted in the Cork accent she'd never lost.

'Evening, Mrs C. This whitefella here's about to rob your car.' The big man gave a triumphant wipe of his nose with an already dirty sleeve.

'Tyson, let me introduce you to my old friend from Ireland, Gerry Clancy.' She was standing between them now, hands on her hips. 'Gerry, this is Tyson, my good neighbour.' She sent Tyson a dagger of a look.

'Sorry, Mrs C. I'll be going home directly.' He turned to Gerry and, without looking him in the eye, gave a grunt of what sounded like an apology.

'Go home and get some sleep, Tyson,' Ellen told him. 'I'll come and see you tomorrow.'

Gerry registered the pain creeping across his jaw.

'Let's get some ice on that before it swells up.' Ellen took his arm and led him back to the house.

—

'So you've met my neighbour,' said Ellen with a smirk as she joined Gerry on the sofa and positioned the icepack against his face.

'Ah, that's sore.' He groaned but didn't pull away, breathing in the sweet scent of her, maybe soap or a perfume she'd applied before she'd gone to the shed to join him. He hoped the latter.

'Do you feel safe living beside a guy like that?'

Ellen sat straight and looked him in the eye.

'You couldn't meet a better person than Tyson. He was one of the first blokes Nick worked with when we moved from Sydney and Nick took a job as a deckhand. Great worker. As Nick gradually built up his fish-farming business, Tyson was there with him every step of the way.'

He put up his hand to hold the icepack and felt Ellen slip hers away.

'What exactly did Nick do?' He could see her struggle with the question as she sat back against the sofa, her fingers finding her wedding ring. Slowly, she filled him in on some of the detail that had been missing from her letters.

'When I met him he was grafting in Sydney, working two jobs, at the fish market and in one of the Greek restaurants. His family were bass and bream fishermen in Santorini. He'd come to Australia for adventure, but fishing was in his blood. The nineties were when they started to farm southern bluefin tuna in South Australia,' she explained. 'He wanted to be part of it so we moved here.'

As she spoke, her body started to relax. It was nice to see her animated and hear her talk, unrestrained for the first time since he'd come here.

'The boats would go out in December and catch the good-sized fish that had been feeding in the Great Australian Bight and bring them back in tow pens. That could go on for months with boats going in and out, sometimes for weeks at a time. They'd bring the fish back to the farm just off the coast here and grow them on to selling size.' She pointed in the direction of the sea. 'Nick started as a deckhand

and worked his way up, buying his own boat and eventually a business. He took on more and more staff. When we bought the block with two houses already on it, Nick offered Tyson the smaller house as a bonus.'

She paused, dropping her chin toward her chest and rubbing her palm with her thumb.

'Tyson's wife and children lived here with him, but when Nick died he was in bits. He was the offsider in the business, I suppose, never the frontman. He could turn his hand to anything practical, but never got involved in the book work. I sometimes wish I could have stepped up . . .' She shook her head. 'The man I sold it to wouldn't keep him on. He got very down and started drinking more than the usual few beers. It was the worst time for Sheryleen to find a new partner. When she took the kids and moved to another town, I think it all got too much for him.'

Gerry listened, the tale a sad one, but the voice as soothing as the cold against his bruised skin. He wanted to reach out to her right then and kiss her deeply.

'Tyson would have done anything for Nick,' she continued. 'I guess he sees it as his duty to protect me now that Nick's not here.'

'Someone should tell him he's taking the job a tad too seriously,' said Gerry with a smile that hurt his face. She got up and fetched their wineglasses.

'Would you prefer something stronger?' she asked as she set them on the coffee table.

'What did you have in mind?'

'Well there's a drop of ouzo in the cupboard, or a whiskey?'

'I'll be in no state to drive if I overdo it. Maybe—' But before he could suggest they leave it to another time, Ellen interrupted.

'I can't let you stay in a motel after the shock you've had. There's plenty of room.'

Gerry didn't want to impose, but despite being nearly pulverised by the next-door neighbour, he was eager to prolong this time with Ellen, to sustain whatever they were sharing, like a campfire you might try building in a late Irish summer, despite a stiff breeze and the threat of autumnal rain.

'Ah sure, I'll have a whiskey so.'

—

Ellen came back from the kitchen with the wine bottle and a tumbler of the Jameson's her brother had brought with him when he'd come to attend Nick's funeral. 'You might need that for the guests,' Aidan had said, 'or even a drop for yourself on occasion.' Gerry had set the icepack down and was leaning back in the sofa. He took the glass and watched as Ellen sat down with her back against an armrest, knees bent up to her chest, holding her drink in the dip of her body.

'To Aidan,' she said, raising her glass.

'I'll have to tell him we drank to him when I get back,' said Gerry.

They sat in silence for a moment.

'When are you going back exactly?'

'Sure aren't I only after arriving and you're trying to get rid of me.'

She looked at him for a second and then threw her head back and laughed. Nearly twenty years later and she still couldn't be sure when he was being serious.

'No, I promised Kieran I'd spend a few days with him before I fly back,' he told her. 'So I've got another week before I go home. Then it'll be back to the grind. And if you think my father was a slave driver, you should try working for Donal.'

'I thought you all had an equal share, were running it together.' She didn't mean to pry, but she had an overwhelming need to know he was being looked after.

Gerry gave a tut. 'With the divorce and everything, I couldn't put in as big a share. Donal was always the businessman of the family, so my father gave the responsibility of managing the place to him.'

Ellen couldn't say she knew Donal well. He was a few years older than Gerry. Fond of himself, she would have said. Always left the bakery in smart clothes when Gerry and his dad would leave in their overalls. He'd been civil to her, yes, but she always felt he thought he was better than the rest of them.

'And is your dad still working there?'

'Ah not so much now. He's taken up golf, so you're more likely to see him at the nineteenth hole than you are in the Stables.'

He laughed, but Ellen couldn't help thinking Gerry had been a bit hard done by.

'Do you think you'll work there long-term, or will you try your hand at something else?'

'I actually quite like the madness of helping run the place,' said Gerry, 'but Donal gets me down at times. Must be the big brother thing, always thinks he has to be showing me how it's done.' He shook his head and took another sip of his drink before setting his glass on the table. When he sat back, she felt he'd moved a little closer.

'What about you and work?'

She bristled at the direct hit. She hadn't been back to the social work office since the accident. Officially she was on extended compassionate leave, but she knew they wouldn't hold her job forever if she couldn't get behind the wheel of a car. She looked away and took a long sip of her wine, aware of Gerry's eyes on her face.

Work had been a huge part of her life. Three years of university had given her a good grounding in subjects like sociology and philosophy, and she'd wanted to do something practical to help people facing challenges in their everyday lives. Some of her professors in Ireland were encouraging students to go overseas, gain the experience that would guarantee good jobs and salaries on their return home. She'd thought her relations in Sydney were her ticket to that kind of future. No one could have predicted it would be her job in Port Lincoln that would provide the job satisfaction she'd craved. Family services was a tough gig, but the wins made it worthwhile. Seeing children's lives improve and adults strive to better themselves made up for the hard, sometimes harrowing work.

'I haven't driven in some months,' she said quietly.

'Pete told me as much.'

It annoyed her that the men had spoken of her in this way. What other issues had Pete made Gerry party to, issues she only ever discussed with Tracey?

'You're lucky to have such good friends,' said Gerry reading her mind.

'I am.'

It was true. Without them she would have become a recluse after Nick died. They were the inner circle to which she wasn't yet sure if Gerry should be allowed entry. Looking down into her glass, she felt his hand slip around her calf. Her breath caught in her throat. She'd wanted him to touch her from the moment she'd seen him from her living room window.

'Come here.'

He moved closer, gently unfolding her legs and placing them across his lap. He took the glass from her hands and set it down as he leaned in, stroked her hair and tilted her chin towards him. Their lips met with a gentle brushing at first, then passionately with the abandon she'd longed for all day. Her body tingled under her clothes, but she stopped herself. This was a man she'd betrayed. It would be selfish to go further.

'Gerry, there's so much I have to tell you,' she said, applying pressure on his shoulder to slow him down.

'It's okay, Ellen. I'm here for you. I know what happened, what you've been through.'

The wine had made her brave. She wanted to be held, loved, reassured that there was life after loss, the possibility of happiness after grief, but she'd kept her secret too long, and before there could be any comfort, there would have to be honesty.

'We're a long way from the HiAce,' said Gerry.

She smiled, remembering the old van. 'That's what I need to talk to you about.'

⸺

It was Ellen's last day before she left for Australia. She'd been out with a bunch of friends the night before and thought she'd seen the last of Gerry Clancy. They hadn't parted on the best of terms. Even though they'd had a happy couple of months together, there'd been no romantic send-off. Instead he'd sulked all night in the pub, making everyone uncomfortable and spoiling her night. Ellen knew he begrudged her moving away and leaving him behind. She'd resigned herself to spending her last night in Ireland at home with her parents when he'd shown up asking her to go for a drive. Grateful to get away from her mother's constant stream of advice, and the sad expression on her father's face, she went with him. They headed out of town and took a walk on the long stretch of beach at Garretstown.

'Sorry for being such a party pooper last night,' he said. 'I can't believe you're going and this is all coming to an end.'

He'd looked so lonesome.

'You know I have to do this, Gerry,' she told him. 'It's the chance of a lifetime.'

'I'll miss you, kiddo,' he'd said, reaching out an arm and gathering her closer to him as they trudged through the cooling sand.

Afterwards, they made love in the back of the van and he asked her again why she couldn't just stay. It had been such an anticlimax, one minute he was treating her like a goddess and the next asking her to shove aside her dreams, her one chance to get away and experience life on her own terms. No matter what she said, he couldn't see past his own agenda. And if Gerry's words had helped convince her she was doing the right thing, her mother's comments when she caught her sneaking in the back door, hair dishevelled and bra in hand, confirmed that conviction one hundred percent.

'Where were you?' her mother asked, standing arms akimbo in the kitchen and scanning Ellen from head to toe.

She didn't even give Ellen a chance to respond.

'Are you out of your mind doing that carry-on and you going to Australia in the morning?'

Ellen hung her head and took the lecture that followed, like the one she'd heard when she'd come home excited after one of her professors had put her forward for the scholarship. Maureen O'Shea had been underwhelmed. What business did Ellen have going all the way to Australia for one year when she could finish her degree in Cork and get a good job without having to leave home? She still remembered her mother's parting shot that night before being allowed to retreat to her room.

'If you get pregnant down there, don't come crying to me, young lady.'

—

Gerry was sitting up straighter, looking at pains to hear what she would say next. Twenty years later and she still hadn't let him in on the secret that was rightfully his to know. Nick was dead. She didn't have to keep it from him any longer.

'Louise is your daughter.'

He pulled back and looked at her open-mouthed. She'd never seen him speechless.

He pushed her legs out of the way and went to the photo of Louise with Spots.

'Why didn't you tell me?' he asked eventually.

She went to him but didn't dare touch him.

'I'm so sorry, Gerry. I didn't know for sure for a time, but I want you to know Nick was a wonderful father to her.'

'She's mine,' he said softly. He drew a hand through his hair and began to pace, trying to take it all in.

'I'll make us some tea.' She couldn't bear to watch the emotions raging in him, nor could she stand her own guilt at having kept this secret for so long.

Water splashed in the bathroom. When he came into the kitchen, his eyes were red and his cheeks ruddy.

'Why didn't you tell me?' he asked again, a tremor in his voice. 'If I hadn't come to Australia, would you ever have told me?'

She set the mugs of steaming tea on the table and sat down.

'When I saw you at my mother's funeral, I began to regret never having told you.' She paused as he stood with a hand to his good cheek, staring at the floor. 'I tried to put it in that first letter, but . . . Louise doesn't know.'

He pulled out a chair and almost fell into it. 'Jesus, that's a lot of stuff to deal with.' He lifted a hand to decline the tea. 'What was Nick's reaction when you told him?' His voice was stronger now. 'You did tell *him*, didn't you?'

'He came to know eventually,' she began, 'but he loved Lou, adored the ground she walked on.'

'Wait a minute. Go back a step. How soon after leaving Ireland did you . . . did you get together with Nick?'

It was a logical question, but one that made her feel uncomfortable. She took a deep breath. Gerry was here, sitting at her kitchen table. He'd be gone before she knew it. What needed to be said needed to be said now.

'I missed you from the moment I landed,' she began. 'Everything was new and different. Sydney was massive, for a start. To say the whole thing was a culture shock would be an understatement. I'd only met my mother's sister once when I was small. When Mam said Auntie Vera would look after me, I'd thought she'd be as much a buddy as an aunt.'

She smiled at the thought of her own naivety. Over the years she'd often revisited the day she landed in Sydney.

Queuing for what felt like an age to have her suitcase ransacked by immigration. Emerging through the arrivals gate to a sea of strange faces in a range of get-ups – suits, sarongs – and searching for someone she barely remembered. In the end it was Uncle Ronnie who recognised her. He hugged her self-consciously and introduced her to her cousin Jimmy, a boy her own age. When she enquired as to the whereabouts of her aunt, Jimmy told her she was getting the place ready. She misread the burning of his cheeks as proud embarrassment rather than shame. There were no such expressions of emotion from Vera. From the moment Ellen set foot in the door of her new home, it was clear her aunt was the boss and she ran the place like a battleship. Ellen's efforts to compliment her aunt on the immaculate state of the house only made Vera launch into the strict regimen that ensured it stayed that way. Vera was a busy woman with her job as secretary in the local Catholic primary, three children to run around after and a house to keep. Ellen would need to pull her weight. She would be sharing with the girls. Her dirty laundry could be placed in the basket in the upstairs bathroom and it would be laundered on a Friday. Shopping was done on a Thursday and anything she wanted that wasn't on the list by Wednesday teatime would have to be bought out of Ellen's own pocket. They went to mass on a Sunday at 10.30 a.m. She would be expected to attend. If she made any friends, she could see them in town on a Saturday. God knew Vera was house full here with the entourage of her own three. There were train and bus timetables on her bedside table, but if she needed clarification about anything, she could ask Jimmy. It wouldn't be the first time she thanked God for Jimmy.

'The two youngest cousins weren't exactly impressed by my arrival,' she told Gerry, 'but the eldest, Jimmy, was a different character, more like his father. He introduced me to lots of people and took me out to pubs and parties. Auntie Vera objected, but Uncle Ronnie would tell her to let me go out and enjoy myself.' She looked down at the table where Gerry's hands were clasped together. She couldn't meet his eyes. 'I'd been feeling queasy on and off since I'd arrived. Put it down to jet lag of course. The university course started and that kept me busy. It was all new and exciting. On a night out with Jimmy, I met Nick.'

It came back to her again, as it so often did, the first time she saw him. Jimmy had taken her to a Greek night, promising to introduce her to some of his pals from his work at the fish markets. The ouzo was flowing and plates of food just kept coming, and the music – she'd never heard anything so evocative in her life. A trio with a gifted bouzouki player entertained the crowd. As the night went on, people relaxed, clapping in time and getting to their feet. When a circle of men formed on the dance floor, she watched, fascinated as they linked arms at shoulder height and began to dip and sway in time with the music. Even before Jimmy pointed him out, she'd been captivated by Nick's presence. Later, when Jimmy introduced them, she stood gazing up into the beautiful dark eyes that looked back at her as if there were no one else in the room.

Gerry sighed and leaned back in his chair, but painful or not, she had to keep going.

'He told me afterwards that for him it was love at first sight. It wasn't like I forgot about you, but I was lonely.' She shrugged and looked away. 'He asked me out on a date, I accepted and we began seeing a lot of each other.' She wanted to say how handsome and kind Nick was, how on their early dates he insisted on taking a bus and a train to get from his tiny shared flat in Rockdale all the way to her aunt's place in Penrith, but she thought she would spare Gerry such details. 'I guess he was my first friend in Australia, and I was a bit green and wide-eyed. The culture was alien to both of us. Even though I'd never been to Greece, nor he to Ireland, we were taking on this new culture together.'

Nick's difference had been part of his appeal. The good looks, that accent were aspects she never tired of, but they had more in common than most people realised. They'd both flown in the face of family expectations. She remembered Nick telling her how he'd gone against his father's wishes to continue the family business. An only son, he'd been expected to follow the fishing tradition, plying his trade up and down the Aegean as his father and forefathers had done for generations. There'd been honesty about how he'd wanted to break with tradition and find out if there was more to life than following in his father's footsteps, but also a deep respect for his family and not a small amount of regret for the rift this Australian adventure had caused. If anything, their mutual lack of family support had brought them closer.

'Anyway, to spare you the details, Nick and I had been going out for a few weeks when I realised I'd missed a period. He'd been responsible, using protection and everything, but I was worried. I couldn't say a word to my aunt, and the girl cousins were only in their early teens, so I just waited for the next month to come round.'

She sniffed back tears and continued. 'My course was full on and helped keep my mind off things. I saw Nick nearly every day. The other students were nice, but they'd all been together since first year and had established friendships. I suppose I relied on Nick as a friend as well as a lover.'

Gerry grabbed a mug and drank deeply from the tea they'd almost forgotten.

'When I missed the second period, I bought a pregnancy test. I never felt so lonely in all my life, afraid to phone home, afraid to tell Auntie Vera, and afraid to tell Nick. After I'd avoided his calls for a few days, he finally came round and took me to his flat. I couldn't believe his reaction when I told him. He was positively stoked.' She couldn't help smiling at the memory of his manly embrace when he'd scooped her off her feet and spun her round in a kind of happy dance. 'Only then did I realise how much more mature he was than me. He was ready to settle down and have children. For him, me and the baby were a dream come true. He reckoned a condom had burst somewhere along the line without our realising.'

'So you never told him about us?' Gerry asked.

'Well, I wasn't sure, and I'd heard about yourself and Jessica in a letter from Colette Barry. It wasn't like you'd let the grass grow under your own feet.'

He raised an eyebrow.

'Anyway, the shit really hit the fan when I eventually told my aunt. She went ape.'

Nick had come with her when she'd sat her aunt and uncle down, without the cousins, and told them the news. He may as well have been invisible. She still remembered the tirade.

'How could you do this to us?' Vera shouted in indignation. 'How can I tell your mother you've gone and got yourself pregnant, and you only here a wet weekend?'

Uncle Ronnie tried to calm her down, but she wasn't having any of it.

'I'm not having that slut of a niece living under my roof giving our young daughters ideas. The ingratitude,' she bawled. 'I take her in out of the goodness of my heart and this is the thanks.'

Vera took it upon herself to phone her mother and father to break the news. Smash the news more like. By the sound of the silence that resonated between them over the airwaves, it was clear that her mother was dumbstruck. Her dad had the grace to ask to speak to her, but when he tried to say it would all work out fine, her mother found her voice and took the phone off him.

'Vera's right,' she told Ellen. 'You've disgraced us. What'll I tell the priests? Granny Keane will be rolling in her grave.'

Oh, yes, Granny Keane, the family's very own iron lady who, Ellen realised then, had raised both Maureen and Vera to be the pillars of society they fancied themselves. How differently Granny O'Shea had reacted later with a letter of love and reassurance.

After her mother hung up on her, Ellen was bereft. She remembered going up the stairs of that house and clearing the room of her things, imagining her aunt's satisfaction at being rid of her like she'd wiped an ugly stain from her precious carpet. It was obvious she could neither stay nor go home. Nick was gobsmacked. Together, they retreated to his flat where he held her close and wiped her tears long into the night. With his support, she picked up the pieces and got on with her life. Uncle Ronnie came by once a week to make sure she was okay and slip her some dollars. They both knew if Auntie Vera found out, there'd be a divorce. 'Vera will come round,' Uncle Ronnie used to say, but she never did.

Gerry was looking at her now in disbelief.

'I can't believe your mother was so cruel. It was the nineties, for God's sake. Sure, we didn't even go to mass half the time.'

She shook her head. 'I know. It was only families like mine and the Polish workers who came on the back of the Celtic Tiger that kept the churches full. I used to be so jealous of my friends who'd pretend they were going to mass but would be off gallivanting somewhere or smoking behind the churchyard.'

His sad smile confirmed he'd been one of those friends. 'We all thought you never came home because you were having the life of Reilly.' He was shaking his head. 'When anyone asked after you, we were all told you were grand, getting on great.'

Going home was hardly an option given the cold war with her mother. After the initial shock, her mother had gone through a phase of crying, Aidan told her. Eventually she resigned herself to the situation, but it was never the same. Oh yes, Ellen phoned regularly and did her daughterly duty, but it was her father and Aidan she spoke to most. Her mother either kept their conversations brief or claimed to be indisposed. Early on her parents had quizzed her about whether she and Nick would get married. Once Louise arrived they were concerned about baptism. After the birth, they sent photos to both families, and while her brother was delighted to be an uncle, she couldn't say the same for her mother's reaction to being promoted to grandmother. And her dad, well, he had to live with her. Looking back, he must have only been trying to keep the peace. She'd always wished they could have come to Australia to get to know Nick and Louise, see the life they'd built, but her mother had always hated flying. In hindsight, Ellen knew she could have tried harder to make a trip home. Going there for the funeral hadn't been without some shame in not having been the one to forgive.

It was late when Ellen noticed how pale and exhausted Gerry looked. The shock of being assaulted by her overprotective neighbour and finding out he'd fathered a child he'd never met had taken its toll.

'I think you need a good sleep, Gerry.'

She organised a glass of water and some painkillers and showed him to the guest room. Standing in the doorway, she looked into his tired eyes.

'I'm so sorry, Gerry.'

He gave a heavy sigh.

'We'll talk in the morning, Ellen.'

Climbing into her own bed, she felt a strange mix of regret and relief. Secrets were exhausting things to keep.

Chapter Nine

The renewed throbbing in his face woke Gerry and drove him to the bathroom in search of Ellen's painkillers. Her bedroom door was ajar, and he couldn't help standing for a minute and staring in at her. It was hard to believe how close he'd come to her after an absence of so many years. Part of him wanted to pad softly across the carpet and slip under the covers to spoon his body beside hers. Then he thought of Louise and the havoc that might cause. He went to the guest room and pulled on yesterday's clothes. He'd go back to the motel and think things through.

On Tasman Terrace, he did a double-take. Just where he'd walked with Ellen along the foreshore were two racehorses churning up the sand at a gallop. Captivated by the scene, Gerry pulled over and took a seat on a bench just metres away from the frisky thoroughbreds. As he watched the trainers put the horses through their paces, he thought of Donal and took out his mobile.

'G'day, mate,' he said in his best Australian accent.

'G'day me eye,' was Donal's response. ''Tis nearly closing time here and it's been a bloody long day. What's up with you, bro?' Gerry could hear the buzz of the pub in the background.

'Oh, nothing much. Just thought I'd touch base and see if you're coping.'

'Without you, you mean? Enjoying the rest, I'd say. Although a few of the customers are missing you. And the new barmaid I hired keeps asking when you'll be back.'

Hearing Donal's belly laugh made him smile. He didn't know what Bronwyn Fennelly saw in him, but it was flattering to be fancied by someone still young enough to dye their hair out of vanity as opposed to necessity.

'So whereabouts are you?' asked Donal.

'Port Lincoln. Just watching a couple of racehorses exercising on the beach. Thought of you, of course. Had a flutter lately?'

'Nah. Seeing a bit of Ellen O'Shea then, are we?'

'Oh, is that the line breaking up?' Gerry said. 'Better go. Be good.'

The big story of his daughter could wait until they were face to face. He shook his head as he watched the horses. A beautiful bay was being led into the shallows. Although Gerry couldn't hear a word, he could see the trainer communicating with her charge, encouraging him further out into the water until they were both swimming. When they reached the small boats moored a little offshore, the trainer turned the horse around, climbed on and rode it back to land. Then it was away up the beach at a canter as the other horse took its turn in the water. When the bay came to a stop and the trainer dismounted, Gerry watched it circle restlessly round her. The horse eventually halted and looked out to sea, whinnying at the other.

Typical temperamental racehorse. Ready for the off. Donal would have his money on him.

As the horses were loaded onto the truck, Gerry wondered if Louise had ever aspired to be a professional rider. Horses would definitely give her and Donal something to talk about, that was if they ever met. Ellen said she would fly in from Adelaide this evening. How strange it would be to meet one of his own children when she was already grown up. He left the car and walked the short distance to his motel where he would run a deep bath.

Ellen opened her eyes as she heard a car turning in the driveway. *Gerry's leaving.* She pushed off the duvet and went to the landing where she could see the guest room door open and the bedclothes pulled back.

Shite! I've driven him away with the concrete block I landed on him last night.

She found a note in the kitchen. *Had to go and clear my head. Talk later. G.*

'Oh God, I hope he comes back.'

The only small comfort was that Paddy had trusted him enough not to bark. She looked around for the dog. Gerry would have let him out to pee, but it wasn't like him to be wandering. He was like her shadow, especially in the mornings when he would plague her with little yelps and nudges of his cold nose under the covers until she got up and gave him his morning meal. She found the dog bowl in the laundry and poured out his food ration. Still no sign of him.

'Come on, Pads,' she called, stepping out the back door and expecting him to be standing there. Something made her stop. Then she heard it – a low whine coming from under the house.

'What are you doing under there, boy?' She hurried to the corner of the veranda and jumped off the two steps to find the dog lying in the shade, his back legs trembling and eyes half closed.

'Paddy, come out of there, boy.' She tried to coax him with the food bowl. He didn't lift his head.

She had to get him to the vet. On any other day, Tracey would have come in a flash, but she'd said she had a string of appointments with Lars at the hospital and Pete would be on his own at the roadhouse. Tyson would take her to the vet later, but after one of his nightly benders he'd be comatose till noon. Even if she managed to wake him, he'd still be over the limit. And Gerry . . . she ran into the house and found her phone. No answer. She tried again, still nothing. She didn't have time to wait around. Paddy might die if she didn't pull herself together.

She fetched her fleece jacket and the car keys that had hardly left their hook in almost a year. As gently as she could, she eased Paddy out from under the veranda and carried him to the garage.

'You'll be fine, boy. I'll get you there. The vet will know what to do.'

She put him on the back seat of the Chrysler and willed herself to get behind the wheel. She was sure the battery would have been dead if it hadn't been for Tyson turning the engine over for her every now and again. As she turned the key in the ignition, the sound of the engine coming to life sent a nervous ripple through her. She placed her foot on the accelerator and checked over her shoulder, praying to God she'd back straight out without hitting the garage doors. Her foot pressed tentatively at first, then more forcefully until the car lurched into the driveway.

Grateful to be out in the open, she worked the steering wheel to turn and face the road. Braking for long enough to take a few deep breaths and steel herself for the journey, she looked at Paddy. His eyes were fixed on her with a beseeching look.

'Okay, Pads,' she soothed. 'Hang in there.'

At the junction with the highway, she noticed the strangulated feeling in her gut and the bloodless white of her knuckles. As much as she would have liked to abandon the mission, she willed herself to think only of Paddy and of getting him well.

In the surgery, as the vet carried out her examination, Ellen wondered how she'd managed to get them there and how she would drive home again.

'I'm afraid it's bad news,' the vet began. 'How old is Paddy?'

'Thirteen, thirteen and a half . . .'

The woman gave one of those hopeless smiles that told Ellen all she needed to know. She only half heard the vet explain why Paddy had come to the end of his life. '. . . kidney failure . . . common in older dogs . . . you gave him a good life . . .'

She tried to be brave and stifle the tears, but a cold lonesome feeling took over and she started to sob. She wished she could just give Paddy the kiss of life, as she'd heard a farmer had done with his dog, and take him home with her again, as good as new.

'I'll give you a minute so you can say goodbye,' said the vet. 'Then I'll come and give him his injection. He'll hardly feel anything, and it will all be over very quickly.'

She put her hand on Ellen's shoulder. It was of little comfort. Alone with Paddy, she touched his warm coat and bent to kiss his silken face one last time. Nick used to shake his head when he'd see her doing that and threaten not to kiss her until she'd washed her mouth. But he'd loved the dog in his own way, telling him he was good and stealing a pat when he thought no one was looking. Paddy pined for weeks after Nick died, hardly leaving the spot on the veranda where he'd wait for him to come home at the end of the day.

'We love you, Paddy,' she said as she buried her face in the thick ruff of fur at his neck and wept.

—

With shaking fingers, Ellen scrolled through her mobile phone. Driving here was one thing, but driving back with

Paddy in a refuse sack defeated her. She went to Phonebook and pressed G.

At vets on Windsor. It's Paddy. Can't drive home.

The house would be entirely empty without him, her one remaining companion.

—

The Chrysler was parked at an angle with its doors unlocked. In the waiting room, a girl in her twenties was busy mopping up a large puddle of straw-coloured urine. A young staffy sat against its owner's legs looking embarrassed. There was no sign of Ellen.

'Can I help you?' the girl asked him.

Gerry spotted the vet's logo on her polo shirt.

'Yes thanks. I'm looking for a friend. She came in with a blue . . . something or other . . .'

'Take a seat and I'll find out what's happening.' She abandoned the mop and let herself into a consulting room.

'You're from Ireland,' said the woman with the staffy.

'That's right.' Gerry smiled.

'I love Ireland,' she said.

'Where did you get to in Ireland yourself?' he asked.

'Oh I haven't been yet. One day I'll get there. I just love everything Irish. That accent gives me goosebumps.'

He thought of Kieran and hoped the accent would open doors for his brave unassuming son.

The vet nurse came back carrying something heavy in a black disposal bag. Ellen was a few steps behind, head down and hands dug into her pockets. Gerry noticed the bed hair and was sure those trousers she had on were pyjama bottoms.

'Could you open up her car?' the vet nurse asked him. When Ellen looked up, he saw the red-ringed eyes.

'I'll get that for you,' he said to the girl.

Ellen went to the counter to settle the bill. With Paddy's body safely deposited in the boot of the Chrysler, Gerry thanked the nurse and leaned on the car to wait.

'Thanks . . . for coming,' said Ellen as she walked along the path towards him. He thought she looked smaller, thinner than before. He had an urge to hold her, to look after her. His hands, almost involuntarily, left his jeans pockets and reached for her. She let her body drop against him and he held her close until his face hurt again.

'Ow! Wrong side,' he said.

She drew back from him. 'I'm so sorry, Gerry. I forgot . . .'

'No, it's me. I keep forgetting I've had my face rearranged by your neighbour.' The attempt to make her smile was useless. 'So,' he said, 'how would you like me to help?'

She fished in her pockets and thrust her keys at him. 'I don't know how I managed to drive here, but I sure as hell can't make it home.'

Under normal circumstances, Gerry would have been thrilled to get behind the wheel of a fancy car, but today it was more of a mercy mission than a pleasure trip. He let the staff in the clinic know he'd be back later for the jeep, and sat in beside Ellen, feeling very much out of place.

Chapter Ten

'Heading home for the weekend?'

Louise turned to see her friend Mark Waller's dad standing beside her. That was so typical of the small pre-boarding area in Adelaide Airport. Everyone was travelling to Lincoln, and the anonymity to be enjoyed in the city disappeared. But the small talk with Mr Waller made the waiting go quickly. When she later sat down and fastened her safety belt in the Q400, she plugged her earphones in and tried to catch up on some of the sleep she'd been deprived of the night before. Once Maxine had left, Louise had finished her last assignment and gone to bed, her mind racing with doubts about the quality of her work and images of Toby Scott with the skinny second year. Wishing she could go home and offload it all on her dad, she dozed off to the rumble of the engines.

On the tarmac at Port Lincoln, Mr Waller checked if she needed a lift home, but she told him Jennifer was on her way. His kindness and fatherly smile saddened her. She spotted Mark in arrivals and gave him as wide a berth as possible to avoid the father–son reunion. If only her big handsome Greek dad were there to welcome her home with one of his bear hugs.

Outside in the cool breeze, Louise scanned the twilight for Jennifer's blue Barina. She'd just started texting *where are you?* when the Barina came trundling past the roundabout and bumped to a halt. Jennifer leaned over to open the passenger door.

'Soooo sorry I'm late, Lou.'

The sight of her friend evaporated the discomfort Louise had felt on arriving. She jumped in and gave Jennifer as much of a hug as the humungous bag on her lap would allow.

'We're going to Mum's if that's okay.' Jennifer looked apologetic as she swung onto the highway and headed towards town. 'She's making us a special dinner to welcome you home, and to give your mum a hand entertaining that Irish bloke.'

'Do we have to?' Louise gave a mock whimper like a child about to throw a tantrum. 'I know I should be the good daughter and race home to help Mum, but I'm desperate to catch up with *you*.'

'Me too, but I promised Mum we'd go straight there. Haven't exactly been massive on spending time with the olds lately.'

'Things going well with you and Beanie then?'

Jennifer shot her a disapproving look and turned back to watching the road.

'I call him Theo now. He prefers it.'

'It must be serious,' said Louise, stifling a giggle.

Theo Moran had moved to Port Lincoln from Adelaide for the last year of high school. Louise didn't know what Jennifer saw in the boy and his affected habit of wearing a woollen hat in all weathers, which had earned him his nickname. She remembered feeling quite jealous when the two got together at the end of Year 12. As she moped around the house one summer afternoon, her dad had asked why she looked so glum. After she'd fessed up to feeling her best friend had been stolen from her, he had delivered one of his life lessons on the power of love, peppered with anecdotes from his own experience that made her blush. She'd imagined his teenage girlfriends holding him tight around the waist as they zoomed around Santorini on motorbikes. But there was nothing like the glistening that came over his smiling eyes when he talked about falling in love with her mother. How precious those insights had become, even if it meant all the men in her life would be measured against him. Thankfully things had calmed down with Beanie and Jennifer by the end of that summer, but it wasn't the same. Their grand plans to be in uni together were on hold. Jennifer had deferred her place on a journalism degree and announced she was taking a gap year.

'Can we go out later, after your mum's?' Louise asked.

'Felicity's invited a few of the crew to her place, so we can escape there once we've eaten.'

'Sweet.'

She would manage to see her mum, meet the visitor and still squeeze in a night out with her friends. She would have the next two days to help out at home.

⁓

Ellen found herself behind the wheel of the Chrysler again as she drove down Ocean Road towards town. She'd offered to let Gerry drive, but when he'd declined she knew he was handing her another opportunity to keep going. Despite her best efforts, he'd had more of an insight into how much she'd struggled these past months than she'd meant to give him. It was hard to believe Paddy was gone, but he'd had a good life, a long life. It was only selfish to have expected him to live forever. If it hadn't been for Gerry, though, she would have fallen in a heap.

Gerry had driven them straight home, parked the Chrysler in the shed and placed Paddy's body in the chest freezer that was empty now that Ellen lived mostly alone. 'Better to let Louise help bury him,' he'd said. 'They say it helps with the grieving process.'

She'd wanted to snap at him then and ask what exactly he knew about grieving, but she was long enough in the tooth to realise there was more to grief than missing the dead. He'd had his own share of loss with divorce, losing the bakery and his son moving to the other side of the world. Despite how she'd treated him this week, he was still here. Whatever else happened, she was grateful for that.

A long, hot shower soothed her and when she came downstairs, the house was filled with the aroma of fresh toast.

'Have a seat, madame,' said Gerry, setting two sumptuous toasted sandwiches on the table. 'I'm sure there was no time for breakfast this morning . . . judging by the pyjamas.'

Ellen had to smile. 'It's okay, Gerry. They're fairly casual here in the country. Pyjamas are nothing. I remember being horrified at seeing Aussies barefoot in shops, but you get used to it.' She sat down and breathed in the homely smell. 'Aren't you great making toasties . . .'

'Croque monsieur,' he corrected in a terrible French accent. 'There's bechamel sauce an' all on that, girl.'

It was quite possible she could grow accustomed to being waited on by a man who could turn a toasted ham and cheese sandwich into a culinary experience. God, it felt good to have company. As they sat and ate together, she reminded herself that her time with Gerry was precious. He'd be gone soon enough, and she'd be alone again, without even Paddy for consolation.

'How will I break it to Louise?' she thought aloud.

Gerry looked at her seriously. 'About me or Paddy?'

She closed her eyes wishing it would all go away, this trouble.

'When does she get home?'

'Not till tonight, but Jennifer's collecting her. We'll see them at Tracey's.'

'Why don't you leave it until the pair of you get home tonight? You can tell her all that's happened gently, if that's possible, and have a good chat, just the two of you.'

It suddenly dawned on Ellen what she'd left behind in Cork all those years ago. When the flippant, playful exterior was peeled back, this man was solid as a rock.

'And what about you?' she asked. 'Aren't you angry with me?'

He set down his knife and fork and reached for her hand.

'Ellen, I'm a lot of things right now, but angry isn't one of them.' The brows rose above his lovely blue eyes. 'Still shocked maybe, nervous as hell about meeting Louise, but I'm here aren't I?'

He unclasped his hand from hers and took up his cutlery. 'Anyway, this talk won't get you fed. Eat up, and don't be letting my good *cuisine* go to waste.'

It was late morning by the time Ellen felt up to the double task of smoothing the waters with Tyson after the shed incident and letting him know about Paddy. Tyson and Sheryleen's had been a second home for the dog. Their children adored him and could always be relied upon to give him plenty of exercise, chasing him around the paddock. The place was so quiet without them. Less than a year ago she might have found Sheryleen and Robbie singing a children's song in her native Pitjantjatjara as she hung out washing, or sat playing with him on the front porch if the girls were at school. Today the only sound was the drawn-out caw of a crow from one of the ghost gums.

She found Tyson in the backyard tinkering with a rusty generator. 'Howdy,' she said.

Tyson took off a worn baseball cap and set it under his arm.

'It's Paddy, Tyson. They had to put him down.'

'Sorry, Mrs C,' he said, his big lumbering frame shrinking a little at the news.

'I'm keeping him until I get a chance to tell Louise and have a proper burial. I'd like you to join us if that wouldn't offend you.'

'I'd be honoured, Mrs C.'

'Right. Well, I'd better be getting back to my injured guest.'

'Tell him sorry.' He cast his eyes to the ground. 'Just somethin' came over me.' And he left it at that.

'He's a good bloke, Tyson . . .' Ellen began.

'None of anyone's business, Mrs C.' He shrugged but didn't look up. 'I was just looking out for you, that's all.'

'Thanks, Tyson. That's what old friends do.' And as she walked back up the path between the houses, Ellen felt a deep gratitude for her good neighbour, even if he had some peculiar ways of showing he cared.

Through the open shed door, she heard whistling. Gerry was filling a bucket of soapy water at the big steel sink.

'Where do you keep your sponges?' he asked.

Not trusting herself to speak her surprise, she went to a plastic box on one of the shelves lining the far wall. He took the sponges and cloths from her hands and gave her the car keys.

'Could you back her out for me so I don't cover your garage in suds?' Without waiting for an answer, he turned back to his task.

Confounded man! Not wanting to drive home with a dead dog was one thing, but not wanting to do a simple thing like back your own car out of the garage was another. Unable to think of an excuse, she found herself behind the wheel for a second time that day. She took a deep breath and turned the key in the ignition. The week hadn't gone so badly. With any luck, by the time he left he might even think she was quite normal. She could climb back into the safety of her reclusive life when he was gone and lick her wounds.

꩜

Gerry watched out of the corner of his eye as Ellen reversed into the driveway. Before he'd been taken by surprise by Tyson, he'd noticed how dusty the car had been, more like an abandoned antique than the smart vintage Ellen would have used as a runabout. In fact, he wondered whether it had sat unused for months, even as many months as she'd been widowed. The anxiety in her face confirmed his suspicions as the car lurched into the sunlight. He wasn't sure how she'd managed to get Paddy to the vet, but one thing was certain, it hadn't been easy for her.

'A beauty to drive, isn't she?' he said.

'Yeah. Terrific.' He watched her lean against the door to steady herself.

'Mind there while I get her soaped up.'

He emptied the bucket over the roof and began rubbing vigorously as the suds ran in rivulets along the windows and dulled bodywork.

—

Ellen watched the Chrysler's colours coming to life as Gerry put his back into the job.

Not afraid to get his hands dirty either.

'Are you ready with that bucket or do I have to go in and fill it myself?' he called.

'Patience is a virtue.' She went to refill the bucket and hid a clean sponge in the pocket of her fleece.

'Another bucket load should do it. Then we can wipe her down and give her a good polish,' said Gerry.

Although happier to be washing the car than driving it, she had to admit it was no small achievement to have bitten the bullet and driven Paddy to the vet. At least she hadn't let him suffer. Such a loyal companion. In a way, there were times when he'd cared about her more than she'd cared about herself. Even in dying, he'd helped her overcome her fear.

Gerry was on the other side of the car, making faces at her through the windows. She loaded her sponge in the cool frothy water.

'Hey, Gerryo, you missed a bit,' she told him, pointing to the roof. When he popped his head up, she let the wet sponge fly, getting him right in the face.

'Pwww . . . what are you doing?' he shouted. But recovering quickly, he soaked his cloth and flung it at her. She managed to duck, but before she could load up again, he was round to her side, another sodden missile ready to launch.

'Ah, you big child. Stop it,' she begged.

'No way. You started it.'

They were fencing now, lashing out playfully, until Gerry proved too much for her. She ran around the car to get away from him, but he wasn't giving up. Grabbing her in one arm, he squeezed his wet cloth down the neck of her jacket.

'You rotter!'

—

Gerry wasn't sure if he should draw his arm away, but the feel of Ellen so close to him was like dreaming. He tightened his hold on her waist and felt her hands find the back of his neck. Bending down, he scooped her up and kissed her.

'We should maybe take this inside,' she whispered.

In that moment, Gerry was twenty-one again, holding the girl he'd loved more than anything in the world.

—

Making love that early afternoon was one of the most intense moments of Ellen's life. Barely inside the back door, they began kissing the deep kisses she'd longed for last night. Raising her arms, she let Gerry peel off her wet shirt and slowly work those strong, familiar hands over her breasts. They didn't get further than the laundry.

He hesitated just once, pulling his hands away and resting them on the bench behind him. But she boldly reached for him, desperate to hold this man, who right now felt like her only hope of surfacing from the depths of her grief. He stroked her shoulders gently, then lifted her up and swooped her round onto the bench. Pushing fears to the back of her mind, she gave herself up to the moment. As she cried out, the exquisite physical pleasure turned to emotional pain. Hot tears smarted at the corners of her eyes.

'It's okay,' he soothed, holding her tight. 'Let it out all you want.'

And she did, sobbing into his shoulder as he drew a big soft blanket from the shelf behind her and wrapped it round them like a cocoon.

Chapter Eleven

There were already three cars in Tracey's driveway when they pulled up in the Chrysler.

'She's here,' said Ellen, pointing to the Barina with the P plates he knew must be Jennifer's. As they walked to the door, he took her hand and gave it a squeeze.

'Don't worry,' he said. 'I'll say nothing. Just let me be an old friend for tonight and enjoy the hospitality.'

She took a deep breath and nodded.

The Pope household was alive with country music and dinner preparations.

'Come in, come in,' said Pete before stopping to take a closer look at Gerry's face where a blue stripe stretched along his cheek bone and a purple-black smudge glared above his jaw. 'What happened to *you?*'

'Tyson thought he was a burglar when he caught him having a look at the Chrysler,' said Ellen.

Pete shook his head and laughed. Beer in hand, he took them past the living room where they could see Louise and Old Lars chatting by the fire. Ellen smiled with pride as her daughter acknowledged their arrival without interrupting the old man's flow of speech. 'She's brought the old bloke out of himself,' Pete whispered. 'He can go for days without a word, and here he is gasbagging. Come and grab a beer, Gerry. Or are you driving?' He gave a furtive glance at Ellen.

'*I'm* driving tonight,' she told him.

Pete opened his mouth in surprise, but promptly shut it again, much to her relief.

'I'd love a beer,' said Gerry, rescuing them. 'We can maybe have these with dinner.' He proffered the wine bottles they'd brought and the two men disappeared into the kitchen.

Ellen went into the living room and sat beside Louise.

'Is that you, Martha?' Lars asked, eyeing her with uncertainty.

'It's me, Ellen, Lars. Louise's mum, Tracey's friend. Remember?'

'Oh, yes, yes, of course. I've just been chatting to your sister here. A lovely young woman. Tells me she's from Adelaide.'

It had been months since she'd spoken to Lars. Tracey had mentioned her father was getting confused, but she had no idea he was this far gone. She put an arm around Louise and squeezed her to her side. Louise drew back and took a long look at her.

'Your hair, Mum!'

Ellen patted her head self-consciously.

'Do you like it?'

'It's lovely.' Louise was still looking her over like she couldn't believe her eyes.

'I haven't seen her in about eight weeks,' she told Lars.

'Sydney is very far away.' The old man sat back in his chair and rested his hands in his lap.

Tracey put her head around the door. 'They told me you drove tonight?' Louise sat up straight.

'Good on you, Mum,' she said, her expression a mix of shock and admiration.

Ellen flushed with embarrassment.

'I'll just have to keep it up now that I've started again,' she heard herself tell them.

'Oh, we can help you there. Can't we, Lou?' Tracey gave Louise a wink. 'I could do with a shopping trip to Adelaide.'

'Wait a minute,' Ellen protested. 'There's a big difference between driving a few country roads around Lincoln and a marathon journey to Adelaide.'

'Carpe diem, darl.'

Before there could be any further discussion, Jennifer was shouting from the kitchen. 'Come and eat, guys.'

'Has Jennifer been slaving over the stove all day?' asked Ellen.

Tracey rolled her eyes. 'If only,' she said. 'I haven't seen her all week and all she's done since she got here is nag about what time we're eating. They're going to Felicity's later.'

Louise flashed a guilty glance at Ellen.

'Is that okay, Mum? It's just that I'm desperate to catch up . . .'

'It's fine, love. We've got the whole weekend to catch up ourselves.' She put an arm around her daughter again and kissed her fire-warmed cheek. 'Come on. I haven't even introduced you to Gerry.'

Pete was easy company, as Gerry had discovered on their fishing trip. His daughter, Jennifer, seemed like a character, full of energy. Gerry had only been in the house five minutes and she'd quizzed him on where he was from in Ireland, how long his son had been in Australia, what he thought of Port Lincoln and how he knew Ellen. He'd stuck to the old friend routine on the last query and was grateful to be rescued by the girl's father.

'I don't know why you're working in that newspaper office dispatching orders,' said Pete with a touch of exasperation. 'With your nose for information, you should be writing the bloody things.'

Gerry watched as the Popes and Constantinopouloses settled themselves around the dining table as one big family.

'Alfie!' Tracey shouted down the corridor that led to the bedrooms, and a boy of about twelve appeared.

'This is Alfie,' she announced. 'Usually only found in front of his Xbox.'

The boy grinned and took his seat without looking at them.

Gerry noticed his grandfather struggling to decide whether he should sit or stand at one end of the table.

'Let me give you a hand there, Lars,' he said.

'You're not Nick,' said Lars, and for a split second Gerry thought he heard the entire company gasp in unison.

'That's Gerry, Pop,' Tracey told her father as she made a big deal of setting large bowls of salad and bread on the table.

Ellen asked if she could help.

'No, darl,' said Tracey. 'Jennifer's my helper tonight. Isn't that right, Jen?'

'Anything to get this show on the road,' said Jennifer. 'Me and Louise have a lot to catch up on, you know.'

Gerry had caught Louise eyeing him as she'd taken her place at the table opposite him and her mother. She was fair-haired, like Ellen, but with a broader face and stronger build. *My side*, he thought. He'd known what she looked like from the photos in Ellen's house, but being here with her in person made her all the more real.

'You must be Louise,' he said quietly, smiling at her.

⸺

Louise took Gerry's outstretched hand and felt the warm manly grip. She searched his smiling face, trying her best to ignore the scary bruises. There was a kindness in his eyes, she thought, mixed with playfulness. A twinkle, her mother would have called it. Yes, definitely a twinkle. Maybe she'd met him before, on their trip to Ireland for her grandmother's funeral. But she'd met a lot of people then. Her mother seemed to have had a whole other life she knew very little about.

Jennifer passed a huge dish of lasagne around the table and everyone fell into easy conversation over the delicious meal. Gerry said he felt he was among old friends and wished he could stick around for longer. Even Alfie joined in halfway through his plateful and told them all about his upcoming school trip to Canberra. Her mother was a bit quiet, she noticed, but social gatherings were probably still a challenge without her father.

'Have you been to the east coast yet?' Pete asked Gerry, who shook his head having just taken a mouthful.

'You still got family there, Ellen?' Pete continued.

'Yes. They're still there as far as I know.'

When Louise caught her mother's eye, she looked down at her plate. It had always been a mystery to her how her mother could have an aunt, an uncle and first cousins in Sydney and never see them. Once on a trip to the city, she'd asked if they could visit. Her mother had said they didn't exactly get along. Even so, her cousin Jimmy always sent a card at Christmas. He was the only one to attend her father's funeral and had seemed lovely. She made a mental note to bring up the subject again when they were alone. Hadn't her parents said on numerous occasions that life was too short for grudges?

'Sydney's a great city,' Pete was saying. 'You'll have to put it on your list next time you come, Gerry.'

Again her mother's eyes were focused on her plate. Louise glanced up and noticed that Tracey too was watching for her mother's reaction.

'Forget the east coast,' said Tracey when neither Gerry nor her mother responded. 'With these two Irish here, I want to go overseas. Any plans for a trip to Ireland, Ellen?'

It was Gerry who answered.

'It's probably not the best time to go with the economy the way it is,' he said. 'The government doesn't know whether it's coming or going . . .'

Louise didn't think the state of the Irish economy was the kind of topic that would make her mother's cheeks turn a deep shade of pink. Surely she'd have told her if Gerry was more than some random visitor. She gave herself a mental shake and told herself to calm down. This was her mum's first outing in months. She should be grateful she was out of the house.

＊

When Jennifer started clearing their plates, Louise got up to help.

'You girls wouldn't be in a rush or anything?' asked Tracey.

Ellen and Tracey gathered the rest of the dishes and followed them to the kitchen.

'Ah, Tracey, weren't we the very same at that age?' said Ellen.

'Mm . . . I suppose,' said Tracey. 'So Louise, what do you think of your mother's visitor?'

'He seems really nice actually,' said Louise as she helped Jennifer load the dishwasher.

'Did you two have a thing when you were young, Ellen?' asked Jennifer. The deep pink was back in her mother's cheeks.

'Just a short romance, once,' she said.

This is news to me, thought Louise. She'd always believed her dad was her mum's first and only love. *My God!* Her mind was racing now. *Why didn't Mum say? Is that what the haircut is all about?*

'And did you have to break up with him to come to Australia?' Jennifer was relentless.

'Yes,' said Ellen, the answer barely audible.

'I bet he was hot back in the day,' said Jennifer, shoving the plates in carelessly.

That might be stretching it a bit, Louise thought, but take away the grey, the wrinkles and the beginnings of a middle-aged spread, and Gerry might have been attractive. Attractive enough for her mother to fall for 'once', in that life before Australia she rarely talked about.

'Hot?' Tracey was giggling as she pressed a hand on Louise's arm. 'Do you know he's old enough to be Louise's father?'

Louise didn't laugh. Her brain was in overdrive. Years, dates, human gestation periods swirled in her head. Her parents had told her she'd been conceived within weeks of her mother arriving from Ireland. But what if she'd arrived already pregnant? She turned and looked her mother squarely in the eye, searching for a sign that might substantiate or refute the suspicion that Tracey had just planted in her head, but that she would later admit had set seed the moment she'd shaken Gerry Clancy's hand.

—

Ellen was rooted to the spot, willing her burning cheeks to cool down. She'd never been a good liar. If only she could have said, 'Don't be ridiculous' or 'Tracey, don't be putting stupid ideas in my child's head' or even 'Shut up, woman.' But the only thing she could do was stand there, gripping the lasagne dish to keep it from crashing to the floor. She felt the blood drain from her face as Louise's expression turned from suspicion to incredulity.

'Is it true, Mum?'

Ellen tried to move, to take her daughter in her arms, but the damned lasagne dish stood between them like a brick wall. Her silence was answer enough. Louise backed away from her, one hand on her stomach, the other covering her mouth.

'We need to talk, Lou . . .'

Louise shook her head. 'Jennifer, let's get out of here.'

Jennifer stirred from where she'd been leaning against the sink with her mouth open.

'Louise, can we—' Ellen tried again.

'Don't talk to me, Mum.'

The two young women picked up their handbags and headed for the back door. Ellen realised there wasn't a sound from the dining room. When she finally moved, she set the dish on the worktop before her knees could buckle under her.

'I'm so sorry, darl,' Tracey was saying. 'I had no idea . . .'

—

At the table, Pete tried to pretend the overheard segment of conversation had never happened. 'So how is old Paddy doing these days?'

Gerry looked at him and tried to hide his disbelief.

'Well actually,' he began, 'there's some sad news on that front.'

'Crikey. There's always some drama.'

'Can I go back on my Xbox, Dad?' Alfie broke in.

'Go on, mate. I'll let you know when it's dessert.'

Somehow Gerry didn't think they'd be serving the bread and butter pudding he and Ellen had put together in the late afternoon when a sense of politeness had roused them from their lovemaking.

Chapter Twelve

'I'm not going and you can't make me.'

Louise buzzed round the kitchen, avoiding eye contact with Ellen. After last night's debacle at the Popes', Ellen knew her daughter had every right to be upset, but the fact remained, Gerry was her biological father and in a few short hours he'd be back in Adelaide. In a matter of days, he'd return to Ireland. She needed to talk Louise into seeing him before he left Port Lincoln.

'Listen, Lou. I know what I did was wrong.' She moved cautiously closer to where Louise was sawing into a loaf of bread. 'I should have told you all this long ago, but please try to understand why I kept it from you . . .'

'Oh fuck off, Mum!' The knife zipped through crust.

'Louise, don't speak to me like that.'

'Jesus, Mum! Do you even get it?' Ellen took a step back as Louise slammed down the knife and shoved the chopping board, bread and all, across the bench. 'My dad is dead and so is my dog, and now this dropkick from your past shows up and you tell me he's my father.'

'I'm so sorry Lou . . .' Ellen began, but Louise had grabbed her phone from the counter and was storming toward the back door.

She raised a hand behind her. 'Too late for talking, Mum. You've ruined everything.'

✌

Louise was right. She'd opened her very own Pandora's box and would have to deal with the consequences. The wise advice of her husband echoed in Ellen's mind. 'Choose your battles,' he'd say on those occasions when she and her headstrong daughter locked horns. There was nothing for it, but to give Louise space and hope they could talk it out later. She sat down at the table but couldn't touch the tea she'd made. It was all too hard. A whirlwind week after months of just existing; what on earth had she unleashed?

✌

Gerry put his case in the boot of his hire car. He'd waited as agreed to hear from Ellen. After the shock that jolted everyone at Tracey's the night before, they'd stayed for an awkward ten minutes before deciding to leave their hosts to recover. Only Old Lars was oblivious to the ramifications of what had gone on in the kitchen.

Ellen had promised to text once she'd spoken to Louise and agreed a time for the three of them to meet. He'd been disappointed when the text came saying Louise didn't want to see him, but he wasn't surprised.

So sorry, Gerry. She's adamant she doesn't want to meet you.

He wanted to at least hear Ellen's voice before he left, but he daren't add fuel to the fire by phoning, with the two of them there in the house already at loggerheads. Better to leave them alone.

I'll just go, Ellen, he replied. *She's got enough to deal with. Me hanging around isn't going to help.*

Oh Gerry, I wish it didn't have to end this way.

Same here. Just bad timing. You take care, kiddo.

The receptionist was scanning her computer screen through the bottoms of her bifocals.

'Had enough of Port Lincoln, Mr Clancy?' she asked.

Right now, for Louise's sake, he wished he'd never come. But for selfish reasons, he wished he could stay. When he'd planned the trip to the coastal town, he'd told himself it would be an excuse to see a bit more of the country, and that visiting Ellen would be like catching up with any old school friend. Instead, he'd realised that in the intervening years, his love for her had never diminished. How different their lives might have been if she hadn't gone away.

'Oh, I'm not sure if I could ever get enough of Port Lincoln,' he said, 'but duty calls. I'll be back to the grind in Ireland by the end of next week.'

'I'm afraid I'll have to charge you for the night you weren't here,' she said, looking at him over her glasses.

Gerry fought the reddening of his cheeks.

'You were safely tucked up somewhere, I trust?'

He managed a smile.

'As long as you weren't out bush . . .' She gave a satisfied laugh.

That's one face I won't miss. He jumped in his car and made for the highway, but the closer he got to Ocean Road, the more uneasy he felt. He wanted to take the turn-off and climb the curving hill once more, and tell Ellen O'Shea Constantinopoulos, whatever her name was, that he loved her and hated leaving, but his visit had caused enough trouble.

The car in front slowed as a horse appeared at the turn-off. Gerry thought he recognised Spots, but squinted to make out the rider. *Louise!* The driver in front had stopped and was letting the horse and rider cross. The children in the back seat looked on in delight. Louise waved at them, but her face was stony. She didn't notice him as she made her way to the grassy verge on the opposite side and steered Spots towards town. He had a split second to make up his mind. He did a U-turn and went after her.

At the small country school of Poonindie, Gerry parked the jeep and watched in his rear-view mirror as Louise turned onto Hirschausen Road, her face set in a frown. He took a deep breath and got out of the car.

'Nice day for a ride,' he called out. She hesitated, Spots giving a backward step in response to the shortened rein. Gerry dug his hands in his pockets and leaned against the car. He preferred horses at a safe distance. As if reading his mind, Louise urged Spots closer and let him stretch out his head and touch his muzzle to Gerry's shirt.

'You shouldn't have come,' she began.

'I didn't come here to find you.'

'So why did you come? To ruin my life?'

Spots shifted his hooves and shook his head. Gerry wished she'd get down off him and keep that head under control.

'I never knew you existed until a couple of days ago. How do you think *I* feel?' He regretted it the minute he'd said it.

'I don't care how you feel,' she snapped. 'You mean nothing to me. I have a father, or had a father. I don't need you. Go back to where you came from and stay out of my life.'

'But your mother and I . . .'

'Spare me. I don't care.' She spoke those words with a finality that stopped him short.

It was like watching the scene from a movie as Louise gathered up her horse and set off at a rising trot. A boy cycled out of the driveway of one of the sleepy-looking houses and stared at him. Yes, he was a stranger in a country far from home, a tourist who didn't belong. The sting of Louise's words brought tears to his eyes. With a heavy sadness, Gerry turned back onto the highway, took one last look at Ocean Road and headed for Adelaide.

Louise wished she could have left Gerry Clancy at a gallop, but the unsealed road was pockmarked with puddles after the recent rain. She longed to get to the beach, to feel the freedom of galloping along the sand, and shake off the shock of finding out that Nick Constantinopoulos wasn't her real dad. She searched her memory for a clear comforting picture of him, but no matter how hard she tried, the image wouldn't come into focus. Why did that Gerry Clancy have to show up? Why couldn't he have just stayed in Ireland? Why couldn't her mother have told her years ago? Even when she turned eighteen? Surely her father would have wanted to tell her. It suddenly dawned on her that he might not have known. If that was the case, she wasn't the only one her mother had cheated.

Last night both she and Jennifer had been so shocked they'd hardly said a word on the drive to Felicity's. The crew were there when they arrived and the punch was flowing. Louise didn't care how bad it tasted as long as it helped her forget about what happened at the Popes'. When she woke the next morning, it all came flooding back. She looked around for Jennifer, but someone said Beanie had collected her earlier. Despite a sore head and a throat like sandpaper, she organised a taxi to take her home, longing for the comfort of her dog, her own bed and the chance to sleep off her hangover. But her mother was waiting when she got there with the awful news of Paddy and some plan about how they could all sit down and talk. She wanted to get as far away as possible from her mother. Adelaide wouldn't be far enough.

A blanket of merino sheep grazed across the flat paddocks stretching from the main road to the sea. She slowed Spots to a walk. *Bad things happen in threes*, her mother often told her. Well, she'd certainly had her three in a short space of time. First, she finds out her boyfriend has probably cheated on her with a skinny second-year, then she's told her mother's old friend from Ireland is actually her father, and then this morning she discovers that her beloved Paddy has been put down. A triple whammy.

She rode on, staring at the horizon where the azure sea emerged from a sandy track at the end of the road and a flock of black swans rested on the water, some with heads nestled under wings, feathers ruffling in the cool breeze. With tears streaming down her cheeks, she tried desperately to remember the last time she'd seen Paddy, to imagine how he'd felt and smelled.

'Get up, Spots.' She urged him into canter. They raced along the empty stretch of coastline, the rhythm of Spots' hooves filling her ears and sending the black swans into flight. They were galloping now and the thrill took over, obliterating all care and worry. Eventually she slowed him back to a canter and steered him gently into the shallows. As his splashing sprayed her jodhpurs, she felt the cool drops soak into her hot skin, matching the salty tears on her face. How she wished she could stay here and never have to face her life that just got more complicated and all the more lonesome without her father in it.

She was untacking Spots at the side of the shed when Tyson appeared.

'How're ya goin, Lou?' he asked, touching the peak of his baseball cap and nodding to her.

Smiling up at him, she felt her shoulders relax. As she undid the girth, Tyson walked round to Spots' head and blew gently on his face.

'You'll be happy to see Lou too,' he told Spots, letting the horse nuzzle and lick at his hands. 'Very sorry to hear about Paddy, Lou.'

Louise lifted the saddle off Spots' back and held it to her chest.

'Thanks, Tyson.'

'When you leavin' to go back to the city?'

'Tomorrow.'

She turned and took the saddle inside the shed. When she returned, Tyson had taken a curry comb and was giving Spots a massage that had the horse falling asleep at the fence post. Louise loved that she didn't have to worry about him when she was away. If her mother couldn't always manage to take care of Spots, she knew Tyson would make time for him.

'Your mum asked me to help bury Old Paddy,' he said, feeling over Spots' coat with his free hand as he brushed.

Louise didn't know if she could face putting her dog in the ground after everything that had happened, but neither did she wish to knock back Tyson's kind offer.

'Any news from the kids or Sheryleen?' she asked, gathering the bridle from the fence.

He shrugged his broad shoulders, returned the brush to the tack box and carried it for her.

'I might have to get your mum's help,' he said, 'to sort things out.'

She set the bridle on its nail and took the box from Tyson. *Oh yes, her mother the saint! Helping out those in need while lying through her teeth to her own daughter.*

When Louise had tidied everything away, Tyson was standing by the freezer.

'You reckon we get this over with and get him in the ground?' he asked.

She stared at the freezer.

'I can have a good grave dug in no time,' he continued. 'You and Mrs C only have to tell me where you'd like him put.'

She went to the door of the shed and looked out over the lawn, down past the paddocks and out to sea.

'Down there, in that corner.' She pointed to a place in the garden where she used to have a trampoline. Paddy had loved to bounce along beside her. She could see him now, jumping to catch a ball, skidding and bouncing until they'd both end up lying in a heap, him licking her to death as she squealed in delight.

Tyson took a spade from the collection of tools Louise knew hadn't been touched since her dad was alive. Another reminder of his absence, as if she needed one. With tears trickling down her cheeks, she went to the house and called out to her mother.

Louise watched wordlessly as her mother lifted the black bag from the freezer. A part of her wanted to grab it from her and run away, cradle Paddy in her arms. But it was no longer her Paddy. She pinched at two corners of the bag and looked away as her mother took most of the weight. They carried him to where Tyson was breaking a sweat at the end of the garden.

When the hole was deep enough, he rested one arm on the spade and held his cap to his chest. Louise and her mother manoeuvred the bag into the grave and stood back to let Tyson cover it with earth. Her mother began to say something about a prayer, but it was all too much.

'I'm sorry, I can't . . .' said Louise, her voice cracking.

Her mother stretched out a hand, but before she could touch her, Louise ran into the house, up the stairs, locked her bedroom door and threw her sobbing self on the bed.

Chapter Thirteen

Ellen found herself home alone for most of the weekend. By Sunday afternoon, Louise had already packed her bag and left with Jennifer. There'd been no mention of the fact that her flight wasn't until the evening, or of anything else for that matter. Louise wasn't speaking to her. Even Jennifer had been unusually quiet. She'd said hello, disappeared into Louise's bedroom and left with a bare 'See ya'. It would have been good to phone Tracey, but how could she justify turning to her friend for comfort when she'd kept the secret from her all these years too? Losing Tracey's friendship would be unbearable.

She'd tried phoning Gerry but only got voicemail. 'Let me know you're safe,' she'd said. His response came as a text hours later. *I'm in Adelaide. It was great to see you and to meet Louise. Sorry things couldn't have turned out better for us.* It had sounded so final. *Us?* Yes, there had been moments in their short reunion when she had imagined them having a relationship, starting again. But she'd ruined it. It was back to square one. He was gone and Ellen felt the hole that had been filled in by his visit opening up all over again.

—

She needn't have doubted her friend. Tracey's Ford bumped along the driveway less than an hour later after the girls had left.

'I would have phoned yesterday, but we were flat out at work and to be honest . . .' Tracey hesitated as she came up onto the veranda, 'I was a bit emotional after Friday night. I didn't want to say the wrong thing again.'

Ellen swallowed hard. She reached out, and as Tracey's arms enfolded her, the tears flowed.

'I'm so sorry, Tracey.'

'Oh stop it, you silly Irishwoman. You'll get me started.' Tracey searched her shiny crocodile handbag and pulled out a couple of tissues. 'Are you going to stand here blubbering or are you going to invite me in?'

'She's hardly spoken to me since Friday night,' said Ellen as they sat in the kitchen. 'I've wrecked everything. She idolised Nick.'

Tracey took Ellen's hand in her own. 'Louise is young. She'll come round. They think they know everything at that age. We're the baddies no matter what we do.'

'Don't you think I've handled it badly, keeping it from her all these years?' Ellen needed an honest answer.

'Oh darl, I wish I could turn the clock back for you. Louise has a right to be upset. Give her time to take it in. She knows you love her. Nick and you both gave her a wonderful life.'

'Nick is probably rolling in his grave.'

'Nick would want you both to be happy.'

Ellen remembered his acceptance of her pregnancy. 'He was so cool about it,' she told Tracey. 'He didn't have any of the hang-ups you hear about guys who can't get enough and then bail out once a girl falls pregnant.'

Tracey frowned. 'I always wondered why you didn't have more kids. You never really talked about it and I didn't want to ask. When Alfie came as a bit of a surprise, I felt guilty as you and Nick only had Louise.'

Ellen remembered the day Tracey told her she was pregnant with Alfie. She and Pete had come back from a holiday on the Gold Coast. 'It must have been all that surf, sand and well . . . you know what I mean,' Tracey had said. Ellen had been overjoyed to hear the news, but Nick had been more reserved. He'd never said as much, but Ellen knew he was jealous of Tracey and Pete and how easily it had happened for them. She told Tracey what she and Nick had kept to themselves all these years.

They'd stopped using condoms once Louise turned two, but as the months went by, they became more and more frustrated as nothing was happening.

'Maybe it's me,' Ellen suggested, knowing how devastated Nick would be if it was him. She tried to convince herself something inside her had changed since having Louise. 'I've heard of women whose hormones go all weird after child-birth,' she told him. 'Their levels change and they need help to conceive.'

Nick went to the appointments with her, holding her hand while she had those blood tests she'd dreaded. What she didn't tell him was that she'd phoned her obstetrician in advance, explaining her fears to the doctor and almost begging her to test her fertility before even mentioning her husband's. If Nick was infertile, Louise's paternity would be thrown into question. The three of them were so happy. He'd be devastated if he found out Louise wasn't his own. She couldn't bear the thought of hurting him. Aileen Dreever was accommodating. She'd looked after Ellen when she'd arrived in Lincoln eight months pregnant, and much to Ellen's relief had been on call the night of Louise's arrival.

It had been a complicated delivery with Louise's head turned the wrong way and forceps having to be used to avoid an emergency c-section. Nick had been stoic, not flinching when she'd squeezed his hand and dug her nails into him. Once it was over, the midwife went to hand the wriggling cone-headed baby to him. He hesitated and looked to her for permission. Exhausted, she just smiled her consent and watched him enfold the tiny girl in his huge hands. As he brought Louise to her, Ellen saw a tear fall on the baby's cheek. Her big brave Nick was crying.

It couldn't have been easy for Dr Dreever to sit across her desk from the pair of them once the test results were back. 'Your levels are normal, Ellen. There are no barriers to conception on your side.'

Nick unlocked his fingers from Ellen's, leaned forward and buried his head in his hands.

—

'But you stayed together?' Tracey was saying. 'You must have loved each other so much.'

'He was very quiet at first, unable to take it in,' said Ellen. 'Then he was angry . . .' She started to cry again and Tracey had to bring the tissue box to the table for the two of them. 'I told him about Gerry. I wasn't so naive as to not suspect the baby might be Gerry's when I fell pregnant, but I'd left Ireland without the blessing of either Gerry or my mother. From the minute I got on that plane, I'd been determined not to look back. Whatever Australia threw at me, I was going to manage.' She swiped at the tears leaking down her cheeks.

'Nick took off on the boat for a couple of weeks. I thought I'd lost him, that he wouldn't come back. But he did. He said he loved me and Louise and didn't want to tear our family apart.'

'So did you ever tell Gerry?'

'No. That was the one thing Nick asked of me.'

Ellen looked down at her hands and squeezed hard on the tissue.

'I'm not proud of myself, Tracey, but that's what's brought all this about. When I realised Gerry still had feelings for me, I had to be honest with him before we . . .'

Tracey raised her newly threaded brows.

'I wondered if you and Gerry had been up to anything,' she said, her face lighting up with the first smile of the afternoon. 'I could sense the chemistry on Friday night.'

Ellen started to laugh but caught herself. 'I'm an idiot, Trace. I should never have . . . Nick isn't even gone a year.'

'Oh God, Ellen. You can be so old-fashioned.' Tracey shook her auburn mop. 'Gerry must have meant a lot to you. I know there wouldn't have been any shaggin' if it had been some other bloke.'

'Tracey!'

'Oh excuse me, miss, but a shag is a shag no matter what you call it. So when are you two ever going to catch up if he's going back to Ireland?'

Ellen took a deep breath and let out a heavy sigh. 'I don't think that's going anywhere. Besides, right now I need to focus on getting back on an even keel with Louise and hope I haven't completely stuffed things up.'

'She'll be right,' Tracey soothed.

They boiled the kettle for another cuppa.

'So now that you're driving again,' said Tracey, her tone cautious, 'will you go back to work?'

It was funny with close friends, Ellen thought; they could almost read your mind for you. 'This weekend is the first time I've considered it possible. I've missed being that person who gets up each day, puts on the smart clothes and turns up at the desk ready for whatever challenges work brings. It might sound stupid, but Gerry made me realise that.'

'You don't have to convince me, Ellen. In a couple of days that man has done what Pete and I have spent the last nine months trying to do. You always loved your job. We'd hate to see your talents wasted.'

Ellen's cheeks burned. It had only been on the night of the dinner party when she'd realised how much Lars had deteriorated that she fully appreciated the sacrifices Tracey made to be available to help her even though she already had so much on her plate. 'You've both been brilliant, Trace. I don't know what I'd have done . . .'

'Don't mention it. We're BFFs, mate.'

Ellen was grateful to know their friendship could withstand the tsunami that had just hit. She could only hope her relationship with Louise was strong enough to do the same. Losing Nick was bad enough. A life without Louise wouldn't be worth living.

Chapter Fourteen

In her room in Adelaide, Louise started to unpack. Her phone was hopping, but she wasn't in the mood to be communicative. She made herself a cup of peppermint tea and abandoning the travel bag, she climbed into bed. The phone rang again. She checked the screen, the photo of Paddy threatening to unravel her. It was her mum. She'd text in a minute to let her know she'd arrived, but there was no way she was going to speak to her.

There were three missed calls from Toby and a message saying, *Are you back yet, babe? Can we hook up?*

'I don't think so, mate.'

Jennifer had messaged her. *Just watched that finding your family show on TV. So excited. We could go overseas and meet up with the Clancys. Meet all the cousins you didn't know you have. Call me x.*

That was the problem with Jennifer. It was all about the adventure, the story. Sure, her friend had agreed her mother had been a cow, but she was already on to the next thing. *Bugger meeting the Clancys*, thought Louise, *I already have plenty of cousins, aunts, uncles, even grandparents in Ireland and Greece.* But if this nightmare were a reality, then she really had nothing to do with Greece. Memories of her only trip to her father's homeland came flooding back. They'd travelled to Santorini on the way back from the funeral of her grandmother in Ireland, a grandmother she'd never met. Despite the sadness of the occasion, everyone in Cork had been welcoming, delighting in meeting her mother's little family. Santorini had been different. There'd been a distance between her cousins and herself which she'd put down to the language barrier. At ten, she hadn't cared why she didn't look like them. She'd thought she took after her mother's side, but the pieces were beginning to fall into place. The heated arguments she'd overheard between her father and grandfather, the silences at mealtimes. Her grandmother had been a mediating force between her son and her husband, but what Louise mostly remembered about her was the strange sweets with funny wrappers she gave her when her mother wasn't looking. And there was that lovely aunt who took her to her house and taught her to make kourabiedes while her young son crawled about on the tiled floor.

She'd told everyone she met she was half Greek. It seemed more exotic than being half Irish. How could she even go back to Stavros and Kristina's restaurant? She'd be a fraud, an impostor. What right did she have to stand at tables with her notepad recommending souvlakia or spanakopita like she was a native. God, she'd been cheated. Cheated on all fronts. She thought about Toby and how they might make up. He'd seemed like the perfect antidote to her grief: bright, vibrant, warm in and out of her single bed. But she didn't need someone she couldn't trust. In fact, right now, she didn't need a boyfriend at all. Her life was complicated enough. She set down her mug on the bedside table, switched off her phone and slipped under the duvet. Tomorrow she would dump Toby Scott.

—

By the end of the following day, Louise had decided on a plan of action. She'd texted Toby and asked him to meet her outside the canteen. There would be no more lies. She was determined to get her university degree and have the life she wanted on her terms. Boyfriends were strictly off the agenda. She was damned if she was going to let history repeat itself. Any children she might have would be born long into the future and they would know exactly who their father was right from the start. Her friends could have all the sex they wanted, from now on she would avoid it until she was well and truly ready.

Toby Scott was devastated. The jungle drums hadn't taken long to reach him.

'I can't believe you'd think I'd cheat on you,' he told her as they sat in the late afternoon sunshine. 'That girl's just a mate.'

'Yeah, sorry about that.' She sensed the hurt, but willed herself not to feel sorry for him. A boy like Toby could have any girl he wanted. She needed to be firm. 'I'm breaking up with you because I want to focus on my studies. This is really important to me, you know.' She almost had herself convinced.

'It's important to most of the people here, Lou. But that doesn't mean we can't have fun and go out together.'

'I'm not going to stop going out,' she insisted. 'I just can't handle a boyfriend right now.' She pulled the strap of her bag over her shoulder and got up to leave.

'Is there a boy from home you're not telling me about?' he pleaded.

'Don't be ridiculous.'

Toby caught her hand to make her stay, but she pulled away.

'I'll see you around,' she told him and set off across the lawn at a brisk pace, telling herself she'd done the right thing.

━

Gerry checked his flight details as he sat in the lounge room at Kieran's.

'You sure you're all right, Dad?' Kieran asked.

Gerry had to admit he'd been a bit quiet since he'd returned to Adelaide. He'd hoped Kieran wouldn't notice, but should have credited his son with more empathy. Kieran had always had a way of reading people. Gerry looked up from where he was checking his travel documents and took a deep breath. 'There's something I'd like to chat to you about before I go home.'

'We haven't had dinner yet,' said Kieran. 'Why don't I shout you on your last night?'

Gerry was grateful for the offer. 'Okay, you can take me out, but I'm paying.'

'Ah now, Dad, shouldn't you be watching the pennies for your retirement?'

'Get out o' that, you cheeky divil.'

In Olsen's they ordered steak sandwiches and drank a cold beer while they waited. It was quiet even for a Monday night, giving Gerry the much-needed space to talk man to man and open up about events of the previous week.

'I've been a bit vague about my trip to Port Lincoln, Kieran, but I want to tell you something very important that I found out there.'

Kieran hunched his shoulders and leaned in towards his dad.

'Well, the woman I went to see, Ellen Constantinopoulos. She was Ellen O'Shea when I knew her ...' Gerry willed himself to find the right words. 'She and I were in love before you were born, before your mother and I got together.' He paused, gathering his thoughts in an effort to say this clearly without hurting his son. 'Anyway, she emigrated to Sydney while she was pregnant with our baby.' He paused again to gauge Kieran's reaction, but his son was concentrating, taking it all in. 'I never knew the child existed until last week. I don't even think Ellen meant to tell me, but we were getting close again.' He felt his face and neck burn.

He watched as Kieran processed the information.

'So you're telling me,' said Kieran, 'you're in a relationship with a woman in Port Lincoln who is the mother of your child who must be what, nineteen or twenty years old?'

Gerry sighed and looked around. At least his son had measured his response instead of shouting out in shock or laughing incredulously at him.

'I don't know about being in a relationship, son,' he said, feeling a little exasperated. 'What's important is, I have another daughter.' He crossed his arms and looked down at the table. 'She doesn't want to know me.'

'So you met her?'

'Yes, she's a lovely girl. You'd like her. Unfortunately, she didn't know I was her father before she met me. It's a bit complicated.' He clasped and unclasped his hands as he spoke. 'I was having dinner at friends of Ellen's and she found out in an indirect way.'

'So she's traumatised?'

'Well, yes, I guess she must be.' He sat back in his chair almost wishing he'd driven out of Port Lincoln and left the matter behind him.

'Gee, Dad, that's a bit full on.'

'And that's the understatement of the year.'

Gerry took a swig of his beer. He was grateful when the waitress came and set two huge plates in front of them. He began to eat, more to take a break from the conversation than to satisfy any appetite he had for the food. Kieran fooled with his chips as the silence between them allowed the news to sink in. Then his face broke into a smile.

'I'm not sure if I can take another sister.' He gave a wry laugh. 'I can't cope with the one I have.'

'Now, now, Stephanie has her good points,' Gerry scolded.

With only two years between them, Kieran and Stephanie had been the best of frenemies, fighting like cats one minute, thick as thieves the next. Gerry hoped they would always be there for each other. After meeting Louise, he was more grateful than ever that he and Jessica had had a second child. How lonely it must be for Louise without a close sibling to thrash all this out. He took consolation in knowing that Jennifer and the Popes would be there for her.

'When do I get to meet her?'

Gerry set down his knife. 'She doesn't want anything to do with me. Maybe in time you'll get to meet one another, but for now, keep it in the back of your mind. I just wanted to be open with you, son. I'll tell Stephanie in my own good time. It's not like I can go home to Cork and put it in *The Examiner.*'

'Ah, that's a shame,' said Kieran, but a few bites of his steak sandwich later, he'd agreed to keep the information to himself and respect his father's wishes.

'Thanks, son.'

Gerry was relieved he'd confided in Kieran, but this was a story that for now would stay in Australia. In a few short days, he would be heading home. He hoped more than anything that Ellen and Louise's relationship would survive in the aftermath of his visit.

On the bus to Glenelg, Louise rehearsed her excuses for finishing at the restaurant. Assignments were piling up, exams were approaching; she needed every spare hour to put into her studies. Students all over the city would be doing the same. But as she walked down Jetty Road, her thoughts turned to her father, at least the only father she'd known and the only one she ever wanted. He would be ashamed if she lied to his friends. A tram rattled past; pedestrians were making their way home or coming out for the night. At the end of the street the jetty stretched out into the ocean. Part of her wanted to keep walking towards it. If her dad was still alive this wouldn't be happening. What would he want her to do? Was she to spend her life feeling this incomplete every time she tried to make a decision without him? He used to tell her the Greeks sometimes had a different take on things. Instead of *I miss you*, they said something that meant *You are missing from me*. Right now, his absence felt so acute, she could hardly bear it.

She was at the restaurant before she could agonise over it any longer. The bright blue and white frontage and bunting of mini Greek flags in the windows made her shudder. As she pushed open the front door, the smells of fresh olive bread and frying fish enveloped her, but with none of the warmth of all the other times she'd walked in here. Even the music failed to uplift her.

'Louise,' Stavros's son, Christos, called out over the early evening buzz, 'you working or just hungry?'

She shook her head and sidled between the tables on the quieter side of the restaurant. She pushed through the beaded curtain and waited. Stavros glanced up from where he was frying batches of calamari as fast as Kristina was assembling beds of salad. They always worked like a double act. Louise imagined that, despite their animated exchanges, they'd never kept secrets.

'Louise!' In one swift movement Stavros passed the pan handle to Kristina who gave her a broad smile and seamlessly continued the work.

'You come to help out?' asked Stavros.

She couldn't bear to look into his huge brown eyes. As he wiped his dark hirsute hands on his apron, she noticed the wedding ring on his right hand where her father had worn his. Had she noticed that before? She wasn't sure. She went to speak, but the speech she'd practised all the way here stuck in her throat. There was a stinging in her nose and her eyes leaked involuntarily. She hadn't wanted to make a scene. She'd wanted to walk in and walk out having done the deed. How hard could it be to quit?

Stavros looked over his shoulder to Kristina, but she was busy plating up and calling out through the hatch to Christos to take the meals to customers. He bent down to look Louise in the eye.

'What is it, Lou?'

When she didn't respond, he put an arm around her shoulder and led her out to the patio at the back where they took their breaks.

'I'm a fake, Stavros,' she began. 'I'm not Niko's daughter.'

As she told him how she had found out, the kindly barrel of a man said nothing, but crossed himself three times. For a moment Louise was reminded of the Catholic confession her mother told her about. But it wasn't she who had sinned.

When she finished, Stavros took her hands in his own and leaned his head on one side.

'To me and Kristina, you are Niko's.' A tear glistened in his eye at the mention of his friend. 'You want break, you take break. You study hard. Do Niko proud.' He paused and, releasing her hands, straightened his shoulders. 'When you ready, we here. Me and Kristina.'

He crossed himself again, but this time it felt like a blessing. In somebody's eyes at least, she really was Louise Constantinopoulos.

—

Ellen replaced the phone in its cradle and looked absently at the television. For the third night in a row, Louise's phone had gone to voicemail. There was nothing she could do except keep trying. She'd given the house the once-over, determined to keep to the standard Tracey had helped her reset. She'd followed through on her promise to get back to work. There was a position becoming available in a month's time. She would be required to attend an interview and a series of workshops. Her boss would ensure as easy a transition as possible. The team would all be delighted to have her back. She was blessed to have friends and colleagues that would keep her on track. Her life would take on a rhythm again, a routine of work and social events, but it was the time on her own she would dread. The time when she rattled around in her home, mourning the loss of a good husband, a beautiful daughter and the chance of a future with an old friend. In her kitchen she'd hung a plaque Tracey had given her that said, *Life isn't about waiting for the storm to pass, it's about learning to dance in the rain.* Yes, she would dance and keep dancing. If only in the hope that, like Gerry's visit, there'd be an occasional break in the clouds.

Chapter Fifteen

Ellen pushed the glass door and let herself in to Abeona House. First full week back at work and she wasn't convinced she'd ever get used to the smell of the old people's home. But it was a minor complaint. Her boss had been sensitive and given her some of the easier cases to help her find her feet in her new role in aged care. The old role she'd loved, working with families, had been filled in her absence, but she was grateful to still have a job. It was Friday already and the week had gone well. Just a follow-up appointment with a lady who'd recently moved into the home and then she could relax and recover for two whole days.

Walking through the dementia ward, she was reminded of how each patient was different. Some became aggressive and demanded that staff remove fellow inmates they imagined were threatening them. Others turned in on themselves, the disease having shut off their personalities. And then there were those who had a perpetual smile that made them look almost happy. It was partly her job to find nursing home places for them after a lengthy assessment on what level of care their families could, or couldn't, manage to provide. Tracey was taking good care of Lars, despite all her other commitments, and Ellen admired her for that, but she couldn't help wondering how long her friend could sustain the care work if her dad's dementia progressed.

Violet Harris was sitting at the window that overlooked the town and the sea that glistened in the warm October sunshine. Ellen couldn't tell if the view was of any comfort to her partially sighted client. A care worker reminded the old woman who Ellen was, then left them alone.

'Do you like it here, Mrs Harris?' Ellen asked.

Her answer was a bewildered smile.

Violet presented as clean and cared for, she noted. The room was certainly bright and airy with flowers in the window and a jug of fresh water beside the bed. The television was on but muted in one corner. Ellen knew the woman no longer had much use for the box and couldn't help thinking it was more for the carers' benefit. As much as she admired caregivers, it was her job to be on the alert for elder abuse. In the short time she'd been back on the job, she'd already come across cases of neglect. Violet Harris was one of the lucky ones with a family who'd made sacrifices to put her here.

'How're all the family?'

Ellen picked up a framed photograph of a younger Mrs Harris and her late husband surrounded by their children and grandchildren. Violet's eyes passed over it as though it were full of strangers. Then something in the image held her gaze and she slowly raised a finger to the glass. She smiled as her translucent digit settled on her husband's face. Ellen couldn't help but feel a stab of sadness at their common loss.

'He was a handsome man, wasn't he, Mrs Harris?'

She placed the picture in the woman's frail hands and finished her case note. There may not have been conversation, but the flicker in the old lady's eyes told Ellen her love for her husband was still intact.

'I'll see you soon,' she said as she left with a sense of comfort, knowing her love for Nick would stay with her for the rest of her life.

⌁

Tracey was perched on the leather lounge in front of the fireplace at the Port Lincoln Hotel.

'Sorry I'm late.' Ellen plonked herself down, unravelling a cheesecloth scarf and pulling up the sleeves of her smart black top. 'Thank God that week's over.'

'I bet you're glad to be in amongst it.'

Ellen took a sip of the wine Tracey had bought her and tucked her feet under her.

'So how's your week been?'

Tracey gave her the gory details of another hectic week at the roadhouse.

'I told Pete if I didn't have some me time, I'd walk off the job.'

Ellen laughed at the thought of Pete raising his eyebrows and willing Friday to come so *he* could have some peace to enjoy a few beers once he'd shut up shop. She listened contentedly as Tracey let off steam about the joys, or rather the drawbacks, of running a business with her spouse.

'I love him to bits,' she was saying, 'but at times I wish I could walk out the door in the morning and not see him again until tea.' She gasped. 'Sorry, Ellen. I should be grateful I have a husband to—'

Ellen put a hand on her arm. 'Stop right there,' she said. 'You don't have to vet everything you say because of Nick. We had a good life, Tracey. Look at me. I'm back at work, getting sorted. I couldn't have done it without yourself and that husband of yours who drives you crazy.'

'Oh, you've reminded me how lucky I am now, and I was looking forward to complaining about him.' Tracey pretended to sulk.

They ordered some food and another couple of glasses of wine.

'So, tell me,' said Ellen, 'is he recovered from the shock I gave him that night at your place?'

Tracey shook her head. 'Oh, you know Pete. Takes it all in his stride. At least he got to know Gerry a bit with their fishing trip before the news broke about Louise.'

Ellen wasn't sure which topic of conversation would be less painful, her daughter or Gerry Clancy, but Tracey didn't give her a chance to decide.

'So what's happening with Louise?'

Ellen sucked in a breath. Six weeks without speaking to her only child wasn't something she was proud of. 'Still not speaking to me. I just got a text when she went back to uni to say she'd arrived. Every time I ring, I get her voicemail and she doesn't reply to my messages.'

'Well, Jennifer's been chatting to her on Facebook and it sounds like she's getting stuck into her study. Even dumped the boyfriend, Jen said.'

'Mm . . .' Ellen wasn't sure if dumping the boyfriend was a kneejerk reaction to finding out about Gerry, but Louise hadn't even mentioned this boy. The thought disturbed her. 'I didn't even know she was seeing someone,' she said, half to herself.

'Oh, I don't think it was anything serious. Probably just a uni fling.'

Ellen wasn't convinced, but she kept her reservations to herself.

'You know what they're like at that age, always meeting new people – social butterflies. They can't all be like Jennifer.' Tracey rolled her eyes. 'I swear she spends that much time with Theo . . .' She took a gulp of her wine.

'I suppose with them both working, it doesn't seem like they have a lot of time together.'

Tracey shrugged.

'It's probably a phase,' said Ellen. 'She'll be in uni next year with Lou and the two of them will be sorted.' She wasn't sure whether she was trying to reassure Tracey or herself.

'At this rate, she may not even go.'

'It's still a few weeks away, but would you and Jennifer come to Adelaide with me to bring Louise back for Christmas?'

'Of course.' Tracey jumped at the idea. 'It might even put Jennifer in the mood for going to uni next year.'

Ellen was relieved. 'Thanks, Tracey. I couldn't have faced the journey on my own, let alone the wrath of my daughter.'

Tracey dipped a triangle of pita bread into a bowl of fresh hummus. 'Have you heard from Gerry?' she asked without looking up.

Ellen had tried to put Gerry out of her mind once he'd left, without much success. He'd made her feel vital again, but she couldn't help wishing events had unfolded differently. The 'if onlys' plagued her. *If only we'd told Louise when she turned sixteen or eighteen. If only I hadn't been such a recluse and had collected my mail regularly. If only Tracey hadn't opened her big mouth . . .* But deep down Ellen knew she was solely responsible for her daughter's shock, and if their relationship was never repaired, she would only have herself to blame.

'No,' she said. 'I suspect he's gone back to Ireland and has decided to put me to the back of his mind. I've caused him enough grief. Poor man is probably shell-shocked.'

'I bet he misses you like hell,' said Tracey.

Part of Ellen wished she was right, but missing someone on the other side of the world was no cake walk, as she'd just begun to find out.

On the drive home, Ellen listened to the news and weather on the radio. A hot northerly was forecast for tomorrow. She feared these weather conditions, the signature of bushfire season. Nick would have been prepared, clearing overgrowth a good distance from the house, cleaning gutters and making sure the hosepipes and rainwater tanks were in good order. Maybe Tyson would help. Although she'd grown more independent in recent months, there were still things she didn't have the confidence to do herself and relied on her neighbour to help sort out.

As she pulled into the driveway, Tyson was sitting on her veranda holding a white envelope in his hands. *Another letter to read*, she thought. At least there was some way she could help and all the neighbourly support wasn't one way.

'I hope that's not the taxman after you, Tyson,' she joked as she got out of the car. Tyson didn't smile. He looked terrified. She set her handbag on the veranda and sat beside him.

'It's from one of my kids,' he said, passing her the envelope with a shaky hand.

'What lovely colouring,' she said, noticing the hand-drawn pink love hearts and purple pussycats. She pushed her finger under the seal, careful not to wreck the child's artwork. 'Let's see what we've got here.' Unfolding the single lined sheet that had been torn from an exercise book, she began to read aloud.

Hello, Dad,
I miss you. My teacher said if I wrote you a letter, she'd
send it. It's my first letter ever so I hope you get it. I's in

*year four now and Kaleesha's in year two. Robbie's goin to
kindy and Mum's got a job there. She says she likes being
with the kids cos she gets to play with them all day. The
Port Augusta mob is all right but they're different to the
mob in Lincoln. It would be good if you could let us visit
in the holidays. Is Louise and Mrs C doin okay? She must
miss Mr. C. I miss him sometimes. We got neighbours but
they're nothin like Mr. and Mrs C and Louise. Write back
when you get this. Happy Christmas. Lots of love, Sarah.*

Ellen put an arm around Tyson as he squeezed his eyes
against the tears.

'How am I gonna get 'em back, Mrs C?'

In all the years they'd lived side by side on Ocean Road,
Tyson and Sheryleen had been good neighbours. Without
being in each other's pockets, they'd been there for each
other. When Ellen needed a babysitter, Sheryleen would
have Louise, and when Lou was old enough, she'd mind
the three small children to give Sheryleen a break or let the
couple have a night out. No money was ever exchanged. It
was just what they did.

While Ellen was falling apart after Nick's death, she
was largely unaware of the ramifications of the event in the
house next door. She'd managed to sell the business and had
fully expected the new owner to keep Tyson on as part of
the crew. If she'd known the colour of his skin had been an
issue, she'd have found a worthier buyer, but settling Nick's
affairs had taken it out of her. She didn't have the energy for

a fight over what was a done deal. Anyway, Tyson had his pride and she was sure he'd get work on another fishing boat before too long. But it didn't happen overnight and certainly not in the timeframe that Sheryleen would have liked. The more time Tyson spent at home, it seemed to Ellen, the more time Sheryleen spent away. In fact, sometimes Ellen's day was punctuated only by the need to let Paddy out and feed him and the sound of Sheryleen's car driving past her driveway. To be fair, in the initial weeks after the accident, Sheryleen had called with cooked meals and a little shopping, but as time went on, Ellen saw less and less of her neighbour until one day she came and announced they were leaving. 'I can't stand it,' she said. 'I can't stand him.'

She'd held out hope that Sheryleen would be back, but Ellen had to admit it was looking less and less likely. As a social worker, she knew only too well that hope wasn't always the best help.

'Look, Tyson, I know you don't like talking about what Sheryleen did, but you have a right to see your kids.'

'She wouldn't do nothin' bad to them, Mrs C,' he said defensively.

'I know what you're saying, Tyson, but not letting them see you is bad in itself.' She paused as he took in what she was saying. 'If you and Sheryleen can't sort it out between yourselves, would you consider contacting our office to try and arrange visits?'

He shook his head.

'I don't want no social worker, with respect, Mrs C, prying into my business. Sheryleen wouldn't take too kindly to someone meddlin' in our affairs neither.'

'We're not all meddlers, Tyson, but I know where you're coming from. Why don't I make enquiries and find you someone you could work with?'

'Could *you* do it, Mrs C?'

'Conflict of interest, Tyson. I'm the next-door neighbour. I wouldn't be impartial.'

Her heart went out to the neighbour who would do all he could to help if the shoe were on the other foot. For most of her career, Ellen had worked in family reunification. Although hugely challenging, she'd relished navigating the complex and often long road that saw parents who'd had children taken away from them rehabilitate and equip themselves to engage positively in their children's lives. So many didn't make the effort, or failed trying to conquer addictions and destructive behaviours, but it was worth it for the ones that did. She wished she'd done something to help Tyson sooner. If Gerry hadn't come, she might still be living in her own little world.

'Let me see if one of my mob can help.'

'Okay, Mrs C.' He didn't look hopeful.

'In the meantime, come in and I'll help you reply to Sarah.'

Although his face brightened, he was hesitant about going inside.

'We'll think better with some food in us,' she said.

It was enough to convince him. He devoured the quiche she warmed up and gratefully accepted seconds. When he'd finished, she went to a drawer and pulled out a notepad and pen.

'Now, Tyson, what would you like to say?'

He began slowly and a bit formally at first, but as Ellen wrote down his words, he gained confidence and added some news about the town and his daughter's old schoolfriends. He promised he'd try to sort things out with her mum so that she and the other children could come and visit. When he'd finished, Ellen carefully pulled the page from the notepad and set them both in front of him.

'Have a try,' she urged. Tyson nervously took the pen and began to copy the words. She watched his big hand command the pen to form neat printed letters, and silently lamented the fact that his schooling was piecemeal at best. Somewhere along the line he'd learned the alphabet but never quite managed to string the letters together. When he'd finished, Tyson stretched his fingers back and forth. 'I should practise,' he said.

'Maybe now that you and Sarah are in touch, you'll have more reason to.' Her encouragement was rewarded with a broad smile.

'You're one smart lady, Mrs C.'

'Oh, just lucky, Tyson. Just lucky.'

Long after her neighbour had left, the words stayed with Ellen. She *was* lucky. She'd had a happy childhood, a good education, married a man she loved and had a wonderful daughter and good friends. Surely it was selfish to want more.

—

'A bit fond of the grog?' Sharon asked as they sat in one of the small interview rooms Ellen had chosen to avoid the embarrassment of a public dressing-down if things didn't go well.

Sharon McGuire was a social worker of legendary proportions. With a great booming voice that matched her formidable figure, she was known in the office, and indeed the town, as a battler. Even the boss, Dawn, was a little in awe of her. Aboriginal herself, Sharon was well versed in the cultural norms and entitlements of her community, but her real passion was the children, black or white, that got stuck in the middle of dysfunctional relationships. Get Sharon on your side and your case had more than a fighting chance. Get her offside and your case could crash and burn as fast as you'd stub out a cigarette.

'It's only a symptom,' said Ellen. 'He took Nick's death very hard and now that his wife has taken his kids away, the grog is only an escape.'

'So you're telling me,' said Sharon looking her squarely in the eye, 'if I intervene and get him access to his kids, he'll stop drinking?'

Ellen was cornered. How could she vouch for Tyson's ability to stay off alcohol long enough to get his life back on track? She thought about Gerry and how those few days had given her a new lease of life, enough to pull herself together and get back to work.

'Look at me, Sharon. You know how much of a mess I was after Nick died.'

Her experienced colleague wasn't going to fall for a sob story, but at least she was listening. 'I had a friend visit from Ireland and that meant so much to me. It made me want to live again. Tyson needs a reason to stay dry.'

Sharon shifted her wide frame in the armchair that looked less than comfortable.

'You know I don't like losing, Ellen. If I go in to bat for this man, he'd better meet me more than halfway.'

Sharon was seriously considering taking Tyson's case. Ellen wanted to phone Tracey right then and ask her to share a bottle of champagne. But it was early days. She'd wait until Sarah, Kaleesha and little Robbie were running around the property before she'd break open the bubbly.

Chapter Sixteen

November was nearly over. With the end of year exams out of the way, Louise turned her attention to the long summer holidays and what she might do to occupy her time. She'd decided to stay at Stavros and Kristina's for the remainder of semester where she continued to be treated like family. Nothing was said, but she knew Stavros had explained everything to Kristina. Instead of the usual rushed goodnights at the end of her Saturday shifts, Kristina made a point of sending her on her way with a hug and a smacker of a lipstick kiss to each cheek. The summer might be uncertain, but at least she had a job to come back to in second year.

'Looking forward to getting back to Lincoln?' Maxine asked from where she was stretched out on Louise's bed, leafing through the pages of a magazine.

'Not really.' Louise didn't look up from the pile of clothes she was bundling into her suitcase.

'Why's that?' Maxine asked absently.

'Oh, just because I have to live with my mother for three months.'

Maxine sat up and crossed her feet under her knees.

'I thought your mother was cool. I met her when she came to move you in.'

'That was then.' Louise slammed down the lid of the case, sat on it and forced the zip to close.

'You want to talk about it?'

'No.'

There was silence. Apart from her conversation with Stavros, Louise had kept her problems to herself. She had focused on study, work and hanging out with friends. Part of her wished it didn't have to end. She cursed the authorities that closed the halls to students in the summer and opened them to conference delegates. Her mother would arrive tomorrow and all that nonsense about her and Gerry Clancy would rear its ugly head again.

'What do you say to one last blast at the Den before you head off?' Maxine was sitting at the edge of the bed like someone ready to leap from a diving board, that signature mix of mischief and excitement in her eyes.

'I'll be in bits tomorrow when my mother comes.'

'Darcy's having a party later. Maybe we could crash it?'

Did Maxine ever listen?

'I'll do the Den, but no promises on your brother's party.'

'We could wear those hot dresses we bought at Harbour Town.' She was on a roll. Although Louise would rather have pulled on an old cardigan and leggings and sat watching a DVD on her last night of freedom, her friend wouldn't be swayed. The prospect of having to avoid Toby Scott for the hundredth time made her cringe.

—

The Den was heaving. Louise regretted following Maxine's wardrobe advice when she walked into the bar and saw the rest of the crew in jeans and T-shirts. Demi, a student from Louise's course, was the first to comment.

'What a beautiful dress,' she said. 'I feel like such a dag.'

Louise went to explain, but as she turned the words evaporated. Toby Scott was heading straight towards her. Judging by the unkempt hair and silly grin, his end-of-year celebrations had started much earlier in the day.

Oh my God. Louise looked everywhere but in his direction.

'So, Demi, what are your plans for the summer?' She needed a focus, but Demi didn't get a chance to reply. Toby pointed his beer glass like an unwieldy sword and cut in between them.

'Hello, Lou,' he slurred. 'I'm not here to harass you. I just . . .' He staggered slightly. 'I just wanted to tell you . . .' The group went quiet. 'To tell you how . . . ravishing you look in that black number.' If the ground opened and swallowed her right then, it wouldn't be too soon. There was nothing for it but to stand, arms folded, and hope he'd finish what he had to say and go. 'I hope you have a pleasant summer,' he said in a posh accent before bowing with a flourish of his free hand, the glass listing to one side like a boat in high seas.

Her friends' circle widened as they dodged the spillage. Louise stood incredulous, the beer soaking down the front of her new dress.

'Jesus, Lou, I'm so sorry,' said Toby as he righted himself and realised what he'd done.

Her friend Adam set his chunky frame between them. 'Okay, you can piss off now,' he told Toby, who took a wobbly step back and slinked off to find his mates.

Maxine came back from the toilets and stared at Louise who was using the hoodie Adam had kindly offered to wipe down her dress.

'What the . . .'

Demi got in before Louise could speak.

'You just missed the hottest boy in first year wishing Lou a *pleasant summer*,' she mocked, 'while spilling beer all over her.'

'What a dick.' Maxine didn't hide her disgust. 'Come and we'll dry that off with the hand dryer.'

Demi joined them in the bathroom.

'That guy has it bad for you, Lou,' she said. 'I can't understand why you ever broke up with him. He's the full package – hot *and* smart.'

Louise just rolled her eyes.

'My mumma says never trust a man who can't hold his drink,' Maxine joked. But Louise was in no mood for laughing. Toby Scott had just ruined her night. She went back to the bar and drank all the free vodka she could manage.

—

'Ah, Maxine. You came to keep an eye on me. Good on ya.' Darcy held out his arms to his twin sister, but Maxine brushed past him in her rush to suss out who else was at this party. He ignored her and turned his attention to Louise. 'You're looking hot tonight.' He slipped his arm around her and was leading her down the hallway. 'Are you still with that uni bloke, or am I in with a chance?'

Maxine spun round.

'Paws off her, bro. She's too good for you.' She pulled Louise toward her and glared at her brother. 'I hope that's not dope I can smell or I'll dob you in with Dad.'

Darcy let out a nervous laugh. 'My friends are here to enjoy themselves, sis. Give me a break.'

Louise felt skittish. The drink had gone to her legs and she needed to sit down. Leaving the siblings to it, she went into the kitchen.

'Can I help you there?'

Drunk or not, she picked the Irish accent. She looked at the tall sandy-haired boy standing beside her. There was something easy, unthreatening about him.

'Sorry, I just wanted a glass of water.'

'No worries.' The boy reached up to one of the cupboards and took down a large tumbler. She watched him take it to the water filter and fill it for her.

'I live here,' he said. 'That's how I know where everything is.'

As much as she'd like to have stood there and chatted, her stomach had other ideas.

'I think I might be going to . . .'

'This way.'

He took hold of her hand as he might a child's and led her to the bathroom.

Why didn't I quit while I was ahead? she thought as she waited for the next wave of nausea to do its worst. She flushed away the half-digested contents of her stomach and washed her face. In the mirror, she dabbed at the panda marks around her eyes and cursed Maxine for talking her into coming out. Her hair had come undone. There was no sign of her hair tie. Her fingers would have to do as a brush. It didn't feel right wearing her hair down. She looked like her old self.

The Irish boy was waiting when she came out.

'You didn't lock it,' he said. 'I thought I'd better wait.'

'Oh, thanks.' Mortified at what he must have heard, she thought to make a beeline for the lounge and beg Maxine to leave, but something about his easy manner made her want to stay with him. 'I wouldn't mind some air,' she said.

'I'll grab your glass and meet you outside.' He gestured to a set of patio doors.

Cars whizzed past on the city street below the balcony, Adelaide still alive in the early hours of the morning. It wouldn't be like this in Lincoln.

'Here you are.' He returned with her glass and sat in the chair beside her. 'I'm Kieran, by the way.' She shook his outstretched hand and marvelled at the maturity of the boy who must have been about the same age as herself.

'Louise.' She sculled back the water in the hope that it might freshen her breath and sober her up. 'I'm just finished first year uni and my mother is coming to take me home tomorrow.' She checked her phone. Two a.m. 'No, today actually. She won't be happy if she catches me in this state.'

'Ah, you'll be fine. What time is she coming?'

Louise wasn't sure how this guy she'd never met before could be so reassuring, but as they talked, she felt herself relax. He told her he was working and travelling for a year. When he asked if she understood his accent, she said it was easy. He sounded just like her mother. When Maxine eventually joined them, they were getting on like a house on fire.

'I see you've met Saint Kieran, my brother's housemate,' she said. 'Anyone who'd share with Darcy would have to be a saint.'

Darcy appeared, making ugly faces behind her back. Kieran and Louise looked at each other and cracked up laughing. Maxine chased her brother back into the house, shouting after him, 'You . . . I'll get you!'

'Sisterly love,' said Kieran. 'They're a riot. My sister wouldn't be seen dead with me at a party.'

'I wouldn't know,' said Louise. 'I'm an only child.'

'They say what you don't have, you don't miss.'

'I don't know about that.' She looked across the street to the blackened windows of empty offices. 'It sucks being an only child. Especially when you're a teenager and it's just you they get to ground.'

'You've got strict parents then?' asked Kieran.

She took a deep breath. So many of her Adelaide friends had made the same assumption.

'Actually, my dad is dead. Just Mum and me now.'

'Oh, I'm so sorry, I just . . .'

'Don't worry. Everyone does it.' Those pesky tears that often snuck up on her welled in her eyes. She should have been used to this by now. They sat in awkward silence. Thankfully Maxine was back before long.

'Come on, Miss Constantinopoulos. I've had enough of this mob and you have to get your butt back to Port Lincoln in a few hours.'

Kieran sat forward in his chair. 'Are you from Port Lincoln?'

'She is,' Maxine answered. 'And her mother won't be happy if she finds her daughter hungover.'

Louise dragged herself up from the chair. 'Oh, Max. Did you have to remind me?' She said goodbye to Kieran, feeling as though she could have talked to him all night. Funny how some people made you feel like you'd known them for years.

Chapter Seventeen

Gerry was behind the bar waiting for a pint of Guinness to settle when the phone vibrated in his pocket. He read the text.

Hey, Dad. Ring me when you get a chance.

'The son in Australia,' he told the customer.

'It'll be money he's after no doubt,' said the man at the bar. 'My fella went off for a year a while back. Wasn't there three months and he was tapping me for a loan. Living it up out there, that's all they want. In my day it was hard graft . . .'

Gerry let him rant, only half listening as he carefully ran a knife over the head of the pint. He wanted to tell this eejit how different it was with *his* son, how proud he was of Kieran, and how it had just made his day to hear from him. Feigning a smile, he set the pint on the bar. The grumpy old goat wasn't going to ruin it for him.

Bronwyn Fennelly was coming back from the restaurant with an order for the kitchen. Gerry silently admired her smart black miniskirt and the silver satin shirt that made the most of her assets. She smiled at him with dark chocolaty eyes that matched the tones in the strands that slipped from her smooth ponytail.

'Hey, Bron.' He beckoned to her with his head.

'What is it, Big Boy?' she said in a voice just low enough not to be heard by the whole bar. He blushed as she came and stood beside him, close enough to feel the satin of her sleeve on his bare arm and see the swell of her breasts at the shirt's plunging neckline.

'Any chance you could serve while I nip out the back?' he asked. 'I want to call Kieran.'

'Sure,' she said, flashing a smile at the next male customer. 'But it'll cost ya,' she whispered, handing him the food order and pulling it back playfully before he could take it.

Gerry shook his head as he went into the kitchen and passed the order to Noely.

'From Bronwyn,' he said.

Noely wiped a hand down the tea towel he had slung over his shoulder and took the paper. 'You'd want to watch out for that one, boss,' he said with a toothy grin.

Gerry thought about responding but, eager to talk to his son, he let it go. He went out the back door and stood in the alleyway. It was the middle of the night in Australia, but Kieran must need to speak to him to text at this hour.

'Hello, Dad?'

'Hi, son. I wasn't sure if you'd be awake. What's the story?'

'I met her, Dad. I met Louise.' Kieran sounded wide awake. Gerry could hear loud music in the background. 'She came here to a party with the flatmate's sister. You know the sporty guy, Darcy? *His* sister. They're in uni together.'

'How did you know it was her?' Gerry was a little in shock that Kieran had met the half-sister that he himself had only just discovered existed.

'Funny thing is we were talking for ages, getting on really well and everything. Then her friend came along and called her Miss Constantinopoulos. She didn't look very Greek. I swear I could see a family resemblance. When she mentioned having to head back to Port Lincoln, it didn't take a genius to work out who she was.' There was a pause as Gerry took in what he was hearing.

'So did you tell her who you were?'

'No, that's the thing,' said Kieran, frustration in his voice. 'Her friend whisked her away before I got a chance.'

Gerry put a hand to his ear to block out the noise of the kitchen and the bar beyond. 'Are you likely to see her again?'

'I doubt it. She's heading home for the summer and I might have moved on by the time she starts uni next year.' Gerry could hear the disappointment.

'Well, at least you know what she looks like, and you got a chance to talk to her a bit.'

'Yeah, I guess. But the weird thing is, Dad, I really liked her. I felt I'd known her for years. Seems a shame not to have some contact with the girl.'

'Things have a funny way of sorting themselves out,' said Gerry, wishing he had more than the platitude to offer his son.

Standing for a minute after hanging up, Gerry registered the cold of the late November night. It would be warming up in Port Lincoln. Ellen would be enjoying balmy evenings on her veranda. If only he could see her again and make something of their mixed-up relationship.

⁓

Apart from scary road trains, Ellen coped better with driving to Adelaide than she'd expected. Tracey was perfect company, reassuring her when someone overtook them and keeping up the conversation without distracting her. Jennifer spent most of the hours on her phone. Ellen could never have imagined having to rely on Jennifer to act as go-between, but for over two months now it had been the only way she and Louise had communicated. Although work had kept Ellen busy, it had been lonely in the evenings without her daughter's calls. If they couldn't work things out, the tension in the house might be worse than being alone. She wouldn't say as much aloud, but part of her dreaded Louise coming home.

It was only when Tracey dozed off midway that Ellen's mind turned to thoughts of Gerry. She tried to envisage him making the same trip. Had he been in awe of the Flinders Ranges just like she was, no matter how many times she saw them? Had he marvelled at their undulating folds of ochre rising up to form the rugged skyline? Since he'd left, she'd been racked with guilt. Guilt at pushing him away, and guilt at wanting him again, when her lovely Nick had died so prematurely.

Louise was sitting on her suitcase outside the uni hall when they got there. Jennifer jumped out of the car and ran over to embrace her. Tracey was next for one of those hugs Ellen so longed for.

'How are you, my love?' she asked, holding out an arm ready for her turn, but Louise's arms barely rested on her mother's waist. She placed a cool peck on her cheek and went to organise her belongings with Jennifer. Ellen avoided Tracey's eyes, the chill between the Constantinopoulos women as embarrassing as it was painful. She went to open the boot of the Chrysler.

'Nice wheels.'

A tall blond boy appeared beside them, a huge rucksack on his back and a hold-all with a lava lamp sticking out of the top of it in his arms.

'Thanks,' said Ellen. 'She's a 1957 Chrysler Royal. My husband bought her about ten years ago.'

'Sweet.' He hovered beside them, balancing his cumbersome baggage.

Ellen heard Louise give a sigh that had nothing to do with the full to bursting suitcase she and Jennifer were setting in the boot. The seconds passed, but Louise didn't turn round. Ellen couldn't stand it.

'Do you know Louise?' she asked, intrigued to know why her feisty daughter had seemed to shrink several inches at the sound of this young man's voice.

'This is Toby,' said Louise, shoving a begrudging shoulder in the boy's direction, hands dug deep into the pockets of her cropped jeans. 'My mum,' she told Toby, barely looking him in the eye. 'This is Jennifer and her mum, Tracey.'

'Nice to meet you all,' he said, the rucksack leaning as he bent his head toward them.

Tracey glanced at Ellen with a raised eyebrow.

'I've seen you on Facebook,' said Jennifer, grinning.

'Are you on Louise's course?' asked Ellen, anxious to move the conversation on and get going if her scarlet-faced daughter wasn't going to help.

'No, I'm doing straight science, but I'm in some of Lou's classes.'

'Oh, lovely,' said Ellen. 'So are you heading home for the summer too?'

'Yeah, I'm just gonna grab a bus. I'm taking a flight home to Alice Springs tonight.'

When exactly Louise intended to join in the conversation was a mystery to Ellen. It wasn't like her to be this antisocial, at least with people other than her mother.

'We could take you to the airport,' she offered. 'We're going to Ikea, aren't we, girls? Sure it's only across the road.'

Only Tracey voiced her agreement. Louise bent her head and fiddled with an errant strand of hair. Ellen wished she'd brushed it.

'Hop in,' she told Toby.

'Oh, if you're sure.' He glanced at Louise.

'Of course I'm sure.'

⁓

'Sorry about last night, Lou,' Toby whispered. 'I didn't mean to be so embarrassing.'

Louise looked up into his baby blue eyes, taking in the clean T-shirt and still unkempt hair. *God, why did he have to be so polite and good-looking?*

'Don't worry about it,' she said, forcing herself to sound cross. 'You just entertained the whole bar at my expense.'

He hung his head, but a hopeful smile curled at the corners of his mouth as he peeked at her over the lava lamp. She smiled back despite herself, surprised by the heat that rushed to her cheeks.

'All set?' shouted Ellen.

Louise had no option but to sit in the middle with Toby's hold-all propped on her lap as he balanced the rucksack against the window. Jennifer's elbow dug at her on one side while on the other she felt the cotton of Toby's T-shirt and the warm skin of his perfectly tanned forearm.

They drove past lines of city houses punctuated by the occasional jacaranda tree shedding its mauve blossoms.

'So what will you do with yourself in Alice over the summer?' her mother quizzed.

'I'll get work with my dad,' said Toby. 'He runs a tour company, trips to Uluru and all that.'

Louise couldn't believe her mother. She nearly had his family's life story by the time they got to the airport.

'Well, if you get a chance,' she was saying, 'come and get some surfing in around Lincoln. Louise and Jennifer know all the good spots.'

'Sounds great,' said Toby, beaming as he got out of the car. 'I'd love that.'

'Give him a hand there, Lou.'

Louise sucked in her annoyance at her mother's demand, but got out and helped him with his bags.

'Maybe see you in the summer then, Lou,' he said as he buckled the rucksack round his waist.

'You'll be too busy in Alice.' She pushed the hold-all at him.

'Don't bet on it,' he said with a wink. 'Thanks,' he shouted to Ellen as he jogged toward the departures entrance, rucksack swinging behind him.

'What a nice young man,' said Ellen as they pulled away.

'Indeed,' agreed Tracey.

Jennifer made a face as Louise strapped herself in. She'd expect to get the low down on Toby later. If sitting up close to him for the last twenty minutes had made Louise remember the short but wonderful time they'd shared, it didn't mean she'd changed her mind. Besides, she had bigger things to worry about, like how to survive the summer with her mother.

Ellen had hoped the retail therapy trip to the city would help restore her relationship with Louise and make the long drive back to Lincoln in a couple of days more bearable. But Louise's attitude put a dampener on the whole experience and although nothing was mentioned explicitly, the vibes were enough to relay the message loud and clear that she had in no way forgiven her mother for the way in which she'd found out about her biological father. Jennifer's loyalty to her friend had only served to reinforce any negative behaviour from Louise, and by the middle of the next day, Ellen and Tracey had decided to leave the young ones in Adelaide's city centre and head to the retail outlet at Harbour Town.

'It's still raw for her,' said Tracey as they sat in a cafe enveloped in the aromas of coffee and fresh cakes.

'I don't know what to say to her, Tracey. It's going to be a horrible summer in our house if she can't shake the attitude. And Christmas . . .'

'You'll just have to have it out with her,' said Tracey. 'She can't treat you like a criminal for what you did.'

'I feel so guilty. If I had my time over, I'd have told her when she turned eighteen. Nick and I should have told her together. At least then she would have seen that both of us were to blame.' She added a rare sugar to the coffee that tasted as bitter as Louise's wrath. 'She must be gutted, Tracey. Nick was her world.'

'Come on, Ellen. Louise might as well have been Nick's, he loved her so much. And you've been a great mother to her. She's had a wonderful upbringing. She can't hold this against you forever. You've got to confront her and get it all out of your systems.'

Tracey was right, but what if having it out with her daughter alienated her even further?

Chapter Eighteen

It was midnight when they pulled into the driveway on Ocean Road. Ellen dug deep into what was left of her energy reserves to drag Louise's suitcases onto the veranda.

'We can leave the rest till tomorrow,' she called, but Louise had already gone into the house without even holding the screen door open for her.

'I'm going to bed,' Louise announced.

Ellen registered the chill in her tone and remembered Tracey's advice. She set the case down and closed the front door.

'I think we should talk, Lou.'

'Can't it wait? I'm so tired after that endless journey . . .'

'No,' said Ellen. 'I've waited since September. Two months I've waited already.' Her voice was getting away from her, but they had to have this out. There'd been enough silence. 'We *need* to talk.' She counted to ten as she plumped up a cushion and sat down in Nick's old armchair. *Be with me in this*, she asked him inwardly.

Louise huffed and took a seat on the lounge, arms folded, legs crossed.

'I don't blame you for hating me,' said Ellen. 'I should never have kept the truth from you.'

Louise didn't look at her, but fixed her eyes on the window.

'Myself and your father—'

'Don't mention my father,' Louise cut her off, a clenched fist pounding the couch with each word. 'He was too good for you. He should never have fallen for you. You're just a liar.'

Ellen had seen her daughter through tantrums and mood swings but had never in nineteen years witnessed such anger, such venom.

'Say whatever you want, Louise. I'll hear you out. I just want us to get past this and move on.'

'Move on!' Louise was on her feet. 'Is that what you did when you *moved on* from Dad and invited Gerry over here to hook up with you?'

It was tearing Ellen up inside to hear her daughter speak like this. Tears leaked from the corners of her eyes, but she was determined to listen in an effort to understand how Louise felt.

'You lied to Dad. You let him believe I was his. How could you have been so deceitful?'

She stormed out to the kitchen. Ellen went after her. In the months since all of this had come out, Ellen had agonised over how Louise would be feeling, what would have gone through her mind. More than anything, she'd feared that Louise would think she'd been dishonest with Nick. In her daughter's eyes, that would have been her biggest wrongdoing. She summoned what was left of her energy.

'You've got the wrong end of the stick, Lou.'

'What do you mean?' Louise spun round, her face burning with fury.

'Your father knew you weren't his.'

Louise looked at her, incredulous.

'Nick loved you because you were mine, part of me,' she went on. 'He loved us both more than anything.' The exhaustion came again, threatening to overwhelm her. She slumped into a chair.

'It's all about you, isn't it?' Louise rounded, giving a mock laugh. 'It has always been about you. Dad would have done anything for you. He idolised you. Even when you were unreasonable, making me do chores none of my friends had to do, making me study when my friends were hanging out, he always stood up for you, telling me to go easy on you, about all the sacrifices you'd made for me.'

Ellen smarted at the tirade, only partially soothed by the reminder of Nick's feelings for her.

'Sacrifices!' Louise hadn't finished. 'What about all *I've* done for you? The daily phone calls to make sure *you* were okay. All those times I came home to help you when I could have been having a great time in Adelaide with my friends, like a normal student.'

'I know, Lou. I appreciate everything you've done—' Ellen began, but Louise was spitting fire.

'No, you've moved on. Everything is fine and dandy. You've got Gerry back in your life. You're driving. You're back at work. You won't even need me.'

As Louise stormed out of the kitchen and up the stairs, Ellen thought she might collapse with the pain that clenched at her core. The bedroom door slammed shut. What could she possibly do to make things right?

Louise yawned as she registered the morning sunlight spearing through a crack in her curtains. Her head felt like a cannonball. Any sleep she'd had the night before had come in fits between the hours she'd spent lying awake in the darkness going over the fight with her mother. She'd had fights with her mother before, but this was different. It was like she'd exploded. At times in the night she'd wondered if she'd gone too far. It was starting to sink in. Her dad had known. If her mother was telling the truth, the man she'd looked up to, her hero, had been in on the secret. That hurt more than anything. She may as well have lost him all over again.

There was a light knock on the door. Throwing the duvet over her head, she willed her mother to go away, but she could hear the handle turning and sensed her hovering in the doorway.

'I brought you a cuppa.'

Fighting a childish urge to stay under the covers, she sat up, pushing against the pillows to put the maximum distance between herself and her mother who was standing there with that stupid cup of tea as if it were enough to solve the world's problems.

'So why didn't you guys give me a brother or a sister?' She took the cup but dispensed with manners.

Her mother looked at the edge of the bed, but didn't sit down.

'We wanted that so badly,' she said, lowering her head, 'but your dad couldn't have children.'

At nineteen, Louise may not have had much experience, but she understood the pain suffered by people who couldn't conceive. Tears threatened at the thought of her dad's longing, but there were still parts of this story she needed to be told, and her mother had gotten away without telling them long enough.

'Did you never think to go back to Ireland and just be honest with everybody?'

Her mother pointed to the furthest corner of the bed and looked to her for permission. Louise nodded. Sitting there with bags under her eyes, looking old, her mother let her in on the tale of her conception, a conversation she knew her mother had never wanted to have. It was falling into place: why she hadn't known her grandmother; why they'd never visited their relatives in Sydney; the sad look in her dad's eyes when she'd press for answers and he'd give her a wink that urged her to leave it. The falling-outs with her grandmother and grand-aunt had been about her.

Wringing her hands, her mother looked up at her. 'Maybe I should have tried to make peace with my mother, gone back as you say, but I was young and hurt . . .'

Louise wanted to run outside, jump on Spots and ride far away, but this mess was theirs, her mother's and hers. She had misunderstood. She suddenly realised that her actions over the past months – ignoring her mother's phone calls, vilifying her, breaking up with Toby Scott – had all stemmed from believing her father hadn't known about Gerry Clancy, and blaming her mother for not having told him. But her father had known everything. Even before there was mention of Gerry Clancy, he had been protecting both her and her mother. He'd chosen to be her father in a way that Gerry never could have done. It was an unconditional love, unobscured by duty.

'I never invited Gerry,' her mother was saying almost to herself. 'I hadn't collected my mail in weeks and missed the letter saying he was visiting his son.'

Louise thought of all the nights she'd phoned home to make sure her mother was okay, the change in her when she'd come home that weekend of Gerry's visit, how much better she'd looked and sounded, the fact that she'd been able to go back to work. The man was obviously very special to her. She pushed the duvet away and moved down the bed beside her mother.

'I'm sorry, Mum. I've been so horrible.'

'No, my love. I'm the one who needs to apologise. I should have told you long ago. But to be honest, if your father had lived, I may never have told you. In his mind, you were his and who was I to take that away from him?'

'I know you did it because you loved him, Mum. But I had a right to know.' She reached out and pushed gently at a fallen lock of her mother's hair. 'Gerry had a right to know from the beginning.'

'Oh, my Baby Lou, I'm so sorry.'

Louise enfolded her mother in her arms. She now understood the challenges this woman had faced when she was not much older than she herself was now. Challenges she'd faced without family. They needed to stick together. Holding her mother close, Louise let the tears that had been building up over months finally flow.

Chapter Nineteen

In Cork, Gerry had just woken up in the flat he shared with Donal above the Stables. He was coming through to the kitchen to make his first coffee of the day when the smell of a hard night made him glance toward the living room. Donal lay comatose on the sofa, still dressed and slobbering into one of the cushions, a whiskey bottle empty on the floor. Port Lincoln felt like a lifetime away. He'd get his coffee downstairs.

The new coffee machine was another improvement to the premises Gerry wasn't sure they could afford. But Donal was in charge. Gerry was just the helper as his brother had made patently clear. So far there'd been no sign of the share in the profits Donal had promised. 'Next month will be better. We're still only breaking even,' he'd tell him.

'Morning, Sheila,' he said as he came down the stairs.

Sheila Flannery was backing her sprightly frame out of the female toilets, followed by deliberate sweeps of her mop.

'Ah, 'tis yourself, Gerry. Always up before your big brother.'

She leaned on the mop, ready to expand on her observation, but Gerry strode past her with a smile, happy to be through the wall of citrus disinfectant and leave the gossipmonger to the job she was paid to do. At the bar, he switched on the coffee machine and went to open the back door. The delivery truck was already unloading crates of vegetables. Lately he'd been doing all the donkey work – carrying in the supplies and unloading them into the fridges and boxes that were lined against one wall. Donal had thought it would save money if they did it themselves instead of paying kitchen staff to come in early.

No sooner had Gerry cleared that lot than the bakery van pulled up. The smell always took him back to their old premises and he cursed having to close it in the name of progress. He'd offered to bake fresh bread and scones every morning, but Donal had knocked him back, saying he didn't care if he never baked a single thing again in his life.

Gerry was just finishing in the kitchen when he heard a tapping on the front door.

'Ah, Dad. You're out early this morning.'

Gerry Senior took off his tweed cap and leather gloves as he stepped into the lounge, taking in everything from ceiling to floor as though he'd never been there before.

'The place is looking well, son,' he said. 'Ye're making a great job of it.'

'Yeah. It's taking shape. How do you like the new dance floor?'

'Marvellous,' said Gerry Senior as he skirted round the lacquered floorboards. 'Not that you'll be catching me on it,' he laughed.

'Ah, now sure, you never know, Dad. We might have you tripping the light fantastic yet.'

There was a whimpering from outside.

'Don't tell me you brought that mutt with you again?'

Domingo sat at the glass door, head on one side, using all his cocker spaniel powers of persuasion to be allowed in.

'I told him he'd have to wait,' said Gerry Senior, 'but the bugger won't take any heed.'

'You'll have us closed down by health and safety, Dad.' Gerry opened the door and looked both ways along the street, but before he could decide whether or not to let him in, the spaniel rushed past his legs.

'Is that coffee I smell?' asked Gerry Senior, ignoring his son's frustration and resting his tall frame on a bar stool.

'Cappuccino, I suppose?' said Gerry through pursed lips. 'There's a fresh scone just delivered if you want . . .'

'Fresh scone me eye,' his dad scoffed. 'God be with the days when we'd have scones straight out of the oven with the butter dripping off them.'

Here we go, thought Gerry as he listened to his father lament the demise of the family bakery and the relentless rise of the supermarket. Even Domingo resigned himself to listening to his master's monologue and lay down on the carpet, eyes closed, head between his paws.

'I don't know why ye're not back there in that kitchen baking after the years of good training I gave ye.' Gerry Senior looked around. 'And where's that brother of yours?'

Gerry didn't answer.

'Don't tell me he's back to his old tricks, drinking all night and sleeping all day?'

'It's not quite that bad, Dad.' He didn't want to completely land his brother in it. 'He'll be on the job by lunchtime.'

'And you're left holding the baby while he recovers from yet another hangover? I'll go up there and give him a piece of my mind.' The older man was out of his seat, ready to march upstairs and lambast his eldest son.

'Ah, Dad. Leave him alone.'

'Gerry, sometimes I think he's running this place in name only. 'Tis you're doing most of the work.' He sat back down and leaned on the counter. 'I hope you know I only let him be the boss because I'm getting too old for the stress of it and you've had other things to be looking after.'

It was no secret his parents had been disappointed about his divorce. Not that Gerry Senior would have come right out and said it. He was from a generation that didn't talk much about affairs of the heart. His mother had done the listening and talking for both of them.

'You're doing a great job, moving on and all that,' said his dad.

Gerry wanted to laugh in his face and tell him how wrong he was. He hadn't moved on. He wanted to be back in the bakery, working alongside him, up to his elbows in fresh scones and batch loaves. As for Jessica Sheehy, of course he'd moved on there. When she'd sat him down and told him she wasn't happy and that they'd grown apart, he hadn't been surprised. There'd been nothing for it but to call it quits. But where had it all left him? In a bachelor pad with a wayward brother, a son on the other side of the world, a daughter he hardly saw and two women in Australia he wished had never left Ireland.

'You've always covered for your brother, son,' his dad was saying, 'but don't let that kind heart of yours drive you to an early grave. He has to do his share.' He stood up again and fished in his jacket pockets. 'Now, boy,' he said, putting a red envelope on the bar, 'put an address on that, will ya? I want to send a few bob to my grandson.'

Gerry smiled as he took a pen and wrote down Kieran's address.

'Morning, Mr Clancy.' Sheila came through into the lounge armed with the vacuum.

'How are you, Sheila?' asked Gerry Senior.

'Fair to middling as they say,' Sheila replied. She plugged in the vacuum, but stood up without turning it on. 'You'll have to come out of that semi-retirement and give young Gerry here more of a hand.'

The two of them looked at her.

'And why's that, Sheila?' Gerry Senior asked.

'I'm afraid your other son wasn't bestowed with the gene for hard work you passed on to this lad,' she said without smiling.

Gerry didn't know whether to hug the interfering old bat or fire her on the spot. There was an awkward silence until Sheila turned on the machine and got back to work.

At the door, Gerry went to give Domingo a pat, but thought better of it.

'Leave him home the next time, Dad.'

'Ah, son, would you see me without a pal in my winter years?'

'I thought that's why you had Mam.'

His dad laughed as he pulled on his leather gloves. 'Speaking of Her Loveliness,' he said, lowering his voice, 'can you make sure your brother is sober when he comes for his dinner on Christmas Day, or I'll be hearing about it for the next twelve months.'

Gerry agreed, but didn't feel at all confident in delivering on his promise.

Bronwyn Fennelly came blustering through the main door of the Stables an hour later. Gerry took in the black above-the-knee boots and three-quarter trench coat cinched at the waist. In the couple of months he'd been home, he'd come to like working with the girl. She was usually upbeat and got on with the job, but there was no mistaking the change of mood today.

'Donal still in bed, I suppose?'

She marched through the gap in the bar and straight into the kitchen. He followed her and rested his shoulder against the doorframe, taking in the new streak of red in the sleek forelock that fell over her forehead.

'It's the third week in a row,' she ranted. 'I didn't mind the first while, but Jesus Christ this is beyond a joke.' She stomped around the steel island, flinging her handbag down and unbuttoning her coat. Gerry had never seen this side of Bronwyn before, but even if her anger was aimed at his brother, she looked mighty attractive when she was mad.

'What's on your mind, Bron?' he asked, keeping his voice calm. Bronwyn pulled an apron over her tight wool dress and ripped a head of lettuce from the fridge.

'I'm fed up of it, Gerry. Every time I come in here, it's just you, me and Noely left to do everything.' She raised her voice over the running water as she washed the lettuce leaves. 'We're slaving, day in day out, to put food on the plates of his beloved customers while he's up there lying in his bed.'

Gerry wanted to defend his brother, but Bronwyn had a point. She was a good worker, and although he didn't take kindly to staff members downgrading the man, he had to concede they weren't blind to Donal's behaviour.

'Ah sure I know, Bron. He's an awful man when he lets the old stress get to him, but he has a good heart. Would you like me to have a word with him?'

She looked up from the chopping board. 'If he were my brother, I'd nearly stab him.' She wielded the knife to demonstrate her weapon of choice.

'Ah now, Bron, that's a bit harsh.'

'Do you know what your problem is, Gerry Clancy?' She scooped up the lettuce pieces and dropped them in a bowl. 'You're too nice.' His cheeks burned as she went on. 'If your brother had half your style, he'd have it made. It's not right. He's the one with the cash and you're the one with the good looks and personality.'

'Don't hold back there, Bronwyn,' he laughed.

'I'm only calling a spade a spade,' she said as she tore into the task of chopping tomatoes.

By the time Noely, the kitchen hand, showed up, Gerry was at the bar serving the first customers of the day and Bronwyn was working like a maniac behind the scenes to get the lunch specials prepared.

'The boss had one of his nights?' asked Noely as Gerry came into the kitchen to grab a couple of slices of cheesecake for two women taking a break from a shopping spree. Before he could reply, they heard Donal's voice from the lounge.

'Morning ladies,' Donal was saying. 'Have ye come in to get a bit of warmth? It must be freezing out there.'

That's my brother, ever the charmer, thought Gerry as he set the plates on the table.

'I see Gerry's looking after ye,' said Donal, smiling broadly. At the bar, he helped himself to a double espresso and took it to the kitchen. 'And how are we all this morning?' he asked them.

'Not too bad, boss. Yourself?' said Noely.

Bronwyn didn't look up from the soup pot she was stirring into submission on the cooker.

'Grand,' said Donal, but his bloodshot eyes told them he was anything but. 'What have we for specials today, Bron?'

Bronwyn pointed to the large whiteboard where they planned each day's roster and menu. 'Veggie lasagne and grilled beef burgers,' he read aloud. 'Lovely jovely.' He went to the safe in the small office and took out the takings from the night before.

'I'm off to bank this lot,' he told them and gulped back his coffee, leaving the cup beside the sink for someone else to wash.

'See you when we see you so,' said Bronwyn.

Time for a brotherly chat, thought Gerry. *Man to man.*

Chapter Twenty

Louise couldn't believe her luck when Judy Lawson phoned and asked her to help out at the riding centre. Over the years she'd spent lots of time there, but to be offered a paid job was a dream come true.

'Don't forget to eat breakfast,' she heard her mum shout from the bedroom.

Downstairs, she grabbed a quick slice of toast but had it barely buttered when Judy's ute thundered into the driveway. Boots in one hand, toast in the other, she ran out of the house.

'Ah you've got slack with all those ten o' clock uni starts,' Judy roared to Louise over the barking of a pair of young kelpies nearly spilling out of the back of the ute.

'I'll be waiting on the veranda tomorrow,' Louise promised, not sure how she could manage to get up even earlier.

'First ride's at eight-thirty,' said Judy speeding out of the driveway. 'Less than an hour to have ten horses ready.'

Louise's tummy flipped in anticipation. Ten ponies to catch. Forty sweet-smelling hooves to clean out. Ten bridles, ten saddles and girths to put on . . . Heaven.

—

It was already twenty-five degrees by the time the first clients of the day arrived.

'I'll lead if you bring up the rear, Lou,' said Judy. 'Watch out for any horses trying to duck out of line.'

While Louise handed out helmets, Judy pointed to each rider in turn, shouting a pony's name.

'Meatloaf, Bon Jovi, you're on Elvis . . .'

There were a few giggles, but a pause and a stern look from Judy were enough to restore quiet attention. Louise began helping riders onto ponies and adjusting stirrups. It would be an hour-long ride along the beach. They would break halfway and distribute the small water bottles she and Judy carried in backpacks. The horses stamped and snorted. As she mounted Marvin, she could feel the ripple of excitement in her tummy.

'All set?' Judy led them out of the yard, leaving Louise to sort out the timid riders at the rear. City kids, who'd never been on a horse before, smiled with that mixture of pleasure and anxiety. On the beach, Judy took the experienced riders ahead at a canter. Louise was happy to see them go as she watched her novice charges gain confidence and tried them at a trot.

Midway through the ride, the horses stopped, ears twitching at the sound of Judy's voice. Louise helped her hand out the drinks, making sure everyone was happy and hydrated before heading back on the homeward leg of their circuit.

'This is going to be one great summer,' Louise said into Marvin's ear.

After each day's riding, they'd untack the horses and turn them out to the paddocks. Louise worked flat out, washing bits, hanging up bridles and saddles and cleaning the yard while Judy got on with the office work. On her breaks, she'd sit in a lounger and read a book, but sometimes in the middle of a chapter she found herself thinking of Gerry Clancy.

Louise considered the notion that she could have been brought up in Ireland if her mother had stayed. She might have had brothers and sisters and been part of one of those big Irish families Jennifer talked about, with hundreds of cousins. How different her life might have been, but how much she would have missed out on by not having the father she loved as part of it. Gerry Clancy was a world away. Who knew if he would ever come back or if he and her mother would get back together at some point in the future? They obviously had something special between them. But it was too soon for such thoughts. Gerry Clancy was not a bad person, but no one could take the place of Nick Constantinopoulos, her father.

Ellen was pleased to see Louise happy and her house full of young people again. She didn't even tell them to turn the music down. The barbecue was in constant use. There were no more difficult conversations. Even the odd reminder to Louise to tidy her floordrobe didn't frustrate her as it would have done in the past. She thought of how Gerry's son might be spending Christmas, wondering whether he would be alone, but she daren't upset the apple cart by bringing up all that business again. It had taken long enough to get back on an even keel with her daughter.

Anyway, she hadn't been in touch with Gerry. It wasn't that she hadn't wanted to write or phone, but it had all been so full on. Sure, his visit had shaken her out of the quagmire of her grief and helped her to regain her life, but the guilt of what she'd done such a short time after losing Nick wouldn't go away. If Gerry Clancy had dropped in five or six years down the track, things might have been different, but it hadn't even been a year. She hadn't even spent one Christmas without Nick.

The holiday came and went with the two women filling stockings for one another and placing carefully wrapped presents under the tree. They were bereft without Nick. Louise said they were like a tricycle with two wheels, useless without him. Even Paddy wasn't there for comfort. But Tracey had come to the rescue and invited them for Christmas lunch, which lasted well into the evening. Boxing Day was the worst.

They took out old photos and reminisced. Ellen told Louise again about her early life with Nick; how he used to work at a Greek restaurant in Brighton Le Sands in the evenings and catch a ride to the city with a friend to work the early hours at the fish market; how he would come home and wake her with breakfast in bed before they'd swap places and she would catch her train to get to the university in the city.

She ran her fingers over a photo of their first Christmas. God, she looked so young, sitting on the beach posing for him in her bikini and the oversized Guinness T-shirt she'd given him covering her bump. The craziness of Sydney had been getting to them both. For Ellen, it was partly the over-whelming sprawl of the place, but there was also that lurking sense of homesickness she refused to give in to. Despite the challenges Australia had presented, she wasn't a quitter.

Nick didn't speak much about home. If anything, his Greek contacts in Sydney seemed to serve as too much of a reminder of what he'd left behind. They'd resolved to move once she'd finished her course in early May. They were always looking for workers in the tuna industry in Port Lincoln and she'd be well placed to take up a social work position anywhere once she and the baby were ready. She would miss Jimmy and the friends she'd made, but they wanted a fresh start. Ellen remembered looking out over Botany Bay that Christmas Day, both excited and nervous for what lay ahead. But mostly she remembered the trust she'd always had in Nick and how he'd made her want to be part of what he called their big adventure.

There were tears and laughter as Louise and Ellen pored over family photos and talked about memories. Ellen could feel a new openness between them. Despite the hurt she'd caused her daughter these past months, the wounds were healing. Nick would have been pleased to see it so.

—

Gerry was grateful to have a day off. He'd managed to grab an hour to do his present shopping the day before. He'd been looking forward to the traditional Christmas Eve lunch of door-step sandwiches washed down with pints of Guinness in the Long Valley pub, but even that was knocked on the head when Donal failed to arrive back from an early break. It was already Christmas Day when Gerry got to bed. He slept in and went to twelve o'clock mass. It was weird being alone in the packed church. Although not the most regular churchgoer, he'd enjoyed going to mass with his family on special occasions like his children's baptisms, their first holy communions and confirmations. Of course there'd been the big white wedding Jessica had insisted upon. After Ellen left, he'd only wanted a distraction. It had been a case of lust in the beginning, but when Jessica announced she was pregnant, he'd wanted to do the right thing. The fact that Daddy Sheehy would have broken his balls if he hadn't, sealed the deal. Love, he had naively told himself, would come in time. For a while he thought it had. Worshippers filed past to and from the altar for communion. A little girl in a red satin dress caught his eye. Her legs in woollen tights dangled from where she rested at her father's hip, her feet covered in a pair of patent shoes shining like her ebony ringlets. Stephanie had looked just like that once. He'd have liked her to be sitting beside him now, but Granny and Grandad Sheehy had taken Stephanie and Jessica to New York.

When he arrived back at the Stables, Donal was having a shave in the bathroom. Gerry leaned in the open doorway.

'You're actually up?'

Donal tapped the razor on the edge of the sink and twisted his face from side to side to see if he'd missed any. 'What do you mean, I'm up? Isn't it the one day in the year I don't have to work? Can't a man do what he likes on his day off?'

'You do what you like every other day,' said Gerry, 'why should today be any different?'

Donal towelled the remaining soap from his face and turned to his brother. 'Look, I know I've had a bad few weeks. I'll make it up to you. I'll have a nice day at home and make a fresh start tomorrow.'

Gerry wanted to say how many times he'd heard that before, but remembering the day that it was, decided to leave well enough alone. 'Come on. Mam'll be waiting for us.'

—

The smell of spiced beef hit them the minute they walked in the door. Gerry said a silent prayer of thanks that his mother and father were alive and well and living close by. Gerry Senior was pouring the Palomino into the good Waterford crystal glasses while Pauline slaved in the kitchen, having surpassed herself as usual with a huge roast turkey dinner with all the trimmings.

'Happy Christmas, Mam,' said Gerry.

Pauline set down a dish of crispy roast potatoes, wiped her hands on her apron and gave him a warm hug.

'How are you, son?'

'Grand, Mam.' He rolled up his sleeves and got to work straining Brussels sprouts and julienne carrots and transferring them to serving bowls with generous knobs of butter.

'Did you get mass?'

'I did,' he said. 'The Holy Trinity was packed.'

'What about you, Donal?' she shouted to his brother who was driving Domingo crazy in the living room. 'Did you go to mass?'

'Ah, Mam, you have no idea how busy we are. I hardly got a wink of sleep let alone mass.'

Pauline looked at Gerry and threw her eyes to heaven. When they were all sitting down, she made Donal say grace. Without getting too hot under the collar, his mother always did have a way of making a point.

After the main course, they exchanged gifts. Pauline suggested a walk to make room for the Christmas pudding she'd had steaming overnight.

'I think I'll have a listen to that Bocelli CD Gerry gave me,' said Gerry Senior. Donal feigned interest in hearing it too and said he'd stay put.

Gerry and his mother set off with Domingo at a brisk pace towards the Glen. The late afternoon sun was beginning its steady decline through a curtain of grey cloud. It only seemed like yesterday that he was holding his mother's hand and tripping through puddles in the oasis of streams and lush green hillsides of the ancient glacial valley that had somehow survived in the midst of urban Cork.

'I hope he's not using your father as an excuse to raid the drinks cabinet,' said Pauline. 'Have you heard from Jessica?'

'Ah, she gives me the time of day when I collect Stephanie,' said Gerry. 'Other than that, I only hear from her lawyer when she wants to squeeze another few euro out of me.'

'I'm still mad she took Stephanie away for Christmas.'

Gerry wasn't too pleased either to have both his children in foreign countries at what was supposed to be a time for family, but he couldn't begrudge his teenage daughter spending a week in New York with its famous festive atmosphere. He let his mother rant.

'It's the well-off ones you have to watch, isn't it?' she was saying. 'They never seem to have enough.'

'I loved her once, Mam. I shouldn't be too harsh. I knew what I was doing when I married her.'

'Don't be so down on yourself, Gerry. You were young and that Ellen O'Shea had your head in a spin when she upped and left for Australia.'

Gerry went quiet.

'You never did say much about meeting her again. What was it like after all these years?'

He tried to measure his answer. 'Ah sure, you know yourself. She's got a bit older like the rest of us. Still the same in ways though.'

Pauline pressed a gloved hand on his arm. 'This is your mother you're talking to here, son. How did it *feel*?'

The darkening of his cheeks was answer enough.

'Wouldn't you be better off meeting someone in Cork and saving yourself the hassle of a long-distance relationship?' He was grateful they had the Glen to themselves. 'You must have your pick of them with working in the pub.'

'Ah, Mam. Don't be trying to marry me off again. I'm hardly over the divorce.'

'Who mentioned marriage? I only want you to have a bit of company.' She linked arms with him and pulled her scarf up around her chin. He could only smile at her concern.

‑

Ellen and Louise relaxed in front of the television, Louise flicking through her newsfeed on her phone in that multi-tasking way Ellen still wasn't sure about.

'Guess what, Mum?'

Ellen turned down the TV with the remote and gave her daughter her full attention.

'Maxine and her brother are driving over to Lincoln tomorrow.' Staring incredulously at her phone, she went on, 'Says she's dying of boredom at home.'

'Doesn't she have a summer job?' asked Ellen.

'Her parents own a winery so she helps out there, but it sounds like it's a bit full on being around the olds twenty-four seven.'

Ellen smiled. She wanted to say it must be pretty full on for the parents too, but kept the thought to herself.

'They'll have to stay then.'

Louise looked up. 'Are you sure you don't mind, Mum?'

'Mind? Why would I mind?'

'They'll only be here a night or two, I promise. I'm sure they've got plans for New Year.'

New Year was indeed the next hurdle that would have to be overcome. As Louise went back to snapchatting Maxine, Ellen glanced at the Christmas cards she'd set along the mantelpiece. There were cards from neighbours and friends here in Lincoln, from relatives in Ireland and from her sister-in-law in Greece who never forgot them. Gerry had sent a small handmade card that supported an organisation that helped the homeless. *Ellen and Louise, wishing you both a Happy Christmas. Hope the New Year brings only the best for you both. Gerry.* It didn't say much, but it was something to hold on to. Ellen tried to imagine the urn with Nick's ashes sitting there, in amongst the cards, as the lady at the funeral home had suggested. It made her so mad to think that anyone could confuse the sight of an urn full of ashes with the constant presence of her husband in her mind and heart. Nick would have hated to be kept in the lounge room anyway, she reasoned. But the bottom of their wardrobe wasn't exactly fitting either.

It was almost a year. They'd never discussed their own funerals. No, they'd had plans, to travel when they retired, dreams of returning again to Ireland and Greece, exploring together the places of their youth. When he died, she'd considered a traditional burial at the cemetery in North Shields. But she would have had to pass it every time she drove to and from the town. She might never had gotten further than the cemetery and spent her days hovering over him. At least the urn kept him close in the privacy of their own home. But what would Nick have wanted? He would have wanted her to grieve certainly, but also he would have wanted her to go on with life. To let him go. Her eyes were drawn again to the Greek lettering on the card from her sister-in-law in Santorini. Perhaps they could make that trip they'd talked about after all. Perhaps she should take him home.

'You okay, Mum?'

Louise looked up from her phone and frowned. It was a look filled with the worry Ellen wished her daughter didn't have to feel.

'Yes, my love,' she smiled. 'I think I have just realised where we should spread your dad's ashes.'

─

Louise and Judy were preparing for the last ride of the day when Darcy's four-wheel drive trundled through the gates of the riding centre.

'Your uni pals?' asked Judy, looking up from tying Toyah's girth.

'Yeah. They're a bit early.' She didn't want Judy to think she'd invited them onto her property.

The office phone was ringing. 'I'll just get that,' said Judy. 'Don't let them scare the horses.'

As she walked to the car, Louise noticed they had an extra passenger.

'Hey, horsey person,' Maxine shouted and flung her arms around Louise. 'Ooh you even smell of the country.'

'Thanks, Max. You smell of road trip.'

'Hey, Louise.' Darcy didn't hazard a hug. 'You remember Kieran, my flatmate?'

Of course, the boy from the party. He looked taller than she remembered, but the sandy hair and kind eyes were familiar.

'Oh yeah. Sorry about that night.' She cringed at the memory.

'Hope you don't mind me tagging along,' said Kieran. 'These two sorta twisted my arm.' He glanced sideways at the twins and rolled his eyes.

'He's on his way to Perth for a holiday,' said Darcy. 'We're showing him the scenic route.'

Judy strode back across the yard. 'You city kids want a trail ride?' Louise registered the frustration in her voice. 'Just had a bloody cancellation.'

'That's a great idea,' said Maxine. 'We've horses at home, but we don't get a chance to ride much with work at the winery.'

'I don't know,' Kieran was saying. 'I might just watch ye.'

'Don't be ridiculous,' said Maxine. 'Louise and me will show you how it's done.'

Judy sorted them out for helmets and ponies.

'Have you ever ridden before?' Louise asked Kieran.

'I was on a runaway donkey once at Inchydoney.' He saw the puzzled look on her face. 'You'll go there some time.'

Thoughts of a little sandy-haired boy on a donkey on a beach in Ireland played around in Louise's head as she tried not to laugh. 'Elton's a sweetie. He won't run away with you. But my mother might. She loves meeting people from "home" as she still calls it.'

The boy's face reddened. She hadn't thought he was that shy.

'No more than an hour, you young ones,' Judy shouted after them as they rode out of the yard. 'Time is money in this business.'

'No worries,' Darcy shouted back.

Louise wondered if the twins were really the confident riders they made themselves out to be, but decided she'd better focus on Kieran, who looked absolutely terrified.

'Just relax,' she told him. 'Can you see the sea?' She pointed down the track.

'I was just keeping an eye on this fella,' said Kieran, his body a statue on horseback.

'It's a bit like being car sick,' she explained. 'You're better off looking straight ahead at the horizon.'

'Right.'

The twins were already a good way ahead by the time they reached the beach. Kieran began to relax as they rode along the edge of the water that glistened in the late afternoon sunshine.

'It's beautiful here,' he said. 'You're so lucky to live in a place like this.'

Louise remembered how easy it had been to talk to him that night in Adelaide. He seemed quieter here. Must be the horses, she reasoned.

'You don't have to look so nervous, you know,' she told him. 'Elton could do this trail in his sleep.'

'Can we stop?' he asked.

Surprised at the request, she brought the ponies to a halt.

'What is it?' She hoped he wasn't feeling unwell.

'There's something I need to tell you, Louise, and I may not get another chance with those two.' He looked along the beach to where Darcy and Maxine were racing at a gallop. 'Remember the night you came to the flat?'

She nodded.

'I thought there was something very familiar about you.'

'I felt the same about you.'

'Maxine said your surname and when you heard my accent, you said I sounded like your mother.' He had her full attention now. 'I put two and two together . . .'

She tried to work out what exactly the four in this equation should be, but drew a blank.

'I'm Gerry Clancy's son.'

It took her a second to compute.

'You're my half-brother?'

'Sorry, Louise. When these two asked me to come, I thought it might be the only time I'd ever see you again. I couldn't lie. I had to tell you.'

She sat straighter in the saddle. Gerry would have told him. He must have been as shocked then as she was now.

'Far out!' She felt her shoulders begin to relax as the idea settled over her. 'I knew Gerry had a son, but I never thought about having a brother.' She reached out and touched Kieran's shoulder to make sure he was real. She wanted to give him a big hug, but didn't trust Elton to stand still.

'Aren't you mad?' he asked. 'My dad said you took the news about him and your mother very badly.'

She took a deep breath. 'I was shocked, Kieran. I thought my mother had kept the truth from my father all these years. It's been a hellish few months, but I'm starting to get it.'

'We don't have to be friends if you don't want. There's no pressure. I just wanted to be upfront.'

'Are you kidding? I'm someone's sister. I have a cool brother.' Yes, she could have been mad. But hadn't she learned the hard way where anger could lead? There were so many questions. 'Are there more of you? Didn't you say you had a sister the night of the party?'

'I have a sister, nearly seventeen. Her name's Stephanie.'

'Far out! Is she like you?'

'Not really,' said Kieran. 'I think I'm more like my dad, but Steph takes after my mother.'

'Oh.' Louise wasn't sure what this meant. If Jennifer was right, there could be a whole family tree of personalities yet to be discovered.

The sound of hooves interrupted them as Maxine and Darcy came back at a canter.

'We'll talk about it later,' said Louise. 'Let's tell Mum first.'

⟿

Judy let the twins and Kieran help with putting away the tack and turning the horses into the paddock. Kieran asked how much they owed for the ride, but Judy wouldn't hear of taking money from them and thanked them for their help. Louise was proud he'd offered to pay.

The Chrysler was in the driveway when they got to the house. As her mother appeared on the veranda, Louise wished it was just her and Kieran.

'Hello, Maxine!' Ellen gave the girl a warm hug. 'Nice to see you again.'

Darcy shook her hand and introduced himself while Kieran hung back a little.

'This is Kieran, Mum,' said Louise, nudging him forward. She watched as her mother searched the boy's face.

'We have something to tell you, Mum. You might want to sit down.'

'What are you on about? I have the dinner ready to come out of the oven.'

'Maxine, Darcy,' said Louise, jerking her head toward the front door. 'Would you mind looking after the dinner?'

Maxine frowned, not understanding for a second but then grabbed Darcy by the arm.

Ellen took a seat beside Louise on the top step, looking perplexed.

'Mum, this is Kieran *Clancy*,' Louise said.

'Hello, Missus eh Const . . . Constanti . . . sorry . . .'

The lines of worry disappeared from her mother's face. 'Ellen. Call me Ellen.'

She stood up and reached out both arms to Kieran. He hugged her warmly and when they pulled apart, they were both laughing.

'I can't wait to hear how you two found each other,' said her mother, 'but it's lovely to finally meet you.'

Louise beamed.

'Come in, come in.' Her mother brought Kieran inside. 'Your dad knows this place well.'

Louise had never seen either of the twins lost for words, but they seemed mesmerised over dinner. As they ate, her mother quizzed Kieran on all his family members and Louise listened, enthralled, as she took mental notes on the grandparents, aunt, uncle, cousins and half-sister she had yet to meet. Maybe Jennifer was right. Maybe it could, in fact, be all good.

Chapter Twenty-one

The first thing Ellen did when Louise took the others for drinks in the town was text Tracey.

Can you duck out for a while?

How did you know I need a break? came the reply.

Ellen waited at the lounge room window, too excited to do anything else. At the first sign of the Ford, she took a bottle of wine from the fridge and fetched two glasses.

'Dinner, I'm afraid,' said Tracey, holding up a bulging greasy paper bag. Eyeing the wine, she threw herself into a chair at the veranda table. Ellen ignored the bag and pulled in a chair.

'You'll never guess who just showed up here out of the blue.'

Tracey shrugged, needing food too much to speak.

'Gerry Clancy's son.'

'True?' Tracey held a hand to her mouth to avoid spraying flakes of pastry.

'As true as I'm sitting here, as my mother would say.' Ellen recounted the afternoon's events to a wide-eyed, pasty-chewing Tracey. 'What are the chances?'

'Million to one,' said Tracey, wiping her hands on a serviette and brushing crumbs off her T-shirt. 'Your pasty's going cold.'

'Sorry, Tracey. I'm full up. I gave them all their dinner before they headed in to town to meet Jennifer and the crew. Louise was busting to show him off. He's even agreed to go to Venus Bay with her for New Year.'

'He must be a lovely bloke if he's anything like his father,' said Tracey.

'He is,' Ellen smiled. 'But tell me what's happening in your life to take my mind off all this drama.'

'Well, *my* latest dilemma is of a more practical nature.'

Ellen raised an eyebrow. 'Go on.'

'Pete's put his back out and it couldn't have happened at a worse time of year. Summer holidays. He thought about getting his dad to come down from Roxby, but he's not well enough. His brother's just about to go out prawning, all his mates are working . . .'

Ellen jumped at the opportunity. 'Tyson!'

'What about him?' Tracey looked puzzled.

'He's available for work.' Ellen could see doubt written all over Tracey's face, but knew it only mirrored her husband's sentiments. Pete had, on more than one occasion, voiced his concerns about Ellen living alone beside a man who, in his opinion, failed to look after himself or his property.

'He'd be great,' she went on. 'It would actually get him out of the house. God knows he could do with a job to get back to normal.'

Tracey's eyes were wide again. 'Pete would freak.'

'Does he need the help or not?' Ellen wanted to tell her friend it wasn't just up to her husband who they hired. Tracey did own fifty percent of the business, didn't she? But they'd never discussed finances and, for all she knew, the roadhouse might be in Pete's name. Whatever the arrangements, right now she needed to get Tyson a job. Sharon McGuire would be no help to him if he couldn't get his act together.

'I'll put it to him,' said Tracey, 'but I'm not confident.'

'Be confident,' said Ellen. 'Ask him like he's already said yes.'

'Ooh. Aren't we pushy when it comes to other people's husbands?' Her face changed in a millisecond. 'Sorry, Ellen. I didn't think . . .'

'Don't mention it. Just get Tyson the job.'

—

Ellen was about to go to bed when the phone rang.

'Pete here, Ellen. Can you tell that neighbour of yours to get in here for eight tomorrow morning?'

'No worries, Pete. I'll go over there now and let him know.' She wanted to give a cheer but held it back.

'I'm not promising anything much,' Pete was saying. 'Just a few hours lifting and shifting.'

'That's fine, Pete. I'm sure he'll be grateful for any hours you can give him.'

'He'd better stay sober on the job, Ellen.'

Tyson was sitting out front in near darkness, a beer in one hand and a picture of his kids in the other.

'Hey, Tyson. You doing okay?'

'Have a seat, Mrs C. Just having a little drink to celebrate Robbie's birthday. He's four today.'

'Well hopefully it won't be too long before you can have a celebration with him and the girls.'

'I don't know, Mrs C. I heard nothin' from that social worker.'

'Don't worry. I'm sure Sharon's on the case.' She avoided looking at the beer bottle. 'Anyway, I've got a proposal that might speed things up.'

He straightened in his chair and set down the beer.

'You know my friends, Tracey and Pete, who own the roadhouse?' He nodded. 'They need a helping hand. I told them you were available for work.'

'That was kind of you, Mrs C, but are you sure they'd want a fella like me working for them?'

'Very sure, Tyson. They'll be lucky to have you. Pete said he'll see you at eight tomorrow. He'll show you the ropes.'

⇌

Venus Bay was hot. The beach was littered with umbrellas and tiny shade tents. Small children ran and splashed in the shallows while bigger ones jumped madly off the jetty and swam screeching and laughing to a raft moored a little way offshore. The crew got to work unloading the jet ski and setting up a canvas gazebo. Louise and Kieran carted the big esky from the boot of Mark Waller's father's four-wheel drive. Kieran had been stoked when they'd invited him to celebrate New Year with them. When the twins returned home, he'd mucked in with chores at the house and helped Louise and her friends to get organised for the trip.

Mark shouted to him from the water's edge. 'You been on one of these before, mate?'

'Never,' Kieran called before turning to Louise. 'Looks a lot easier than riding a horse.'

'And less painful,' she laughed.

'Don't remind me,' he said and walked off bow-legged to join Mark.

The girls had stripped down to bikinis and the lads to boardies. Jennifer handed round sunscreen.

'Thanks, Mum,' Beanie teased her.

'Not there, Beanie,' Felicity shouted at him as he set his camping chair beside the gazebo.

'Am I blocking your view or something?'

They all laughed, knowing Felicity would want the camping chairs strategically placed to maximise the view of the beach's talent.

'Nice buns at nine o'clock,' said Felicity, settling in her chair with a cool drink.

Louise followed her stare to the far side of the beach where a tall blond boy their own age was helping a couple of small girls into a two-seater canoe. She did a double-take.

'Oh my God!' She put a hand to her mouth. 'I don't believe it.'

'He's not that good looking,' Felicity mocked. 'Anyway, I saw him first.'

Louise slumped into the chair and tried not to stare in the boy's direction. Instead, she focused on how Kieran was doing on the jet ski.

'It's mad,' he shouted as Mark cut the engine and swerved the machine back to shore.

'Come on, Lou,' Mark called. 'You're up next. Kieran can take you. He's a natural.'

'Wish me luck,' she said to the girls. Jennifer followed her to the water's edge with a lifejacket. 'Thanks, Jen.' She pulled it round her, keeping one eye on the canoe which was heading toward them.

'Come on, Lou.'

Kieran was ready. Toby would have to wait. She jumped up on the ski and wrapped her arms tight about Kieran's waist. She loved the sea. As Kieran revved the ski along the sparkling surface, she let the salty wind unravel her hair and watched the stunning scenery unfold. They whizzed towards the Entrance where a dozen dolphins fished and frolicked over the reef that teemed with life. All this, and to experience it with her brother, took her breath away.

Once they got back, she was so pumped she didn't see the boy watching her from the shallows. In her enthusiasm, she grabbed Kieran and gave him a big hug and a kiss on the cheek. 'You're brilliant,' she told him. 'That was awesome.'

She unbuckled her lifejacket and was handing it to Jennifer when she noticed Toby Scott. He waved in acknowledgement, but his face was serious. She was about to go over to him when he turned the canoe round and pushed it back along the shore, its two occupants squealing in delight. *That's weird,* she thought, but headed off to find a towel and collapse into a camping chair. The short exchange hadn't escaped Felicity.

'Do you know that guy?'

'Yes, actually,' she said, keeping her voice steady. 'He's the one I told you and Jennifer about.'

'The one from uni?'

'Not very friendly, is he?'

'He is usually.' Her mind raced. What was Toby Scott doing in Venus Bay and why on earth hadn't he come and spoken to her?

After several trips with the jet ski, it was time to eat. Louise volunteered to walk up the hill to the small shop to buy lunch. Kieran went with her. At the shop, she spotted Toby again. He was with an older guy who was taking the wrapping off ice creams and handing them to the two little girls who'd been in the canoe.

Kieran, oblivious to Toby, wanted to know why they called them hot chips.

'What would happen if I said I wanted cold chips?' he said, laughing at his own joke. He leaned his elbow on Louise's shoulder as he perused the menu board above the counter.

Toby turned around to check out the person with the accent.

'Hi, Toby,' said Louise as casually as she could.

'Oh, hi, Lou.' He blushed as he pushed his hands into the pockets of his board shorts, seeming suddenly conscious of his naked torso.

'Didn't expect to see you,' she said. 'Are you here with family?' The words came out awkwardly.

'Yeah, yeah . . .' He drew a hand from his pocket and gestured to the man beside him. 'This is my brother, Glen.'

The brother smiled. 'How're ya goin?' he said.

'These are my nieces,' Toby continued, but the small girls, who only had eyes for their ice creams, were heading to the door. 'Maybe see ya later.'

'Yeah,' was all she could manage as she watched them leave.

Walking back along the beach in the searing heat, she could still feel the cool of their exchange. Maybe she'd misread the smile and that wink he'd given her at the airport after all. Perhaps too much time had passed, she'd been too hard and she'd left it far too late for going back.

—

By late evening the atmosphere was building at the jetty. Sensible adults had brought chairs to sit in comfort while they waited for the fireworks to start. A few couples sat dangling their legs over the edge and holding hands as they looked up at the stars. There was a band playing an eclectic mix of cover versions while children danced, delighted to be allowed up so late. Louise scanned the crowd for signs of Toby.

Felicity came and stood beside her. 'Looking for anyone in particular?'

Louise shrugged. 'Let's see what Venus Bay has on offer, shall we?'

They weaved their way through the crowd, stopping to talk to people they knew. It looked like half her hometown was there for the celebrations. Just as they were heading back to the crew, Louise bumped into a camping chair. She tripped and almost fell, dragging Felicity with her in the process.

'Sorry,' she said, trying to look completely sober and cursing the two bottles of cheap wine they'd shared before they went out.

'No worries,' said the grey-haired man they'd almost fallen over. 'It's getting a bit busy here.'

She noticed the lady sitting beside him with a sleeping child in her arms and then, turning around, she saw Toby trying to make himself invisible at the other side of their circle. Felicity noticed him too.

'You're Lou's friend, right?' Felicity wasted no time in introducing herself to the entire family. Louise watched as the man beside her, who must have been Toby's dad, looked to his son for explanation.

'I know Louise from uni,' he said, looking like he wished the ground would open and swallow him.

The woman sat straighter in her chair, careful not to disturb the child, and stretched out a hand from around the small body. 'I'm Claire, Toby's Mum. He's told me lots about you, Louise.'

Felicity let out a snort and quickly put a hand to her mouth to stifle an outburst. Louise about died. Her embarrassing friend was bad enough, but what exactly had Toby told his mother?

'Go with Louise, Toby,' his mum was saying. 'Have fun with some young people.'

Although she was sure Toby wanted to do anything but hang out with her, he got up obediently.

'Come and meet the Lincoln crew,' Felicity said as she turned to lead the way to where their friends were making fools of themselves, dancing and singing out the words of the songs they knew, making up the ones they didn't.

'You're a bit quiet,' said Louise as Toby tagged along, hands in his pockets.

'Yeah,' he mumbled.

The coolness was there again, defying the balmy evening.

'Come and meet my brother,' she said.

Toby looked puzzled.

Louise called to Kieran who danced toward her and caught her hands, making her twirl. She laughed and threw back her head. 'Behave for a minute. This is Toby.'

'Ah, Toby. How are ya, mate?'

Toby looked from one to the other. His face broke into a broad smile.

'Good thanks.'

Kieran, a few beers to the good, was off dancing again. Toby turned to Louise. 'I thought you two were . . . You told me you didn't have any brothers or sisters.'

'I only found out a few months ago. Long story,' she said. 'But you didn't think we were . . . together, did you?'

'What was I supposed to think? You could be with any of those blokes you're here with.'

'Well I'm not,' she said and folded her arms. Now she'd sorted out that misunderstanding, she wasn't sure what to do next. But Dutch courage kicked in. 'Were you jealous?'

'What do you think?' He looked away toward the band.

If that constituted a yes, he still fancied her. Oh God, this was her chance.

'I stuffed up, didn't I?' she said, willing him to look at her.

Without saying anything, he took her hand. At the edge of the crowd he stepped closer and held her. They moved together in a slow dance even though everyone around them was bopping madly to some fast number. It was as though they had their own music, their own rhythm.

~

When the final countdown started, Louise found herself between Toby and Felicity.

'Does this mean you two are back together?' Felicity stage-whispered.

Louise shook her head, but couldn't suppress a broad smile.

The lead singer was revving up the crowd. 'Five, four, three, two, one, Happy New Year.'

The crowd erupted. Rockets exploded and streaks of colour lit up the sky. Everyone was reaching to the person beside them, but before Louise had time to turn to Toby, they were swamped by her friends. 'Hope it's a good one for you, mate,' she heard Kieran say to Toby before turning to give her a massive bear hug. 'Happy New Year, sis.'

As she watched the fireworks shoot up from the jetty and burst into spectacular shapes, Louise felt a hand on her shoulder. Toby bent down and kissed her lips gently, then passionately, as she turned her body toward him and slipped her arms around his neck. Somebody wolf-whistled and when they drew apart, the crew cheered their approval.

'I'll be back in a minute,' he whispered. She watched as he merged with the crowd.

'Have we frightened him away?' asked Jennifer, looking worried.

'No, Jen,' Louise answered. 'This time, I think he's definitely coming back.'

The band had started up again and everyone was dancing. Louise quickly texted her mum who would be with the Popes. In the crowd, she spotted Toby folding his mum's chair as she began heading off with her grandchild still in her arms. His dad took the chair from Toby and pointed toward the band area. She saw him try to protest before walking back toward her, shaking his head.

'Dad wouldn't let me help him with all the gear. Said I should be with that pretty uni girl.' He gave her a wink that made her blush.

'Are you all staying in one of the shacks?' she asked.

'Yeah. My brother bought it just before Julie . . . well, for Julie.'

They strolled along the beach as the crowd slowly dispersed, leaving the party animals to enjoy the music. Louise took off her pumps and let her feet tread on the cool sand. The sounds from the party faded behind them. Toby took her hand and fell in step with her along the water's edge. Frothy ripples swirled at their feet, but it was the warmth of his hand she noticed.

'Feels a bit surreal being here with you,' she said.

'A bit scary, I reckon.'

'What do you mean scary?'

They took a few more steps before Toby answered.

'I thought we had something really good going in uni,' he said quietly.

Louise took a deep breath. It was time she gave Toby the explanation he deserved.

'Mum took Dad's death very badly,' she began. 'I had to step up, be the parent for a while. When you asked me out, I thought our relationship would help me out of my own grief, but it was all too hard. Mum needed me. I'd promised Dad I'd work hard at uni. Then I found out he wasn't my real dad and I just lost it. Didn't want history repeating itself. Couldn't handle a relationship, so I pushed you away.'

Toby didn't say anything, but interlocked his fingers in hers. They walked toward the sand dunes and sat watching the moon shining on the dark sea like a spotlight. Louise cupped the still-warm sand in her hands and let it gush through her fingers.

'Who was Julie?' she asked.

'Glen's wife.' Toby leaned back, propped up on an elbow and explained how his sister-in-law had lost her battle with breast cancer. 'She made Glen buy a place here. Venus was her favourite spot. She wanted the girls to have summers by the sea.'

Tears stung her eyes. 'I'm so glad I had my dad for as long as I did,' she said.

Toby sat up and put his arm around her. She let her head fall on his chest and relaxed as he held her close. When she looked up at him, he too had tears.

'Sorry, Lou,' he sniffed. 'I just get sad when I think about Glen and the girls having to say goodbye.'

It wasn't the romantic reunion she'd expected, but Louise was happy to be spending the first hours of the New Year with Toby Scott. They lay for hours in each other's arms and when they finally said goodnight, Louise felt a whole new chapter awaiting her at uni. She hoped the summer would fly.

Ellen saw in the New Year alone. Tracey and Pete had invited her to share it with them, but she'd declined their kind offer, preferring the honesty of loneliness to the sham of putting on a brave face for her friends. Instead, she'd curled up on the couch in front of the television watching an alien crowd of revellers on Sydney Harbour Bridge. It was where she and Nick had spent their first New Year. A little after midnight when a wave of homesickness had come over her, as it had done that Christmas, he'd held her face in his hands, and looking deep into her eyes he'd said, 'This year we will only look forward.' It would become the vow they made every year. She'd made a terrible job of honouring it without him. This year she would try harder.

Not long after midnight, she propped up her pillows and reached for the half glass of merlot she'd taken to bed. Rolling the glass between her hands, she thought over what the year might have in store. She'd come so far, no longer shutting herself off from the world. Ironically, it was Gerry's visit that had brought her round. She'd overcome obstacles that had seemed insurmountable; that first phone call to her boss requesting to return to work, walking into the office having dreaded the turning of heads and wagging of tongues and the relief of the overwhelming warmth and encouragement from her colleagues and friends. She'd turned it around, but she couldn't have done it without him. And timing aside, too soon after Nick's death perhaps, Gerry had made her question her absolute conviction that no one would ever share her life again.

What if circumstances were different? she asked herself. *What if Gerry had stayed longer? What if he never came back?* Her fond memories of Nick, those years spent building a life together, would always be special, but long term, what would become of her? Would she be content living in her lovely but lonely home on Ocean Road, working until she retired? And then what? Louise was carving out her own life. She would hopefully build a career, eventually settle down. Gerry Clancy might even find someone to share his life with. The thought pulled her up. Hugging her knees tight into her chest, she felt the blood pump harder in her veins. Sure, the timing was terrible, but when had timing ever helped any of them? If she'd gone to Australia earlier, she might never have fallen in love with him. If his son hadn't come to Australia, she might never have met him again. If that kangaroo had decided to forage in the undergrowth for thirty seconds longer instead of jumping out into the path of Nick's ute ... No, she refused to torture herself. She'd come too far for that. She could fantasise about Gerry returning and coming to see her again one day, or she could wait until she got Louise through university and take a trip home then, but she'd had enough of the maudlin and mulling over. Ireland was only a short hop from Santorini. She could book the extra flights and surprise him. Who knew what could happen from there? It was a bridge she'd cross when she came to it.

Chapter Twenty-two

A few days later, they were gathered in the garden overlooking Boston Bay. Ellen was pleased she'd made an effort to keep the lawn mowed and the weeds to a minimum, although it was mostly wild gazanias that decorated the front of the house. Their fiery reds and canary yellows added a measure of cheer to the event. It was the first anniversary of Nick's death and she was nervous as hell.

'Remember you're among friends,' Tracey whispered to her as the group stood waiting for the speech she'd prepared.

Dotted across the lawn were the friends and close colleagues who had supported her in different ways over the years. Despite cutting herself off from most of them over the past twelve months, they'd been there waiting in the wings to be part of her life again. On the veranda, Louise had displayed some of the family photos she had carefully scrapbooked. The Chrysler was freshly cleaned and parked out front, its chrome finishes and white and turquoise paint-work gleaming in the sunshine.

Ellen gave a small cough to clear her throat. 'I didn't want to drag you all to a church service that I know some of you would only have endured for Nick and me.' There was a chuckle from the group. 'But it would be another very lonely day for me and Lou without you all.' Fighting a tremor in her voice, she looked at her beautiful Baby Lou. 'I'm hoping this gets a little easier as time goes on, but it's really hard to speak about someone you loved with all your heart in the past tense, so I'll make it short and sweet.'

They listened in the hush of the lazy country afternoon as she acknowledged their kindness and patience with her, and the strength Louise had shown in supporting her in her weakest moments when Nick's loss had been almost unbear-able. When she finished, there were hugs and handshakes. Louise was in bits. Jennifer comforted her while Tracey helped Ellen serve the afternoon tea they'd been preparing since early morning. The mood was lightened by stories about Nick from people who knew him as a boss, a neighbour, or as a friend. Nick would be pleased, thought Ellen as she was reminded of the many gatherings on the property that were always imbued with Nick's warmth and generosity.

'Thank you so much, Tracey,' Ellen said when everyone was happily tucking in to cakes and sandwiches.

'I did it for Nick too,' said Tracey.

It was obvious her husband was sorely missed, yet there was a collective comfort to be had among these people who'd been their friends for most of their adult lives. Life could be good here, she thought. No matter what happened, she would always feel at home in South Australia.

～

In the late afternoon when everyone had left, Ellen sat with Louise on the sofa listening to the details of the trip to Venus Bay. She couldn't help but delight in having been right about Toby when she'd met him that day in Adelaide. She thought Nick would have liked him too, but even so, no one would ever have been good enough for his Baby Lou.

'I shouldn't be happy, Mum. I should be thinking about Dad.'

Ellen thought her heart might break all over again.

'Oh, sweetheart, Dad would be so proud of you. If he were here, he'd be quizzing me in bed later about the suitability of Toby Scott for his princess.' She laughed at the thought of how old-fashioned Nick could be when it came to raising Louise, and the conversations they'd wait to have in bed for fear she'd overhear. 'He'd want you to be happy, Lou.'

She took her daughter in her arms and stroked her sun-kissed hair.

'I love you, Mum.' Louise gave her a squeeze.

'My gorgeous girl, I love you so much.'

How good it felt to share in the news of her daughter's romance. Her own mother would never have entertained such a conversation even if she had stayed in Ireland.

'You're going to have such a good second year, Lou. That lovely young man and your best friend, both in Adelaide with you.'

'I hope so, Mum.'

'Oh that reminds me, I promised to give your new landlady a call in early January.' Ellen kissed the top of Louise's head and stood up. 'Best to have that organised before we go to Santorini.'

———

Louise had to smile. Her mother was definitely back to her old self. She was more than capable of organising her own accommodation, but if it made her mother happy, she would let her do it. There'd been enough discord between them. She hugged a cushion to her chest, rested her head on the arm rest of the sofa and allowed herself to daydream about their trip. She'd been stoked when her mum had asked if she'd go with her to Santorini to spread her dad's ashes. As sad as it was, it was what he would have wanted. For some reason, they hadn't had many photos of the trip they'd made there when she was ten. It would be good to fill in the blanks on the patchy memories she had of her father's homeland. Ireland would have been great too, but she assured her mother she'd prefer to go there another time. It was too soon. She needed to hang on tight to the memory of her dad at least for now. Her mother was older. Maybe that made the trip to Ireland more urgent, but Louise had years hopefully to explore that whole other family. She'd already met Kieran so the connections were established. She could build on them at her own pace. Besides, the last thing she wanted was to be a third wheel or left with relatives she hardly knew. Thankfully, her mother had already thought of Plan B.

Toby was like someone who'd just won the lottery when she'd phoned and asked him if he wanted to spend a few weeks in Europe before they went back to uni. Her tummy fluttered as she thought of travelling alone with him once her mother left. It seemed like such a grown-up thing to do, but after Venus Bay she was sure they'd get along.

Chapter Twenty-three

Ellen was heading out the door to go to work, thinking about Paddy and how he'd follow her to the car, when Tyson came striding across the path that linked the properties.

'Mrs C, Mrs C,' he said, his breathing heavy. 'Can you come over for a minute? I won't keep you long.'

'Okay, Tyson.' She threw her bag in the car and followed him.

'Your friend got my kids back,' he was saying as he ushered her in through the screen door at the front of the house.

'Is it awright, Mrs C? Clean enough and that?'

She looked around the lounge room. Not only was it clean, but Tyson had erected two sets of multi-coloured streamers along the roof and placed a stack of five or six neatly wrapped boxes beside the fireplace. The whole place smelled fresh and vibrant. Picture frames gleamed and a bunch of freshly cut flowers sat in a jam-jar vase.

'Tyson, you've done a massive job. The kids will be stoked.'

'I can't thank you enough, Mrs C.'

'Don't mention it, Tyson. You and Sharon did all the hard work.'

The big man's cheeks flushed as he lowered his head in a mixture of pride and embarrassment. There was no underestimating the effort it must have taken to transform what had become a bachelor pad back into a family home.

'Speaking of work, I thought you were still at the roadhouse.'

'It's going good, Mrs C. Pete gave me time off to get the place ready for the kids. He's a good bloke, you know.'

Driving to work, Ellen marvelled at how life had a way of setting a new equilibrium no matter what was thrown at it. Tyson would see his children again and with any luck, on a regular basis. Who knew what her trip to Europe would bring? It was enough to know that she had relearned how to look forward.

When Ellen got home at the end of the day, there was noise on the block. Not the usual sounds of birdsong or a header harvesting in the fields, but the bubbling of young voices she hadn't heard in months. She parked the car and hurried toward her neighbour's. Through the gap in the wattle trees, she could see Sarah tearing around the garden with Kaleesha chasing after her armed with a water balloon. Tyson was sitting on the veranda looking like he'd died and gone to heaven, Robbie curled in his arms to avoid the missiles. Before she could say a word, the girls spotted her and came running barefoot with arms ready to wrap around her work-weary body.

'Mrs C, Mrs C,' they chanted, squeezing with all their might.

She squeezed right back, the feel of their skinny arms around her neck unleashing a burst of joyous tears.

'I've missed you little tackers,' she told them.

They took her by the hands and pulled her toward the veranda. Tyson said nothing but gave her the broadest smile. Robbie didn't look too sure and turned his head of curly jet black hair into his father's chest.

'It's Mrs C, Robbie,' said Sarah. 'She'll let ya ride Spots later if you're good.'

Robbie gave her a sideways glance.

'Only if you want to, Robbie,' Ellen assured him. 'He might like it if we gave him a carrot.'

And that was the way the children's visit went; spending time with their dad and popping in to see herself and Louise and ask for a ride on Spots. They brought Ocean Road back to life and warmed her heart.

The date was getting closer. Ellen had let her brother know she was coming and sworn him to secrecy. Her father didn't need to be in the loop until the last minute, she decided. It wasn't as if she owed him anything. Although phone calls to and from the family home had become more frequent since her mother's passing, it was always Ellen who made the effort to ring. Oh yes, conversation topics such as tunnels, by-passes, swimming pool to hotel conversions, the unemployment rate, the value of the euro were all covered enthusiastically by Bill O'Shea when he took a mind to lifting the phone. Subjects of a more personal nature, however, were pretty much avoided. They'd lived very separate lives. Ellen hoped that situation could be righted now that they'd speak face to face. He'd be seventy soon too. Definitely time for reconciliation.

There was a feeling of nostalgia at the prospect of visiting her native city after such a long absence. Ellen allowed herself the luxury of imagining its rediscovery with Gerry Clancy as guide. She'd thought about giving him her itinerary, but despite her optimism, there was a small voice inside her head questioning whether she'd go through with her grand plans. This doing life on her own was still new to her. She would take one step at a time and not get ahead of herself. She'd get through Santorini first. She could contact him from there.

The small going-away party Ellen had organised was in full swing. Their friends had turned up in typical Aussie style, bearing plates of food to share and eskies full of bubbles and beer. The trestle table they'd pulled out of the shed was covered in enough food to feed a small army. Ellen stood at the barbecue in the apron she'd given to Nick for such occasions. He was a good cook anyway, but he especially loved a barbie for the mix of banter and outdoor cooking. She turned a blackened steak and hoped she was doing him proud.

'It's like old times,' she remarked to Tracey, remembering all the family barbecues they'd had when their children were young.

'Except for the playlist,' said Tracey, rolling her eyes and tipping her head in the direction of the speaker Louise had set up on the lawn.

'Ah, Tracey. If it was up to you, we'd be listening to the eighties all night.'

Pete came and topped up their wineglasses. 'All set for your trip, Ellen?'

He looked cautious, but she was emphatic in her answer. 'Definitely, Pete. It's about time I did it.'

He smiled. 'Will be good for Nick's family to be part of it.'

She could only hope he was right.

'I thought I might see Tyson tonight,' he said, skilfully changing the subject.

Ellen looked around, but couldn't see any sign of her neighbour.

'Do me a favour, Pete, and send Louise in to get him.'

She berated herself for not realising he'd be too shy to come of his own accord.

～

Louise found Tyson sitting on his armchair at the front of the house. If it wasn't for the long face, she'd have told him how cool he looked with his freshly washed hair and the clean white shirt and smart boardies.

'You okay, Tyson?'

He gave a soft sigh.

'Sorry, Lou. I just don't know if I can go in there.' He nodded toward her front yard.

'How come?'

He shrugged his broad shoulders. 'I didn't buy nothin' and I can't take any grog as I'm . . .'

'I know,' she said, 'Mum told me you're off it.'

It must have been hard watching the children go back to Sheryleen's, she reasoned. A party with a lot of people he didn't know was probably the last thing he wanted. She'd almost resigned herself to the fact that she couldn't budge him when she remembered the drinks bar in the shed.

'Would you drink alcohol-free beer?'

He looked up, curious if unconvinced. She smiled and beckoned him to follow her.

'Come on.'

Ignoring his groans, she led the way to the back of the shed where they found a few bottles of alcohol-free pilsner still in the fridge.

'Dad used to drink it when he and Mum went out and he was deso.'

He looked at her blankly.

'Designated driver?'

He nodded slowly and let her put two of the bottles in his hands. A smile spread across his face and he gave a deep chuckle.

'If he could see us now, Lou.'

They both laughed and went to join the party.

When the last of the guests had left, Louise and Ellen sat on the veranda looking up at the stars. That was one of the things Ellen loved about Australians and their barbecues: they all mucked in at the end, helping with the clean-up and taking their empty plates and eskies with them, leaving little to do. Louise yawned beside her, succumbing to the effects of several helpings of the beautiful sangria she'd made.

'Do you really think Dad's up there looking down on us?'

It was an impossible question to answer, but Ellen knew her daughter needed a positive response.

'Oh, I think if we hold him in our hearts he can be anywhere.'

She watched as Louise's eyelids started to droop.

'Come on, love. Best get some sleep before our travels.'

After Louise had gone inside, Ellen went to the shed. In the driver's seat of the Chrysler, she let her head lean back on the firm leather.

'I'll never forget you, my love,' she said aloud. 'I hope you understand why I need to see if there's something out there, something like we had, again. I've been so lonely without you.'

After a long time, she locked the doors and ran her hand over the bodywork before going inside to bed.

⌐

Tracey and Jennifer took them to the airport. At the security gate, Jennifer instructed them on the updates she wanted, reminding them to put heaps of photos on Facebook. Tracey and Ellen left them to say their goodbyes and walked a little away.

'You will be okay, won't you, Ellen?'

'I think so, Tracey.' Tracey was like a mother duck watching one of her chicks take flight, literally, Ellen mused. 'Thanks for everything, Trace. You've been fabulous.'

'You take care of yourself,' said Tracey. She paused and Ellen thought she might tear up, but a mischievous smile spread across her face. 'Are you sure I can't text Gerry and let him know when your flight gets in to Cork? It would be so roman—'

'No meddling,' said Ellen. She took a deep breath and, in a serious voice, said, 'I honestly don't know how I'll be in Santorini, Tracey. I need to be able to back out of the Ireland trip if I have a wobble. Just say a prayer it all works out.' They had a last hug. 'I'll miss you.'

'Just tell Gerry Clancy I still have his number and am more than happy to give him a serve if he steps out of line.' They laughed, but their tears weren't far away.

'It's not like you'll never see each other again,' said Jennifer.

Tracey and Ellen just looked at each other and smiled. Despite the periodic frustrations they caused them, they were united in their absolute love of their daughters.

As they waited for the connecting flight at Adelaide, Toby Scott ran toward them, rucksack swinging as he weaved between travellers.

'Sorry I'm late. I had to—'

'You're here, Toby,' said Ellen. 'That's all that matters.' She gave Louise a wink and made a trip to the bathroom to give them a few minutes alone. She'd have twenty-four hours in the boy's company to hear why he was late.

—

On the plane an hour later, Ellen wondered if she wasn't completely mad embarking on this trip. She'd only been to Greece that one time with Nick and Louise. The family may not even want her. There'd been no reply to her letter to Thecla, but she reminded herself of how highly Nick had always spoken of his sister. She'd shown them only kindness when they'd stayed in her home on that otherwise difficult visit. Unlike his parents, Thecla had kept in touch. She'd been the one Ellen had contacted when Nick died. There'd been a lovely card, but no one had come in person. Who knew what Nick's parents thought of Ellen's idea to spread their son's ashes? What if they wouldn't help her? Would she be forced to throw them off the stern of some tourist boat with a bunch of nameless onlookers?

And then, if she had any energy left over, it would be on to Ireland for an overdue reunion with her father. She'd played the scene where she'd meet Gerry Clancy over and over in her mind, but for these other reunions she was unprepared. Would she not have been better off staying in Port Lincoln with Tracey, looking after the girls before they left for uni and putting these fantastic ideas out of her head? She shivered. *I'm beginning to sound like my mother, God rest her soul.*

Ellen put her head back, reclined her seat as far as possible and tried to blank out all the negative thoughts that threatened to ambush her. At one point, half asleep, she reached out to Louise.

'You okay, Mum?'

She nodded and closed her eyes again. It felt good to have Lou by her side.

—

In a washroom at Athens airport, she took a good look in the mirror above the washbasin. Three flights down and one to go before they'd arrive in Santorini. 'You look like shit,' would be Tracey's assessment. Even if Thecla wasn't there to meet them off the next flight, she wanted to look strong enough to take on anyone who recognised her as Nick Constantinopoulos's widow. She took the hairbrush out of her handbag and teased the knotted strands into something that no longer looked like the fleece of a sheep in a wet field. The rub of a dampened cleansing wipe brought her complexion back to life, and a smear of lip gloss at least gave the impression of a woman who cared how she looked.

She listened to the short exchanges going on around her; sounds and rhythms that reminded her of Nick when he spoke to his Greek friends in Australia, or on the phone to his sister, or sometimes in his sleep. She regretted not encouraging him to teach Louise. They'd felt so inadequate, not able to make even the simplest of conversations with his family on that one visit. Nick's sister and cousins had some English from school, but the parents had none. She hoped it wouldn't be as much of a barrier this time. Surely they'd be kinder to her now that they shared Nick's tragic loss.

Chapter Twenty-four

Thecla was standing in the crowd, scanning the steady stream of passengers from the evening flight. Ellen recognised her thick dark hair, the same as Nick's, and her heavy build. *Surely not*, she thought as she saw the tall boy beside her. Could that be little Costas who'd been the sole source of entertainment on their one and only visit? Then a toddler, he'd been immune to family sagas and had given generously of his smiles, infectious laughter and podgy cuddles. She wondered what stories he'd been told about them in the intervening years.

'*E-len*,' Thecla shouted as she recognised her in the crowd.

The arms were stretched out wide. She needn't have worried. When they drew apart from the warm embrace, Ellen turned and beckoned Louise to come closer.

'You remember Louise?'

Thecla took a step toward her and reached out a hand to touch her cheek.

'Oh my child,' she said sadly, 'how my brother loved you.'

Despite the tears at the airport, the journey to the house was a happy one. Thecla glowed with pride when Ellen told her how handsome Costas had become and how like his Uncle Nick. Ellen thought she could feel the heat in the boy's cheeks radiating from the back seat and when she turned around she was happy to see he was indeed embarrassed but smiling. Louise and Toby tried to join in the conversation, but jet lag was already affecting them. She wondered what Toby made of it all, but he was a good lad, helping with baggage and transfers and insisting on paying his own way at every pit stop. He'd asked a few questions of course to make conversation, but he was curious rather than nosey. Besides, if the way he and Louise looked when they were cuddled in together under their plane blankets was anything to go by, he'd look after her.

In Fira, Thecla parked the car at the top of the hill and sent a text to her husband. Ellen recognised the narrow laneway that wound its way down toward the house. In the dim glow of a streetlight, she saw three shapes hurrying up towards them. The two little girls she'd only seen in photographs jumped and swung from their father's arms, hardly able to contain their excitement. She did a mental check and reckoned they must be four and seven. Dimitri unclasped himself from the older one and stretched out a hand to Ellen.

'Welcome to Santorini,' he said, the warm smile she remembered spreading across his weather-beaten face. He'd aged a bit, but hadn't they all?

'You'll remember Louise,' she said.

Again, he was warm in his welcome of Louise and Toby, but as they started down toward the house with the bags, Ellen caught a look between Thecla and Dimitri that made her wonder if this visit would indeed be smooth sailing.

⸺

At the house, a young tabby cat stretched in its bed and yawned before padding over and weaving between their legs. The older of the two girls, Anna, picked him up and showed him off to Toby. Her sister, Alyssa, had already laid claim to the attentions of her cousin and was leading Louise into the living room. Ellen left the young ones to it and followed Thecla.

'You like new kitchen?' Thecla panned a hand one-eighty degrees around the modern room. 'Dimitri do all.'

Ellen admired Dimitri's handiwork, a little distracted by the delicious smell of something cooking in the oven. Her stomach gave a growl as she remembered the beautiful meals Thecla had made on their last visit.

'Don't worry,' Thecla smiled, 'I have the moussaka I know you like.'

In a flash Thecla had covered the table in a spread fit for a king. Dimitri went to the living room to summon the troops. Toby seemed to get a second wind as he took in the bowls of olives, tzatziki, cucumber salad and fresh bread. He didn't need to be asked twice when Dimitri urged him to take a seat. Thecla took the moussaka from the oven and set the steaming clay casserole dish in the centre of the table.

As they ate the delicious supper, Ellen wished Nick had been alive to see how Costas had grown, to sit down to a meal with his beloved sister and the children whose lives he'd missed out on. When Thecla said she'd better put the children to bed, Anna and Alyssa began to protest, but Louise did a theatrical yawn and said she too needed to sleep. They happily took a hand each and led Louise to her bedroom, talking over each other as they planned what to do with their cousin the following day. Before Toby fell into a food coma, Costas politely offered to show him to his room. Finding herself alone with Dimitri, Ellen spoke candidly.

'I hope I did the right thing by bringing Nick's ashes here,' she began.

Dimitri took a bottle of retsina from the only old cupboard in the modern kitchen. Ellen remembered admiring the piece on her last visit when Thecla had shown her around and proudly pointed out those items of her grandmother's she'd inherited. She'd always wished she had something of Granny O'Shea's, something to touch and to look at that would remind her of the woman she'd loved. She pushed her glass a little closer to Dimitri and let him half fill it with the cloudy resinated wine.

'Thecla's father and mother still very sad about Niko,' he said, sitting back down and cradling his own glass in his hands.

'I don't want to offend them in any way . . .'

Dimitri waved a hand. 'No problem. We are proud to help you. I speak to my father-in-law. He want to come with you on boat.'

Thecla came in as he was speaking. Ellen wished she would sit and talk, but instead of joining them, she began clearing away the dishes and stacking them in the dishwasher.

'I'm a bit nervous about seeing them again,' she said.

They both smiled, but she couldn't help feeling she was missing something unspoken that passed between them.

⸺

The day was half over when Ellen woke in the comfort of her sister-in-law's spare room. Rays of bright winter sunshine squeezed through the blue shutters. She checked the small alarm clock on the bedside table and realised she must have been oblivious to the sounds of the children getting ready for school hours earlier. This was the room she'd shared with Nick. It had seemed colder then. They'd hardly slept for the hushed arguments about his parents' behaviour toward herself and Louise. They'd been civil, but there'd been none of the warmth she'd expected. She'd demanded Nick translate the heated exchanges. He'd told her his father was still angry that he'd left the island and not taken over the family business.

Louise stirred beside her.

'What time is it, Mum?'

She was glad Thecla had made up a bed for Toby in Costas's room. This time with Louise was precious. It might indeed be the last time they shared a bed. She turned on her side and spooned her Baby Lou, breathing in the smell of her freckled skin and her bed hair. She kissed the back of Louise's head. 'Time to get up!'

Pushing open the shutters, she squinted at the sight of the sea sparkling beyond the low white wall surrounding the terrace where the friendly tabby was sniffing at a patch of cerise flowers. The town of Fira had woken up long ago. Cars and buses rumbled up the road somewhere above the house. Tourists splashed in heated swimming pools and dined on terraces. As she looked out over the island-studded Aegean, she envied their ease.

She pulled on the dressing gown Thecla had left for her and hurried downstairs. A night and half a day were gone already and there was still so much to organise. Nerves were starting to take hold by the time she reached the kitchen. Thecla sat at the small family table perusing a women's magazine. Seeing Ellen, she set it down and immediately began covering the table with food.

'What would I have done without you?' said Ellen as she helped herself to the creamy yoghurt she remembered. 'I wish you could all come to Australia so I could return the hospitality.'

Thecla smiled, but her silence said it all. Ellen had often urged Nick to let his sister know they were welcome to come to them in Australia. It might have been a dream they'd enjoyed while Nick was alive, but Ellen knew that dream had most likely died with him. She could only hope that one day Costas or his sisters might make the journey in their uncle's footsteps. She chewed the fresh bread and drank the strong coffee gratefully. She needn't have worried about a boat. Dimitri had arranged for one of the fishermen to take them out in his trawler just before sunset. The local priest had heard about the event and volunteered his services. Ellen was afraid it would be too formal, but Thecla assured her the priest was a younger man who didn't go in for fatigue-inducing services. She could meet him if she liked. His church was just up the hill from Thecla's house.

'When would be a good time to see your parents?' Ellen was determined to extend the hand of friendship even if it might be rejected.

'I take you now, when you're dressed,' said Thecla. 'No rush. You have shower. I wait and do some housework.' She must have seen the dread in Ellen's eyes and laid a hand on her shoulder. 'They good people. Last time . . .' She got up and went to close the kitchen door before sitting and speaking again. 'They think you bad person.'

Ellen felt her body stiffen in the chair. What on earth had she done to make them think that?

'They think you take Niko.'

She sat incredulous, watching the colour rise in her sister-in-law's cheeks.

'I'm to blame.' Thecla looked down at her lap, but Ellen could see she'd started to cry.

'It's okay, Thecla.' She leaned in towards her and took her hand. 'Whatever it is, just tell me.'

'When Niko find out Louise not his child, he write me. I tell them . . . they not happy.' She shook her dark curls and sniffed back her tears. 'They think Niko, how you say, trapped.' Without looking at Ellen she continued, 'I tell them he happy in Australia. He love Louise and you.' She lifted her face to Ellen's. 'He no tell you?'

'No, Thecla.' She fought back tears of her own. 'He told me his father was still angry about him not keeping on the business here.'

There it was, out in the open. Her good strong Nick; his loyalty to her and their daughter had never waned.

—

Ellen was glad to be out in the winter sunshine. They'd left Toby and Louise to recover from the journey and have some time alone to take in their surroundings. Besides, any smoothing of waters with her in-laws was best done without Louise, who had been the innocent victim of their prejudice.

As she got her bearings, it began to feel real, that she'd actually made it to Greece. Far below them, the ferry from Piraeus was steaming into shore. The town rose vertically like a seabird colony, jam-packed with houses nestled carefully into the hillside. Whitewashed walls and blue church domes dazzled her and she could almost taste the vibrant reds and yellows of plants adorning small terraces and windowsills.

'Does Santorini always look this good?' she asked. Thecla smiled, but didn't say much as she made her laboured way uphill toward her parents' house. Ellen wondered how the donkeys did it, carrying tourists and their baggage up and down the stepped path to hotels and pensions. Thecla greeted locals on the streets but didn't stop to chat. Eager to get to the Constantinopoulos house, Ellen was grateful to be spared any introductions. It was obvious by the looks on their faces that they already knew exactly who she was.

'They will come later,' Thecla told her. Ellen wasn't sure what she meant, but focused on meeting her in-laws and building bridges.

The front door was open despite the stiff breeze. Thecla walked straight in, beckoning for Ellen to follow. Nick's father was sitting in a wooden chair by the small window. He stood up in a way that looked painful. With one hand supporting a hip and the other outstretched, he came to her. She hesitated for a split second, but when his face broke into a smile that revealed his widely spaced teeth, she dropped her handbag and took his hand in both of her own.

'Mr Constantinopoulos,' she said. Then thinking of one of the few Greek greetings she knew, she blurted out, '*Kalinihta.*'

Laughter erupted from a darkened corner of the room and Nick's mother emerged to receive her guest. Ellen looked to Thecla, but her sister-in-law only smiled. Nick's dad released Ellen's hand and pointed to his watch with a giggle. It dawned on her. She'd just wished the man goodnight at two o'clock in the afternoon. At least her mistake had broken the ice.

Nick's mother's laughter turned to tears as she held out her arms and drew Ellen to her, kissing her on both cheeks. Ellen sensed relief as she touched the plain dark dress Anna

Constantinopoulos wore out of respect for the dead. Nick's presence was almost tangible as they sat around the old wooden table and Thecla helped her mother serve kourabiedes and the strong grainy coffee Ellen remembered.

'*Efharisto*,' she said, thanking them.

As they sipped their coffee in silence, Ellen saw Nick's mother's hand move under the table and nudge her husband's knee. Giorgos Constantinopoulos cleared his throat before speaking. Even before Thecla translated, Ellen registered the sadness and regret in his tone and the painful way he shrugged as he spoke.

He said they were ashamed they hadn't been kinder to her when they'd first met, that Nick had chosen a life in Australia with her and Louise and that they should not have misjudged her. Nick's death had been a huge shock to them both. His mother said it made her realise life was too short for bearing grudges and she should have had more faith in her beautiful son. Ellen hadn't noticed the tension in her shoulders until that moment when they assured her both she and Louise would always be welcome here. She smiled and sat back in her chair, relaxing for the first time in the Constantinopoulos home. Nick would have been so proud that Louise would have the opportunity to spend time with his family. Her university degree might even bring her here for work, but that was all for the future. Right now Ellen was content to make peace with her in-laws and honour the life of the husband she'd loved.

'Hey, babe.' Toby rubbed his eyes as he joined Louise on the terrace and collapsed into the sun lounger beside her. He reached for her hand and held it to his cheek. 'You doin' okay?'

Louise nodded and set the book she'd been reading on her chest, but the presence of her boyfriend and the warmth of his tanned skin unleashed the emotions she'd been trying to suppress since she'd stepped off the plane. She drew back her hand and sat up straight, bending her head to her knees.

'What's up, Lou?' Toby sat sideways on his lounger and stroked her back gently as she began to sob.

'This must be so weird for you,' she said without looking up.

He didn't say anything, but moved a little closer, encircling her in his arms and letting her go on. She spoke to the gap between her crossed arms and drawn-up thighs.

'We hardly know each other and you come halfway around the world with me to spread my father's ashes.'

She shook her head and sniffed. 'Part of me feels I have no right to be here.' She felt like an impostor. She turned her head on one side and looked into Toby's swimming-pool eyes. 'How can I face my father's parents?'

'It'll be right, Lou.' He brushed her hair from her face and let his fingers thread the strands at the nape of her neck. 'I'm here for you, no matter what happens.'

A year ago she would have doubted his sincerity and tried to be stoic. But this gorgeous gentle boy had spent months waiting for her. She knew now that he too had lost someone important in his life. Although it sucked to be so young and to have experienced such grief, it helped to share with someone who understood. She swivelled toward him and slipped her hands around his neck. Holding her close, he bent his head and pressed his parted lips against hers. It was a kiss full of the passion and connection she felt. She wished it could go on forever. It nearly would have if her cousins hadn't appeared, giggling on the terrace. When she opened her eyes and pulled a little away from Toby, poor Costas, with a face like a tomato, was trying to usher the two girls back into the house.

Toby said something about taking a shower and made a beeline for the bathroom. Costas could hardly look her in the eye when she went to the kitchen and asked how his day at school had been, but Anna and Alyssa saved the day. Knowing she wouldn't understand a word they were saying, they took paper and crayons to the table and drew pictures of love hearts and wrote *Louise* and *Toby* in them. When Thecla and her mother returned, she was grateful they retold the story behind their artwork in Greek. At least her mother would only get the gist. Seeing Costas's embarrassed reaction to the retelling, Thecla pulled at his cheek. 'You lucky to be young, my son,' she said in English and turned to give Louise a wink. Toby reappeared to another round of giggles from the girl cousins, but Thecla shushed them and told them to do their homework. Their grandparents had been invited to dinner and there was lots to be done.

Promising to be back to help once she'd showered and dressed, Louise went to the bedroom.

'Everything okay, Lou?'

She jumped as her mother's voice interrupted her thoughts.

'Yes, Mum, just trying to decide on a suitable outfit.'

She stared into the suitcase as her mum came around the side of the bed.

'I thought you'd been crying. Are things okay with you and Toby?'

She nodded, but continued to peer down at her clothes.

'It's okay if you don't want to tell me, Lou. I don't want to pry.'

She drew her hands through her hair. 'Oh, Mum. They're not even my real grandparents. How can I face them?'

Sitting down on the bed, her mother pushed the case a little away to make room for her. She sat down and her mother took her hand.

'They know, Lou,' she began. 'Thecla only told me last night, but they've known for a long time.'

Louise tried to work it out. If her mother didn't have a clue that they knew, then the only person who could have told them was her dad.

'But that time we came,' Louise began, 'it will be the same. They must hate us.'

'Hate is a very strong word, Lou,' her mother cautioned. 'They thought I tricked your dad into keeping you.'

She smiled and gave a shrug, but Louise was gobsmacked.

'How could they . . .' she began, but stopped short. She herself had suspected her mother of doing the same.

'They're getting on in years, Lou. Let's not fight with them. They misjudged your father, but when I spoke with them yesterday they were contrite. Anna herself said how ashamed they were to have treated us so badly.'

'Oh, Mum. Dad gave up so much for us.'

'That he did, love.' She gave her hand a squeeze and stood up. 'Now choose one of your lovely dresses and let's help Thecla prepare what will no doubt be another feast.'

Giorgos and Anna Constantinopoulos looked older than Louise remembered. The dark dress her grandmother wore out of mourning accentuated her white hair. A robust woman, like Thecla, she bustled into the house and took Louise in her arms, kissing her warmly on both cheeks. In the absence of a common language, Louise was sure this overt display of affection was meant, in some way, to make amends. She'd remembered Giorgos being taller. He looked so vulnerable with the cane and the slow way he negotiated the steps down into Thecla's living area. But the pain left his face when he saw her. As he registered what must have been the many changes of the intervening years, a broad smile spread across his face. She only managed a smile in return before he was usurped by his granddaughters. It was hard not to think of them as her grandparents too. But the important thing was that they were her father's parents and she was determined to make the most of the opportunity to get to know them. As they ate another of Thecla's sumptuous meals, Costas translated their questions as she happily filled them in on her life in Adelaide. They were surprised to hear about Stavros and Kristina's restaurant, and when she tried her hand at the phrases she'd learnt and the menu items she'd practised, the approving looks that passed between them made her grateful she'd kept her job.

—

Ellen made a mental note to thank Tracey for her wardrobe advice. It looked like half the island had gathered in a uniform of dark suits and dresses to pay their respects to Nikolas Constantinopoulos. The dark trousers and smart jacket gave her a sense of control which settled the nerves she'd been battling all day. Thecla and Dimitri had driven them round to Kamira on the other side of the island, where the trawler sat at anchor awaiting its grieving passengers.

'Wow,' she thought aloud as she took in the throng of sympathisers gathered on the beach. She'd only expected immediate family.

'No worry,' said Thecla as they got out of the car. 'No all go in boat.'

Ellen wound the black pashmina she'd bought that afternoon round the shoulders of her jacket. The wind was picking up and the early spring temperatures reminded her of South Australia's winter. She walked toward the beach flanked by Thecla and Dimitri on one side and Toby and Louise on the other. The blackness of the sand struck her as it had all those years ago when its luxurious warmth had been a huge comfort after a frosty reception from the Constantinopoulos clan. Ellen remembered how they'd escaped to Kamira's volcanic beach where Nick and Louise swam out to small boats while she lay snoozing in the sizzling sun until Nick returned to massage another layer of sunscreen into her skin. Tonight the beach was cold, devoid of warmth, each grain of sand a sharp reminder of the gaping wound that was Nick's absence. His parents stood close to one another, looking uncertain about what to do. Ellen smiled and beckoned them to follow as Thecla steered her past the crowd toward a man who stood alone at the water's edge.

Dimitri made the formal introductions as the skipper, Yannis, removed a half-smoked cigarette from the side of his mouth before saying something in Greek.

'He say he love Niko,' Dimitri translated. 'Knew him since he was small boy.'

'Good fisherman,' the skipper interrupted. When Ellen looked into his ageing eyes, she thought she saw the sorrow of the whole community reflected in them. If it took a village to raise a child, this was Nick's village right here. As Yannis helped her into the small wooden boat that would ferry them in relays to the Constantinopoulos' trawler, she thought how futile it had all been, rejecting a son because he had chosen to marry outside his culture and raise a child that wasn't his own.

The priest, in his long dress and tall hat, climbed into the boat, his censer jangling, sending trails of pungent incense smoke into the crowd. He sat beside Ellen and gave her a kindly smile. As the skipper revved the outboard motor, she clasped the urn tightly to her chest. The boat bobbed over the short stretch of sea to where they would disembark onto the larger vessel. Ellen reluctantly handed the urn to a deckhand before climbing the rope ladder. She steadied herself against the swell and retrieved the urn. The deckhand motioned to her to take a seat on the fibreglass bench on the port side. Louise joined her and held tight at the crook of her arm.

'Bit of a stink,' she said, more to calm Lou's nerves than to point out the smell of a recent catch.

Louise gave a small laugh but didn't loosen her grip. Together they looked out over the water as the rest of the family were ferried to the trawler. Toby had done them proud, having put on the long black pants and dark long-sleeved top he would have packed specially and lending a hand wherever one was needed.

They watched now as he helped the passengers aboard, taking special care with Nick's parents who he and the deckhand pretty much lifted on board. As Yannis took the helm and revved the trawler's engines, Ellen saw Giorgos take Anna's hand and give it a squeeze.

The fresh wind showed no sign of abating as they headed west into the pink and orange canvas of the Santorini sunset. The black sand of Kamira disappeared as they sailed further away from shore. Ellen cradled the ceramic vessel she'd kept in her wardrobe for over a year. As her stomach lurched with the swell, she pulled a little closer to Louise.

'Dad would be so proud of you, Mum.'

It had been a source of family entertainment that sea legs had never been Ellen's strong point. Nick had often offered to take them out to the sea cages or feeding barges, but Ellen declined after the first couple of experiences when she'd turned shades of green that could have matched the Irish landscape. In her mind, he teased her now, softening his words with a playful wink that always made her heart leap.

About ten kilometres out into the Aegean, the skipper killed the engine. A lonesome chanting rose above the sound of the sea as the priest began the ceremony in a beautiful baritone. Taking a holy book from under his vestments, he continued with readings Ellen didn't understand but trusted to mean well. When he paused, Thecla leaned over to her and whispered, 'It's time.'

Yes, it was indeed time; time to let go, time to let her husband rest in peace in the waters of his homeland. With Louise at her side, she stepped to the side of the boat and unscrewed the lid of the urn. The family and friends looked on, bidding their silent farewells. Tilting the urn, she could smell the ashes as they escaped over the sea, caught up in the invisible clutches of the wind and currents that would determine Nick's final resting place.

It was time to leave Santorini. Rather than the energy-depleting challenge Ellen had feared, it had been a time of healing. She hoped it wouldn't be the last time she'd visit, but she knew enough about life's uncertainties not to be making promises she couldn't keep. She'd already said most of her goodbyes the night before and this morning she'd been given the hugest hugs from the children before they left for school. Even shy Costas had kissed her cheek and thanked her again for the gifts. She'd sent Louise and Toby off on their island adventures earlier to avoid any emotional upsets. As she came downstairs and set her suitcase in the hall, she could hear music coming from the kitchen. It was an operatic piece she recognised but couldn't name. Nick could have told her. He loved all kinds of music.

'Ah, El-len.'

Thecla was standing at the kitchen window, dabbing at her eyes with a tea towel, an old CD player perched on the modern worktop beside her.

'Are you all right?' asked Ellen.

A sad smile broke across Thecla's face, the corners of her mouth trembling as she went to speak.

'I play it for Niko,' she said, fresh tears glistening in her dark eyes. '"*L'amour est un oiseau rebelle*" . . . It's Maria Callas.'

Ellen did her best to translate with her school French. Yes, in Santorini Nick would have been seen as a rebel, leaving his homeland for a new life in Australia.

'We were just children when they spread her ashes, like Niko,' Thecla continued.

'In the Aegean?' asked Ellen, incredulous.

Thecla nodded and dried her eyes again. 'You tell Louise she one of us. Always place for her here.'

'Thank you, sister,' said Ellen.

It felt right. Her big-hearted husband would have approved. Santorini had exceeded her expectations. Louise was in safe hands and she herself was ready for the next leg of her journey.

—

Louise held her arms tight around Toby, happy to let him manoeuvre the ATV they'd borrowed from her uncle. She didn't want to miss any of the sights and wonders of her father's island. Although Santorini was small enough to get around in a day, they took their time. She wished she'd paid more attention when she'd been here with her dad. If she'd known they'd never travel together again, she might have kept a diary, written it all down. But what ten-year-old would have that kind of foresight? At the end of the day, it wasn't the details that mattered to her anyway. Santorini, with its lighthouses, volcano, thermal springs, shops, sunsets, all the things a tourist might come for, would have meant so much less had she not had a father from here. No, she may not have remembered much of the geography but now, as then, she'd come with Santorini already in her heart. When she and Toby climbed Skaros Rock and looked out over the edges of the Aegean in all its sapphire glory, she imagined her father sitting there on his favourite spot and marvelled at what he might have been like at her age; young, full of dreams, hungry for adventures beyond the caldera where the Minoan ancestors he'd told her stories about had fallen into the sea. Maybe he'd even come here with a girl he was in love with who had very different dreams.

She'd expected Toby to be the tourist, making suggestions about things to see and do, Snapchatting selfies back to Australia every ten minutes. But he hadn't done any of that, happy to go with her relatives' suggestions as to what to see and gracious in accepting their invitations to visit for lunches and dinners.

After her mother left for Ireland, there was still the safety net of her father's relatives, but she was about to embark on the part of the journey where she and Toby would have to rely on each other twenty-four-seven. Her whole body tingled with nervous excitement. As she strolled along Red Beach linking arms with Thecla, Louise watched him play effortlessly with Costas and his sisters, drawing the map of Australia in the sand to show them where he lived and teaching them Australian slang. How did someone know when they'd met the person they wanted to spend their life with? Surely that was something that would happen well into her future? Louise took a deep breath of Santorini air with its signature smell of the sea and told herself to enjoy the moment.

Little Alyssa came and tugged at her hand.

'G'day, mate!' she said, looking up at Louise with her beautiful brown eyes. Satisfied with Louise and Thecla's surprised reaction, she ran off and climbed onto Toby's back, wrestling him to the ground with the help of her brother and sister and insisting on burying him up to his neck in the rough sand.

'He love children, no?' said Thecla as they walked.

'He has a couple of nieces,' Louise smiled, thinking back to the day she saw him with them in the canoe in Venus Bay.

Thecla put an arm around her and drew her close. Lowering her voice, she said, 'Your children, you bring them to see Thecla and Dimitri.'

Louise gasped. 'Thecla, that's a long way down the track . . .'

'We be old,' she was serious now, 'but you come.'

Louise thought she saw tears in the eyes of her father's sister. How much the siblings had missed out on: babies they hadn't held, birthdays they hadn't been there for, lessons they hadn't passed on. She hugged tight into her aunt. 'I'll come, Thecla.'

Chapter Twenty-five

In his parents' living room, Gerry flicked through the supplements of the Sunday paper while his father read the main section ensconced in his favourite armchair. Domingo snored in front of the open fire as his namesake sang 'Nessun Dorma' from Gerry Senior's extensive collection of opera.

'You sure I can't set a place for you?' asked Pauline as she came through from the kitchen with plates and cutlery for the roast dinner that wafted tantalisingly from the oven.

Gerry put the paper aside and stood up. 'No thanks, Mam. I promised Stephanie I'd pick her up at one.'

'If I had my way, you'd all be sitting round here every Sunday,' his mother sulked.

'Leave the man alone, Pauline,' said Gerry Senior. 'Isn't it a bonus nowadays that a teenage daughter even wants to be seen in public with her ageing father?'

'Would you listen to the spring chicken in the corner there?' laughed Gerry.

'Like father like son,' said Pauline setting the plates down heavily. 'Never serious for long enough to hold an adult conversation.'

'Only for you, Pauline,' Gerry Senior called after her as she strutted back to the kitchen.

He set down his paper and pushed himself out of the chair. Checking to make sure she wasn't about to come back in, he pulled the wallet from his back pocket and took out a fifty euro note. 'Give that to my granddaughter,' he whispered, handing it to Gerry. 'Tell her to come and see her old granny and granddad soon.'

'Ah, Dad, you don't need to bankroll her. She could open a shop with all the clothes and makeup—'

'Can't you do what you're told now, son, and keep your mouth shut. You'll be a grandfather too one day, please God.' He replaced the wallet and began whistling along to the dramatic tones of Plácido.

Pauline was back, setting the meat in the centre of the table, carving tools at the ready for his father to do the honours as usual. 'And don't forget, you're welcome to bring anyone here, son.'

Gerry Senior rolled his eyes at her.

'I only want the boy to have a bit of company, Gerry,' Pauline argued. 'You can't blame a mother for that. He's too young to be getting set in his ways.'

'I assure you, Mam,' said Gerry, thinking she might need reminding that he was actually in the room, 'you'll be the first to know if there's anything happening on that front, but I hate to disappoint you . . .'

'As bad as your father is, I wouldn't be without him,' she said, addressing him now as if his father weren't there.

'I'm gone,' said Gerry to his dad, 'before she takes matters into her own hands and starts making phone calls.' He laughed good-humouredly and went to kiss his mother's cheek. 'See ye next week if not before.'

'Good luck, son,' said his dad with a wink. Gerry shook his head as he walked to the car. Maybe he'd been on his own longer than he'd realised. And what did his mother mean, 'getting set in his ways'?

⌐

Gerry drove slowly into the suburban housing estate. On the green in the middle of the crescent, a group of young lads having a kick around halted play as the ball rolled onto the road in front of him. He braked and waited as one of them came to retrieve it. The boy waved at him. He'd been a neighbour's child, once.

In the driveway of his former family home, a Mercedes-Benz soft top was taking up the second space, forcing Gerry to park at the kerb. The two-storey suburban dwelling looked immaculate as ever. He was surprised and a little ashamed at having imagined Jessica might have let it go without his help to maintain it. Although he hadn't spent a night under its roof in over two years, the sight of the house always made him feel sentimental.

The curtains twitched at an upstairs window. He rang the bell anyway. After a few minutes he was just about to ring again when he heard Jessica's voice inside.

'Stephanie,' she called out, 'that's your dad. Hurry up.'

She opened the door and stood in a silky salmon dressing gown he'd never seen.

'Gerry.' Tightening the belted garment round her narrow waist, she looked past him, scanning the neighbourhood for who might see her.

'Jessica.' He pulled the collar of his jacket up around his neck. He didn't expect to be invited in. She'd read his mind.

'I'd invite you in,' she said, nodding her head toward the staircase, 'but I've got company.'

Gerry looked away.

'Aren't you lucky,' he said half under his breath.

'Gerry, you'll meet somebody too.'

He smiled. She meant well, but he wasn't prepared to stand there in the cold being reminded of how single he was.

'Go in out of the cold there, Jess. Sure isn't your man waiting for you?'

She gave an embarrassed smile and went back in the house, giving a last call to hurry Stephanie along before disappearing upstairs.

In that moment the September afternoon with Ellen came back to him. Holding her slim body to him, her soft blonde hair brushing against his skin. How warm and natural it had been. How playfully it had begun with the water fight, both of them behaving like the twenty-somethings they might have been if she hadn't gone away.

'Sorry, Dad,' said Stephanie as she came down the hallway, shoving her phone in her jeans pocket. 'I was just messaging someone.' She kissed him quickly and pulled the door shut behind her. 'Awesome car, isn't it?'

Gerry didn't answer, but clenched his fist around the keys he had a churlish urge to scrape along the paintwork.

In the car, he wanted to tell Stephanie she should have worn a raincoat. The tiny made-in-China fake leather jacket would do nothing to keep out the wintry squall. Instead he sucked it in. Time was precious when you only met your daughter for a fortnightly lunch. He would have liked her to stay over at the flat. Donal would probably have behaved himself in his niece's presence, but Jessica wouldn't hear of it. No, the idea of her daughter spending any time in a flat above a pub with an alcoholic uncle wouldn't be entertained. Gerry had thought she'd have been grateful to have the house to herself, but she'd always been a protective mother. He couldn't fault her for that.

With his bank balance dented and copious carrier bags to prove it, Gerry perched himself next to Stephanie on a stool at the smoothie bar. The fumes from the selection of scents she had tested made him cough.

'You okay, Dad?' she asked him, her eyes full of concern.

Gerry waved his hand in front of his face.

'Yes, love.' He covered his mouth to cough again. 'I'm not used to all this perfume wafting about the place.'

'What you need is a girlfriend, Dad.'

The comment made him cough again, but it was more like choking now.

'Mum's new boyfriend's nice. She's not lonely now. It's about time you found someone.'

'Whoa, whoa!' He made a stop sign with one hand and stifled another coughing fit with the other. 'Since when did you become an expert on what I need?'

'Oh, it's not just me, Dad. Granny Pauline agrees with me. You're not too old—'

'Stop right there, Miss Madam, and drink your smoothie. Your grandmother should know better than to meddle in other people's affairs. And as a matter of fact . . .'

Stephanie's phone sent out its ridiculous frog ringtone. She raised one hand and screwed her face up in apology as she took the call.

'What's up, Debs?'

Gerry slumped in his stool and sucked on his homogenised fruit. He could have gotten it all off his chest if it hadn't been for modern technology and Deb's latest boyfriend issue.

It was all a bit sad. Spending a Sunday afternoon in a shopping centre with people falling over themselves to grab a bargain in the sales, when what he really wanted was to have a decent conversation with his daughter and tell her about what had happened in Australia. Kieran had been a rock, but Stephanie was a different animal. Gerry dreaded the melodramatics that would no doubt ensue. She'd be gobsmacked to find out she had a half-sister. She'd go straight home to Jessica and tell her. Given the circumstances of their own marriage, he didn't know how Jessica would take it. By the end, she'd been adamant she didn't want to waste the rest of her life with someone she no longer loved. Would she feel cheated? That half her life had been wasted on someone who'd loved someone else all along?

He watched as Stephanie held the phone to her ear, frowning as she bent her head of dark hair to the straw of her pineapple smoothie, lips glistening with the lip gloss she never left home without. It seemed to him that her made up face belied her natural beauty, but he had long since resigned himself to keeping mum on his thoughts about Stephanie's overgenerous approach to the application of makeup. He tried to imagine Louise joining them on the next stool along. Would they have anything in common? The same taste in music if not in cosmetics? Maybe a day would come when they would find out.

'Have you heard from Kieran?' Stephanie was asking as she replaced the phone in the pocket of her skinny jeans.

'He's back in Adelaide after his travels. Having a ball by all accounts.'

'I might do that when I finish school. You know, take a gap year. Go to Australia with some of the girls.'

Gerry smiled to himself as he watched her scrape the froth from the inside of her glass with her straw. His baby girl and her big plans. It would break his heart if she went away, but he couldn't tell her that.

'I might even go to university there,' she went on. 'Can you do that?'

'You can do whatever you set your mind to, sweetheart.'

The news of Louise could wait. Maybe they could all sit down together when Kieran came home.

—

The usual Sunday night crowd were squeezing the last drops of socialising out of the weekend. Gerry normally liked Sunday nights as the clients were more cooperative than on a Saturday, easier to convince to go home with a whole new week of work and commitments looming. Tonight, he just felt irritated and couldn't wait to see the back of them.

'A couple of cappuccinos for table seven when you're ready.'

He looked up from a line of pints he was finishing off. His face must have had 'Tell the shaggers to go home and make their own coffee' written all over it.

'Under a bit of pressure there, are we, Gerry?' Bronwyn set her shiny teeth on a bottom lip thick with lipstick the colour of a Snow White apple.

He shrugged apologetically. 'I'll have them for you in a sec.' Paul, the new barman, was flat out at the other end of the bar and Donal was nowhere to be seen. *Probably necking some married woman round the side*, Gerry thought before admonishing himself for being so immature.

—

'Night now.'

Gerry couldn't remember a night he was so pleased to see the pub shut. The staff were finishing off in the kitchen. Donal appeared out of nowhere to do the till, as he insisted on doing every night. Gerry went upstairs to the restaurant to take the worst of the mess from the carpet. Sheila would have it looking perfect again in the morning, but she'd only complain if there was too much work involved.

'Tough day?' asked Bronwyn who was clearing the last of the tables.

'I've had better,' he said without looking at her.

'Have a seat there and I'll bring us a drink.'

She was gone before he could say no, but Gerry didn't want to say no tonight. Between his slavedriver of a brother and his mixed-up family, he could do with a drink. Bronwyn set a couple of glasses of red wine on the table in front of him.

'Cheers.' He raised his glass to hers. She took a sip, but instead of sitting, she set down her glass and came behind him. The feel of her hands on his shoulders surprised him, but he suspended his reservations.

'Ooh, that feels good.' He closed his eyes as Bronwyn worked her fingers and thumbs into the tight muscles of his shoulderblades and up the back of his neck.

'You need to relax a little, Gerry.' Her voice was sexy like the black miniskirt she wore with those tights. 'You know what they say about all work and no play . . .'

She was leaning closer to him now. He could feel her breath as she spoke, almost touching his ear with those crimson lips he could see without looking. There were shouts of 'goodnight' from the last of the staff as they left, but he didn't move. She was onto a vigorous head massage, his body sitting heavier in the chair as he gave in to her efforts to de-stress him. When her hands had rubbed for long enough, they pushed under the neck of his T-shirt and came to rest on his clavicles. He felt the rush of blood to his thighs and groin.

'We could take this upstairs,' she said, plunging her arms down his chest and teasing at his earlobe with her tongue.

When he turned, she straddled him, taking his face in both her hands and thrusting her chest at him. The shiny fabric of her shirt pushed against his skin. Her breasts heaved against the buttons. He traced the curve of her waist and moved his hands to touch the stud-like nipples. She groaned with pleasure. He was sure she smelled of one of the expensive perfumes Stephanie had tried on in the shops. The thought brought him up short. Okay, so he was here with a beautiful younger woman sitting astride him, daring him to take her. It wasn't as though he got laid every weekend. In fact, apart from his unforgettable afternoon with Ellen O'Shea, he'd been celibate for what felt like years.

'I need to make a phone call,' he said in a breathless squeal that didn't sound at all like his manly self.

'Can't it wait?' said Bronwyn, intent on getting her tongue past his words.

'Eh, no . . . eh, sorry, Bron.' He pushed her leg gently to one side and eased himself out from under her.

Without as much as a backward glance, or a nod to Donal as he went past the bar, Gerry rushed through the kitchen and out into the teeming rain.

'You have reached the message bank of . . .' was all he got from the mobile. The landline went straight to voicemail.

'Ellen, it's me, Gerry. If you're there, can you pick up please? I need to speak to you.' He dialled the mobile again and again, before leaving a final message. 'Ellen, as you must know by now, I'm desperate to talk. I want us to be together . . . somehow. Can't stop thinking about you . . . Ring me when you get a chance . . . I love you.'

～

'Mobile phones can now be switched on,' the steward announced over the intercom as the 747 taxied along the runway at Cork Airport. Still half asleep, Ellen scrabbled in her handbag and took out her phone before remembering the battery had died in the first few days of her journey. Thecla had taken her to a shop where they could only offer to order a replacement battery from Athens at a ridiculous price. The buzz of Cork city and county accents crescendoed around her, sounding simultaneously familiar and unfamiliar. There was a harmony of other accents too. When a child with beautiful dark skin and the prettiest cornrows popped her head up over the seat in front of her and started speaking in an accent thicker than her own, Ellen had to smile. The child's mother said something in a language foreign to her and the child dropped back into her seat obediently. It was almost ten years since she'd been home. Ireland had changed, but then so had Ellen O'Shea.

Cork Airport had undergone a major facelift since she'd been here last. It was all chrome and teak, a bit like Thecla's kitchen. Ellen decided she liked it. *Life is change*, she thought as she scanned the crowd awaiting arrivals.

It was her father she spotted first. She wanted to stop and take a good look at him before proceeding any further, but the rush of travellers propelled her forward. Aidan was beside him, her once lean brother now a heavier version of their dad.

'Hey Ellen, over here,' he shouted and almost ran to grab her bags like a child welcoming a much-loved parent home.

'Thanks for coming,' she said, gratefully handing over the luggage and kissing his cheek. She turned to her father, relieved to see him looking healthy despite the advancing years.

'Long time no see, Dad.'

Bill O'Shea held out an arm and stretched it round his daughter. Without a word, he drew her to his side and planted a kiss on the top of her head. As he steered her toward the exit, Ellen could almost feel the lump in his throat.

Aidan quizzed her about the journey as he drove them home. Her answers were interrupted at intervals by their dad's nervous commentary. 'Watch out for him, son . . . Look at that bastard . . . sorry, Ellen . . .'

'Who's driving this thing? You or me?' Aidan caught her eye in the rear-view mirror and made a face.

She laughed inwardly at the banter. The details of her trip could wait. She was happy just looking out the window as her native city revealed itself to her in all its night-time splendour. They were taking her the scenic route along the river with its network of quays and bridges: Albert Quay; past the City Hall, its limestone façade and clock tower bathed in golden light; across the river's south channel to Merchant's Quay with its bus station and shopping centre. The comfort of the familiar landmarks enveloped her, like the cross on the Church of the Ascension shining red on the skyline at Gurranabraher. And Patrick's Bridge across the north channel; she must have crossed it a thousand times and yet her clearest memory was crossing it hand in hand with Gerry Clancy. What the coming days might bring filled her with nervous anticipation. She resolved to savour every moment like a bar of chocolate after a strict diet.

～

Their terraced house was looking well. Ellen wouldn't have believed her father could have kept it so tidy. She hovered in the hallway as he changed out of his shoes and set them neatly on a small shoe rack under the stairs before pulling on a pair of fur-lined slippers. She wiped her stockman boots a second time on the doormat and padded as lightly as possible over the new carpet. Aidan, who seemed oblivious to his father's little ceremony, was already boiling the kettle after abandoning her suitcase inside the sitting room. 'I'll take that up for you later,' he'd said.

'You're keeping the place lovely, Dad,' she said as they sat in the sitting room drinking tea and eating leftover Christmas cake from the best china. She wasn't sure whether to be alarmed or flattered at being served supper from the rarely used wedding present that had been her mother's pride and joy.

'I have a woman who does for me a bit,' said Bill looking into his teacup. Ellen wanted to ask who, but the look Aidan shot her made her abandon the idea.

'That's grand tea, son.' Bill set his cup on its gilt-edged saucer and looked at Ellen. 'So what do you think you'll do while you're here, love?'

She would like to have said 'reconnect with my old life', but something told her that her dad was looking for a more practical answer.

'Oh, catch up with yourselves and a few old friends, hopefully.'

'I'm at your beck and call,' said Aidan. 'I have a couple of apprentices with myself and Rob now, so I can get a bit of time off.'

'Thanks a million.' She was glad the building trade had taken a turn for the better. Although hundreds like him had been leaving weekly for Australia in the downturn, it was never an option for her brother the home bird.

'You'll want to visit your mother's grave, God rest her,' said her dad.

'Of course,' said Ellen. 'We could do that together. Tomorrow even.' In truth, she'd had enough of remembering death. She'd already cried buckets in Santorini. A walk around her old haunts, linking arms with her father, was more what she had looked forward to, but maybe her dad hadn't thought of that.

Upstairs, Aidan deposited the suitcase in the single room that had been his own until he renovated an old two-storey townhouse in Blackrock and finally left home.

'Why am I in *your* room?' she asked, following him in reluctantly.

'Don't ask,' he whispered, tapping a finger to the side of his nose. 'I'll talk to you tomorrow.'

She wanted to sit down on the bed beside him right now and talk, but something about the atmosphere in the house made her think it better to wait until they were away from it, alone.

With his signature smile that held more empathy than a bear hug, Aidan went downstairs. There was a comfort in sleeping in her big brother's old bed. It reminded her of childhood holidays in their grandmother's house in West Cork, when they slept in bunks and told each other jokes, trying to giggle quietly, long past the time they should have been asleep.

'Cooee, only me.'

Ellen thought she was hearing things as she lay half dozing the next morning. The shrill voice called out again, 'Cooee.' *Did people even say cooee in real life?* thought Ellen, wondering if she was still dreaming.

'Sorry, Fran. I was out the back.' Her father's voice sounded laboured. There was silence. Ellen imagined he must be gesturing to the woman to be quiet as she was supposed to be asleep upstairs. *Fran*, thought Ellen. *Who the heck is Fran?* The only Fran she knew was Frances Brady, the neighbour who'd barely tolerated Ellen and Aidan as children and wasn't averse to displays of meanness. She would never forget the time she'd put a fork in Aidan's football when the treasured possession had gone over the garden wall one time too many. Her mother hadn't liked her and she certainly would never have had a 'Cooee, I'll just let myself in your front door' relationship with the woman.

Showered and dressed, Ellen ventured downstairs. Her father and their visitor were sitting in the kitchen, their voices hushed. When the woman turned around, the pinched lips and chipmunk cheeks left Ellen in no doubt as to who she was.

'You'll remember Fran,' said her father. 'Fran and Terry used to live in the house behind us. God rest his soul.' As he made the sign of the cross on his chest, the neighbour was making no secret of checking her out from head to toe.

'Eh, of course, Mrs Brady. I'd have known you anywhere. You haven't changed a bit.' The charm offensive had always been Ellen's strategy with the woman, despite only limited success.

'Are you home for long?' asked Frances without any preliminaries like 'How was your trip' or 'How is Australia treating you?'.

Ellen wished her father would say she was welcome to stay as long as she liked, but he had already left the table and was putting on the kettle for another round of tea and toast. Eyeing the butter and marmalade, Ellen realised she was famished.

'I'm not sure, actually,' she heard herself saying. 'Just looking forward to catching up with everyone.'

One of Frances's heavily pencilled eyebrows seemed to rise of its own accord. The port-wine lips may have pinched even tighter together, but Ellen told herself she was imagining things. She was only the next-door neighbour, for God's sake. What business was it of hers? She took a seat at the table.

'Fran does a great job helping me out around the house,' said her dad as he set a plate and knife for her.

'Sorry, Dad. I should be helping myself instead of having you waiting on me hand and foot.'

'We have our own way of doing things, don't we Bill?' said Frances with a look to Bill that softened her features.

We, thought Ellen, mentally biting her tongue. Since when had her father and the old neighbour from hell been a *we*?

'We won't be long, love,' said Bill, getting up from the table, although it seemed to Ellen the man had just sat down. 'We're just nipping down to twelve o'clock mass in town.'

She stopped chewing. 'Oh, right. Say a prayer for me.'

'We will,' said Frances without a smile.

'Will we go to Mam's grave after that, Dad?' She wanted to say, 'You know, the one she's rolling in right now over this carry-on.'

'We'll see,' he said and left her alone in her old home.

In the sitting room, she ran a finger over the picture frames. Not a speck of dust. Her mother's face looked at her from a family photo taken at her confirmation, pride written all over it. She'd been a good girl then. How she must have shattered Maureen O'Shea's sense of propriety when she told her she was pregnant. Her friends in both Ireland and Australia couldn't believe it when she told them how her mother and aunt had reacted. They'd said their attitudes were outdated, that their parents would have welcomed them and their babies with open arms no matter how they were conceived. Yet her mother hadn't been all bad. By the time Ellen was mature enough to build bridges, it was too late. They'd been planning a trip home when the phone call came from Aidan that their mother had died suddenly in her sleep.

Upstairs, she looked at the closed door of her parents' bedroom. It must be lonely for her dad, she thought. The shock he must have got when he found his wife lifeless beside him that morning. Ellen shivered. It reminded her too much of what happened to Nick. She went to brush her teeth in the bathroom that used to be painted apple green. It was wall to wall tiles now. White with a pink rose at intervals. She couldn't resist the urge to trace the rose with her fingers.

Stick on! Her mother would never have allowed stick-on tile designs. Although she didn't need anything from the cupboard under the sink, Ellen found herself opening it out of curiosity. A polka dot toilet bag and matching cosmetic case were pushed in behind the spare toilet rolls and an economy pack of soap bars. Surely to God those bags weren't Frances Brady's.

The door to her old bedroom was closed. She went to open it, but her hand froze on the doorknob. *Get a grip,* she told herself. *This was your bedroom once. Still is really.* Her hand turned and the door swung open. This was definitely her bedroom no more. This wasn't even a bedroom. It was more of a . . . *boudoir.* She put a hand to her mouth, not sure whether to laugh or cry at the four-poster bed complete with princess canopy adorned with satin sheets and all manner of cushions in varying shades of pink from shocking to positively pastel. Two creamy cupids in what looked like marble served as lamp stands on the bedside tables. She lifted one of the lamps. *Plastic!* A key turned in the front door. Her heart pounded as she backed out and closed the door behind her.

'Are you up yet, Ellen?'

'Thank God it's you, Aidan.' She came down the stairs two steps at a time and almost fell into his arms.

'Did you see a ghost up there or what?'

'No. It was worse. Take me out, for God's sake, before I crack up here.'

'Let's walk,' she said as Aidan went to unlock the car. 'Are you okay for time?'

'Yeah. The lads have it all under control so I took the afternoon off.'

'The advantages of self-employment,' said Ellen.

Aidan pulled a woollen scarf tight around his neck and put his hands in the pockets of his fleece jacket. They linked arms as they headed down Wellington Road against a stiff breeze. Ellen drank in the cityscape in daylight now, the River Lee meandering its way under Cork's many bridges, past landmarks like St Fin Barre's Cathedral to the Southside and Shandon to the north. These were the pictures she had etched in her mind since childhood, pictures that came to her whenever she thought about her native city.

'So tell me, Aidan, what exactly is the relationship between Dad and Mrs Brady?'

Out of her peripheral vision, she saw his cheeks redden.

'He's never actually told me straight out, but as far as I know they're . . . a bit of an item.'

'Ah, that explains the *boudoir* that used to be my bedroom.' Ellen bristled. 'But why her? Of all the old biddies in Cork City, why did he have to choose Frances Brady? Mam couldn't stand her.' She pulled her scarf down from her chin, not sure if the increase in her body temperature was due to the exercise or the subject of their conversation.

'You could always stay with me if she makes you feel uncomfortable.'

'Thanks, but I wouldn't do that to Dad. Anyway, it's my family home too.'

'Suit yourself,' he said. 'But behave yourself, or she won't be inviting you to the big seventieth birthday bash she's organising for him.'

Her jaw dropped. 'You're kidding me?'

'I know we talked about taking him out for dinner with a few of the rellies once you were here,' said Aidan, 'but Fran's got a whole other scenario in mind. It's to be a surprise.'

Ellen's mind boggled. 'Is it too early for a drink?'

'Now you're talking. Will we go in to the Valley?'

'No,' she said. 'Just somewhere we're not likely to meet anyone.'

Aidan glanced at her quizzically. 'I thought that was the whole point of your visit, to meet people.'

'Well, not *people* as such. Wait till we sit down and I'll tell you.'

In a quiet corner of Dan Lowry's, Ellen gave her brother the lowdown on Gerry Clancy's visit to Port Lincoln. Like everything else, he took the news of Louise's paternity in his stride, no shock, no judgement. When she explained how she and Gerry had rekindled their old feelings for each other, he smiled.

'I always knew he held a torch for you,' Aidan teased. 'Always asks for you when I run into him. Nice restaurant he runs with the brother. Good tucker as you'd say Down Under. The beer's not bad either.'

'Aidan,' said Ellen losing her patience, 'are you getting this?'

He took a sip of his pint and let her continue.

'So tell me I'm mad to even be here, thinking about a future with him.'

Aidan moved his glass to one side and leaned over the table, arms crossed in front of him. 'Give me one good reason why you wouldn't be?'

'That's a bit rich coming from a confirmed bachelor,' said Ellen before she could help herself.

Aidan sat back in his chair and looked at the stained-glass window. 'Some people don't know how lucky they are.'

She felt ashamed. In the years since she'd moved away, Aidan had had his share of failed relationships. She hadn't been close enough to know the details, but whatever they were, her luck in love had been a lot better than her brother's.

'Carpe bloody diem,' he said and downed the last of his pint. Tracey had told her to do the same.

They sat in silence as she mulled over her brother's comments, but the pub was filling up for lunch. This was no place for quiet reflection. As they got up to leave, she saw a familiar face coming toward her.

'Ellen O'Shea! What are you doing here?'

'Colette Barry. Is it yourself?'

She threw her arms around the old school friend she still kept in touch with. In her excitement, Colette spoke in hurried sentences.

'I'll kill you for not telling me you were coming home. You're looking fantastic. How's Louise?' For a moment her bright smile waned as she looked from Ellen to Aidan. 'Is everything all right?'

'She'll tell you over a pint. Won't you, Ellen?'

'Sounds serious. What are you doing tonight?' That was the Colette Ellen knew and loved. Spontaneous to a fault. 'I'll collect you around seven and we can go for a drink and maybe a bite to eat. Can't wait to hear all the news.'

Ellen couldn't believe she'd just bumped into Colette like that. But then, that was one of the things she loved about Cork. She was sure she spent the afternoon beaming as she strolled around the shops with Aidan indulging her at every stop, even finding a shop where she could buy a replacement battery for her ancient phone.

Chapter Twenty-six

Gerry Clancy felt like a prat. It was days since he'd left that blasted message on Ellen's voicemail. He cringed now as he remembered the desperation in his words. He'd turned over every excuse he could think of, but the fact remained that if she'd wanted him as badly as he wanted her, she'd have phoned him back straightaway. Okay, maybe she'd sleep on it for a night, but then she'd ring. Nothing, not even a text. That was the worst. Maybe his mother was right after all. It was a pipedream to think they had a future. She'd left him once before. How could he have been so foolish as to believe she'd want a life with him after all these years? He could meet someone here easy. Bronwyn Fennelly was already heading up 'the queue' as his mother called it. God knows, he'd met his share of women through the course of his work. Enough of them had flirted. He could have taken it further, but until that trip to Australia, the urge to be with another woman had never been anything other than physical. Call it old-fashioned, but that wasn't enough. He wanted the real deal. He thought he'd found it, or at least won it back.

Bronwyn hadn't waited around for Gerry to finish his call. She'd phoned in sick the two following days. He might have done the decent thing and rung her up if he hadn't been so obsessed with waiting for the reply he now realised would never come. She was due on at seven tonight. He hoped she'd come in. It would give him a chance to make it up to her, if she'd let him. *Time to move on*, he thought. *Get real for once.*

———

Bill and Frances were side by side on the couch watching an episode of *X Factor* when Ellen came downstairs all set to go out with Colette. The anxiety she'd felt in the hour she'd taken to decide what to wear dissipated at the sight of them. Despite her dislike of Frances Brady, she envied their companionship. Hadn't that been the greatest bonus of her life with Nick, indeed what she was searching for in coming here? She had no idea how this was going to pan out, but the message from Gerry was clear. He wanted her in his life. She'd replayed the message over and over, and was so close to calling him, but she was here, she could just walk into the pub and meet him. It would be worth it to see his face. She took another deep breath and grabbed her bag. A drink with Colette would help calm her nerves.

'That'll be Colette,' said Bill as a car tooted out front. 'Watch out for those cowboys down town,' he advised, following her to the hall where he helped her into her woollen coat. She glanced at herself in the mirror. She felt quite trendy in the skinny jeans and floaty top she'd bought especially for the occasion, but what if Gerry thought she was trying to look young?

'You look lovely,' said Bill.

'Thanks, Dad.' She stretched up on her toes and gave her dad a kiss. She mightn't like his choice of 'home help', but he was still her dad.

—

'You're a saint, Colette Barry,' said Ellen as they drove off. 'You have rescued me from a very awkward situation.' She heard herself babbling on about Bill and Frances, but couldn't hide from the truth that her story served only to cover her nerves.

In the Mutton Lane Inn, they filled each other in on the details of infrequent emails. Colette mostly elaborated on her recent divorce. Ellen would never have put Tadhg and Colette together in the first place, but at twenty-five her friend had been convinced that he was the one, and besides, she'd been desperate to have babies. The fact that the latter had never transpired had been a contributing factor to the demise of the marriage. Ellen could empathise. It made it easier to tell Colette about Louise's paternity and how the reunion with Gerry had triggered recent events.

'I always knew you two were meant to be,' said Colette, delighted with the news. 'So what are we doing sitting here, ya eejit? He's no doubt at the Stables right now.' She pulled on her coat. 'From what I hear, he hardly takes a night off. Donal's a fecking waste of space.' Ellen gathered her bag and stood up from the table, caught in the white-water rapids of Colette's spontaneity.

'Are you sure you don't mind coming with me, Colette? I don't want you to feel like a gooseberry when I rush madly into his arms and declare my undying love.' She laughed, buoyed by the glass of Baileys and her friend's company. She was ready to make her move.

'I wouldn't miss it for the world,' said Colette.

They headed out into Patrick Street and, under Colette's umbrella, made their way to the Stables at a brisk pace. It occurred to Ellen why she'd become instant friends with Tracey Pope. She was Colette all over.

⁓

The reception from Bronwyn was icy when she came on at seven. Ignoring him, she sashayed past Gerry in a black number and her knee-high boots. He hated the atmosphere it created. Even a couple of regulars had commented.

'What have you done to Bronwyn?' one asked.

Gerry laughed it off with some flippant remark, but knew he was guilty as charged. Even Noely was on to it. 'Jesus, boss, she's in foul form. Have you two had a tiff?' After an

hour or so, he couldn't handle it any longer and told Paul
to hold the fort at the bar.

'Can I have a word?'

Bronwyn squeezed her mouth to one side in a pout and
slammed her pad and pencil on the counter. Gerry was
already walking to the front door.

'Won't be a minute,' he heard her say to Donal.

'I'm running a business here, not a counselling service,'
said Donal, a tad too loudly for Gerry's liking.

Bronwyn caught up with him a little way down the street
and stood, arms folded. He noticed the drizzling rain seep
into her sharply cut hair as he thought of what to say to
make this quick so they could both get back on the job and
in out of the miserable weather.

'Bron, I owe you an apology for the other night,' he
began. 'I was out of order. I should never have—'

'Ah, you're being a gentleman again, are you?'

He looked down and took an audible breath. 'You're
right. It was very bad of me to interrupt you the way I . . .'

When he looked back up at her she was smiling. She was
toying with him now. He'd been forgiven.

―

As they rounded the corner onto the South Mall, Ellen felt
the rain spit against her skin and realised Colette had stopped
walking. Turning to get back under the umbrella, she saw
the stunned look on her friend's face.

'What is it, Colette?'

'I don't think we should go to the Stables tonight,' said Colette. 'Maybe we should go somewhere . . . quieter.'

Ellen scanned the buildings along the South Mall until she spotted the sign for the Stables Restaurant and Bar. It didn't take long to realise what had made Colette change her mind.

⟿

Gerry leaned an arm against the wall and moved in closer to Bronwyn mainly to shelter her a little from the rain. 'What I'm trying to say is . . . can we start again? I'd like to take you out for dinner.'

Bronwyn let her arms unravel and slipped them round his waist. Before he knew it, she was kissing him.

⟿

Ellen was in shock. She hardly felt her legs as Colette steered her into the nearest side street.

'Will we get a bite to eat and talk it over?' Colette suggested. Ellen nodded. She didn't want to talk. In fact, she hadn't been able to utter a single sound since she'd seen him, but given the choice between going back to her father and Frances or sitting in a restaurant with Colette, she knew which she'd prefer.

'Jesus, Ellen, I swear on my nan's soul Gerry Clancy hasn't had a woman since his divorce.'

Ellen could only sit there stunned.

'Does Aidan know what happened in Port Lincoln?'

Ellen nodded again.

'He can't have known either.' Colette was almost talking to herself, attempting to reason why neither she nor Aidan had been able to shield her from this.

'I can't believe it,' Ellen said eventually as she watched Colette rip off a piece of the pizza she'd ordered for them to share. 'I just assumed he was completely serious . . . committed, you know . . .'

'The bastard!' Colette chewed with a vengeance.

'No. It's my own fault. I should never have expected to just waltz in there . . .'

'He gave you all the signals.' Colette was resolute. 'That's what his message was about, wasn't it? Wanting to be with you? God. If I had him next to me, I'd give him a piece of my mind.' Her jaws worked furiously on another bite.

'Did you recognise her?' The scene was fixed in Ellen's mind like a DVD on pause. The woman with her back to the building, one foot resting on the wall, her dark skirt halfway up her thigh above a pair of long sexy boots, the kind Ellen herself wouldn't wear in a million years.

'No. I didn't get a very good look at her. It was pretty dark.'

Ellen wondered if Colette was being kind. She could have said the woman was a looker, most probably younger than her, and if the passion in their brief sighting was anything to go by, totally into Gerry Clancy.

When she got back to the house, there was a muffled conversation coming from the boudoir. Emotionally and physically exhausted, Ellen climbed into bed and drew the duvet over her head, but it was pointless; jet lag, Baileys, wine, happy thoughts of Ocean Road, nothing could make her sleep. The freeze frame of the pair of them, his hand touching her hip and her, well, eating the face off him as Colette had said, wouldn't disappear. She wished she hadn't seen it. Why couldn't someone else have spotted them and given her the news second-hand? By six a.m. she'd had enough of trying to banish the demons and decided she needed to leave. There'd be no solace here, and right now the whole of Cork City was too small. She'd die if she bumped into him in the street.

Chapter Twenty-seven

Ellen held her smart Cosgrove and Beasley travel bag tight into her as she stamped her stockman boots against the frosty footpath. In the queue, passengers commented on the weather, their breath lingering in the air around them. The bus would be along any minute. The phone buzzed. Her gloved fingers fumbled in the pocket of her woollen coat.

'Hi, Aidan,' she said sharply and immediately regretted sounding curt.

'Hey, sis. How did last night go?'

'Don't ask.' She looked around, scanning the morning's passers-by.

'Ah, that's no good. Where are you?'

'At the bus stop. Dad gave me the key to Gran's house.'

'You're going to West Cork?' He sounded more surprised than disapproving.

'Yeah. I need to get away, clear my head.' There was silence. She could hear her brother struggling to comprehend her hasty departure, but knew he wouldn't pry.

'Okay if I give you a call later?'

'Yes, big brother,' she conceded.

'You'll have to get wood from the Coughlans. And don't forget the shop shuts early and—'

'Aidan,' she interrupted, 'I'm a big girl. I can look after myself.' She smiled. That's why she loved her brother. Never brash or pushy. He minded her in his own way. 'Gotta go. Catch ya.'

The bus pulled in and the grateful passengers began to board. Ellen let them all on ahead of her, glancing round one last time on the off-chance that Gerry would just appear.

She closed her eyes and tried to clear thoughts of Gerry from her mind. She shouldn't have come. What right had she to expect him to wait for her?

~

Gerry heard the tapping on the glass doors as he sorted the morning's deliveries in the kitchen. Striding through the lounge, he saw the woman framing her forehead with a hand against the tinted glass, trying to see in. *Colette Barry.*

'Colette, come in.' He needn't have said anything, she was already in and heading to the bar. 'What can I do for you at this hour of the morning?'

'I'm supposed to be at work, Gerry, so I'll cut to the chase.'

Given the gravity in her voice, Gerry looked around to make sure Sheila hadn't shown up yet. Apart from Donal, no doubt comatose in his bed, they were alone in the building.

'Ellen O'Shea is home.' Colette paused, awaiting his reaction. He couldn't think of anything to say.

'Anyway,' Colette went on, 'we were in the Mutton Lane Inn last night and she told me all about you and her getting cosy in Australia . . .' She looked exasperated now. 'The thing is—'

Bang, bang.

'What the—' Gerry turned to find two guards at the door. 'Hang on, Colette.' He opened up for a second time. 'Can I help you, officers?'

'Are you Donal Clancy?' the older guard asked him.

'No, that's my brother. Will I get him up for you?'

'Is there a rear entrance?' asked the younger guard.

Gerry pointed in the direction of the back door through the kitchen.

'Right, let's be having him then.'

Gerry bristled at the tough-guy language. 'Is there something wrong?'

'Just get him down here. We can go up and get him if you'd prefer.' The look on the older guard's face was enough to get Gerry moving toward the stairs. He held out his palms to Colette to let her know he had no idea what was going on and no option but to do what he was told. Ellen was home. Bloody brilliant! Colette was probably organising a party.

'You might want to leave us to it,' he heard the guard tell Colette.

Upstairs, he shouted in the door of the flat. When there was no sound from his brother, Gerry barged in to the bedroom and shouted again.

'For feck sake, get up, Donal. It's the guards. They want to talk to you.'

Donal opened his bloodshot eyes and frowned at Gerry.

'What do you mean, the guards?'

'They're downstairs waiting. You'd better get up.'

Wordlessly, Donal shoved back the duvet and quickly pulled on a pair of jeans and grabbed a clean shirt from the wardrobe.

'What would they want to talk to *you* about?' asked Gerry.

Donal ignored him as he combed back his hair and checked himself in the mirror. Whatever they wanted with his brother, there was no doubting the effort he was making to look in control.

'Is there anything you want to tell me, Donal?' Gerry hesitated. 'Before we go down?'

'Leave the talking to me, Gerry,' he said, pushing past him. 'Don't say a fucking thing.'

It was no secret Donal could be a ducker and diver, a bully for sure, but a criminal ... Gerry hoped he was as confident as he was obviously trying to sound.

'What can I do for you, gentlemen?' said Donal, striding into the lounge.

'I'm afraid you'll have to come with us to the station, Mr Clancy. Seems you think you're better than the rest of us. Not paying your taxes on this fine establishment here.'

'Are you sure about that, guard?' asked Donal.

Gerry had seen his brother charm his way out of sticky situations before, but something in the body language made him suspect Donal did indeed have something to hide.

'I have it in black and white you defied a court order. Not too clever, Mr Clancy.'

Gerry stood incredulous. Being a bit behind in paying tax was one thing, but letting it get so out of hand that you'd be brought to court was on a whole other level. His parents would be mortified.

'Donal, what the hell . . . Will I come with you?'

Donal shook his head. 'Give Martin Mulcahy a ring for me.' As he left the Stables flanked on either side by a guard, he shouted back, 'And for God's sake, keep this place going.'

Gerry could only look on, wondering what exactly Donal had been doing with the takings he insisted on counting and the books he insisted on keeping himself. Keep this place going? Wasn't that what he'd been doing all along?

Martin Mulcahy, their solicitor, assured Gerry he'd join Donal at the police station right away, leaving Gerry with the unenviable job of phoning his dad.

With Gerry Senior beating a hasty retreat from some golf tournament down the country, Gerry got on with the demands of running the pub, the realisation that Ellen was home starting to sink in. Apart from trying to figure out what could have gone so wrong with the finances, another question kept nagging at him. Why on earth hadn't Ellen returned his calls? He wished Colette hadn't had to leave. Maybe there was a plan to surprise him. He'd be a millionaire by now if he'd worked out how the mind of a woman worked.

—

Ellen registered the motion of the bus as she stirred from a deep sleep. Her bleary eyes took in the winter countryside as they sped past fields of cows and sheep corralled by dry-stone walls and sparsely clad hedgerows. They passed fewer and fewer cars as they neared Crookhaven. She stretched a little in her seat and checked the time on her mobile. Mid morning. The shop would be open. She would purchase her supplies before holing up in her late grandmother's house and licking her wounds.

'Take care now,' the friendly bus driver said as she alighted.

Take care is right, she thought. *I will take care. Take care not to do anything rash like this ever again.*

In the shop, a girl who couldn't have been much older than Louise was serving. As the till opened, Ellen watched her stop the drawer with her hand and noticed the bump she was protecting.

'How far gone are you?'

'Twenty weeks,' the girl answered.

'You're very neat. You look great.'

'Thanks.' The girl beamed. 'It's my first.'

'There's nothing like it,' said Ellen. She gathered up her shopping and headed for the door. 'Take care.'

She thought about the girl all the way along the road out of the village and after she'd turned onto the boreen that led to her grandmother's old farmhouse. It didn't seem so long ago that her own belly had swollen to make room for a growing baby. At least Gerry Clancy had given her that. A life without Louise didn't bear thinking about.

It was strange turning the key in the lock of her grand-mother's front door. The door had always been left unlocked, ready for any caller to let themselves in after a quick knock and hearing, 'Come in, it's open,' from the kitchen where Lizzie O'Shea spent most of her waking hours. Ellen set her bag down in the long narrow hallway and wandered toward the kitchen, wishing she'd find her grandmother baking a batch of her legendary scones to feed her visitor. But there was no comforting smell wafting from the range, only the mustiness of a lifeless house. Her boots echoed along the floorboards once she'd passed over the hall rug her grand-mother insisted was a genuine Persian brought home by the grandfather who'd survived Gallipoli in the First World War.

Her steps softened on the linoleum of the kitchen, but there was a hollowness she had to admit spooked her a little. The ghosts of her grandmother and the bachelor uncle who'd lived with her perhaps. Her grandmother had died when Ellen was still in her twenties, but as far as she could remember, her uncle had only died a few years ago. He'd been a gentle soul, just a demon for the cigarettes that took him in the end. The place was clean though. Her father had said their cousins, the Coughlans, looked after the place, throwing open the windows and giving it an airing when the weather allowed. She drew her coat around her and tucked her hands under her armpits. A fire, she thought. That would get the place warmed up.

The knock startled her.

'Is it yourself, Ellen?' said a voice with an accent as thick as a slice of her grandmother's soda bread.

'Eamon?' She took a cautious look around the kitchen door.

''Tis myself.'

She took in the barrel-shaped paunch of the cousin who appeared in the hallway, removing his tweed cap to reveal a much-receded hairline from when she'd last seen him at her mother's funeral. The ruddy cheeks were the same though, just as when they were children.

'I was over in the far field and I spotted you from the tractor. Thought you'd want a bit of wood.'

The kindness of the gesture, the familiarity, the absence of formalities was enough to replace the warmest hug. Their family had never been big on hugs, the mutual affection unspoken yet almost tangible.

'You're very good,' said Ellen.

As they carried the firewood in from the trailer and set some of it beside the range and the rest on the hearth in the parlour, Eamon confessed he'd had a phone call from Aidan. His embarrassment was palpable. Aidan would have told him she needed a break. It would have been enough information for the older cousin who'd always been reliable, the one who rounded up the gang of children when they were called in for tea, or led their explorations of the shoreline, warning of slippery rocks or an incoming tide.

'I just needed to get away,' she told him, hoping not to sound too melodramatic.

'That was a tough break ye had all right.'

She nodded, marvelling at the volumes spoken in the understatement. Without any elaboration or questioning, he set to work arranging and lighting the beginnings of a beautiful fire in the parlour.

Standing up, he rubbed his hands together and inclined his head toward the kitchen. 'I'll get the range going for you an' all. You'd hardly remember how it's done, yourself,' he teased good-humouredly.

'I wouldn't have a clue where to start,' she laughed.

In the kitchen, Eamon knelt down on one knee and began twisting sheets of old newspaper to light in the firebox as she moved about, storing her groceries in the pull-down compartment of the duck egg blue Formica cupboard she was sure had shrunk and in the small fridge that had been her grandmother's only mod con.

'You'll have seen Bridget in the shop,' he said as he worked.

'Is that Bridget?' She couldn't believe Eamon's youngest daughter was already a woman. 'I was only talking to her. She's a lovely girl.'

'Takes after her mother of course,' he joked.

'How many grandchildren will that be?'

Listening to Eamon reel off the names and ages of his children and grandchildren, Ellen marvelled at what she'd missed. Births, weddings, their uncle's funeral, had been events related to her second-hand. Her aunt's letters, her dad's phone calls, Eamon's own recent foray into Facebook, had all kept her up to date, but it wasn't the same. The thought of reuniting with her relations warmed her now as Eamon's fire-making began to take effect.

'That should warm the place up a bit,' he said. He looked at her a little uncertainly before adding, 'Sure, you could come up to us and have your meals . . . whenever you want, like.'

'That's kind of you, Eamon.' She paused before adding, 'Tell Orla I'll definitely be up. I just need to . . .'

She stopped again as she saw his cheeks redden even more than their natural colour.

'Tell her not to go to any trouble. I'll drop in for a cuppa.'

'Well, you know where we are if you need anything.' The nod and the manly wink said it all. Her big cousin would be looking out for her, just like he used to.

⤜

Noely came on shift not a moment too soon. Although used to running the show without Donal until at least lunchtime, Gerry had the added pressure of having to endure Sheila's nagging on and off all morning. As luck would have it, she'd come in just as Donal was being shown into the back of the police car.

'It'll be in tonight's *Echo* if Sheila has anything to do with it, so I might as well tell you,' Gerry said to Noely as they got down to lunch preparations.

As Gerry relayed the story, Noely just shook his head and gave one of his toothy grins without missing a beat as his knife whizzed over a half-dozen hemispheres of onion.

'I thought you'd be shocked,' said Gerry.

'I feel sorry for you, Gerry. Honestly, I do. But your brother had it coming.' Noely rested the knife. 'When you went to Australia . . .' He looked at Gerry hesitantly.

'Ah Jesus, Noely, now is no time for secrets. What the heck happened while I was away?'

'Donal had a visit from the taxman. Wanted to see the books, till receipts, that kind of thing.' Registering the shock on Gerry's face, he said, 'I never once thought he'd keep it from you.'

'Don't you think you might have told me?'

As Noely tried to explain away his embarrassment, Gerry was hearing alarm bells. He'd never actually seen Donal give a customer a receipt without being asked, although he did so himself as a matter of course. Come to think of it, the other bar staff rarely did it either. Then there was the banking. Or maybe half of that was trips to the bookies. Surely Donal wouldn't have bet the takings on horses. He'd always been known to have a flutter, but serious betting? By now Bronwyn and Paul had come on and were serving customers. Gerry wanted to be the one to tell them, but the Stables was filling with lunchtime trade and whether its future was certain or uncertain, people needed to be fed and watered.

'Two soups for table seven,' said Bronwyn. 'And a smile for your favourite waitress would be good.'

Gerry forced his face into what was more of a grimace than a smile.

Paul put his head round the kitchen doorway. 'Someone at the bar for you.'

'Tell them I'm busy,' said Gerry.

'He's a regular. Looks anxious to speak to you.'

'Shite!' Gerry placed two bowls of steaming soup and a basket of bread on a tray and handed it to Bronwyn. He shouted over his shoulder, 'Won't be a minute, Noely.'

Aidan O'Shea was standing at the bar with a pint of Guinness in front of him. Good news of Ellen was just what Gerry needed.

'How's it goin', Gerry?'

'I've had better days, but I hear Ellen's home.' He put his troubles to one side for a second and smiled in anticipation.

Aidan put his elbows on the bar and inclined his head.

'That's what we need to talk about,' he said softly. 'She saw you last night with . . .' He stopped midsentence as Bronwyn swished past them through the open bar hatch, giving Gerry an air kiss with puckered lips covered in a thick layer of cranberry. 'Ellen and Colette were on their way here,' he continued, looking at pains to get his story out. 'She came all the way from Australia in the hope that you and her, well . . .' Bronwyn passed them again. Gerry drew a hand through his hair and let it rest on his jaw.

'She didn't answer my calls,' he said when Bronwyn was out of earshot.

'Phone battery died. I had to buy her a new one yesterday,' said Aidan. 'She looked pretty happy when she got your messages.'

'Any chance of a pint?' A customer in a business suit wielded a twenty euro note in Gerry's face. He looked up the bar to where Paul was flat out serving.

'Sure, mate. What'll you have?' Gerry turned on his customer-is-always-right face and set a pint glass under a Heineken tap. 'Give me a sec, Aidan.'

Thoughts swirled inside Gerry's head like the frothy liquid filling the glass. She'd come from Australia to see him and he'd made a balls of it. That's what Colette had come to tell him. They must have seen himself and Bronwyn. *What an eejit. What a complete tosser.*

'Is she at home?' he asked as he stole another few seconds to speak to Aidan.

'West Cork. I'll write down the details.'

'Thanks, mate.' Gerry wished he could tell Aidan that Donal had been arrested and he wasn't sure exactly when he could get a break to pee let alone drive to West Cork, but a packed bar was no place for such divulgence. Of all the lousy timing for Donal to get busted.

It was mid afternoon when Ellen decided a walk was in order. There wouldn't be much left of the day now that she was in the northern winter. The thought of the heatwave Adelaide was reported to be experiencing made her smile as she pulled her boots on over two pairs of socks and took the woollen gloves out of her coat pockets. No need to lock the door. She drew it closed and made her way along the boreen, cutting off at the track to the stony beach which, as children, she and her cousins believed was their own. It was desolate now apart from a few oyster catchers probing beaks like pointed carrot sticks at the water's edge.

She wished she'd brought Nick here, shared this and all the other secrets of West Cork with him. Having grown up on an island, he'd always loved the sea. In their early days together, they'd been regulars at Bondi Beach, taking the bus from Sydney's inner city on a Sunday where Nick would borrow a mate's surfboard and show off to her as she sat on the sand, happy to sunbathe. He'd taught Louise to surf at beaches near Port Lincoln, but Ellen's favourite memories were of those lazy days the three of them spent at the foreshore with sandwiches and nappies full of sand, taking Louise by chubby little hands and paddling through the velvety softness of the shallows.

Walking back through fields of wind-flattened grass, she willed herself to remain in the moment. The sense of foolishness and disappointment at having come all this way on false hope threatened to overwhelm her as she dug her hands in her pockets and bent her head against the strong spring gust.

~

Bronwyn was the last to know about Donal's arrest.

'Are we still on for tomorrow night?' she asked Gerry when the lunchtime rush eventually subsided.

Shite. He'd forgotten all about the dinner date they'd set after the snog last night. His head had been buzzing like a blender all day, but he knew he needed to think straight to get out of this one.

'Actually, Bron, something's come up.' As he watched the frown form with the raising of her professionally waxed eyebrows, Gerry wasn't sure he could face the wrath of Bronwyn Fennelly. He reckoned she might never work for them again if he gave her the flick, especially if he did it here on the premises. This was no time to lose staff. Cop-out or no cop-out, he'd blame his brother.

'Donal's in a spot of bother. The police took him in for questioning this morning. Something about tax.' The shock on Bronwyn's face gave him confidence. 'I'm left holding the baby, you see. We'll have to take a raincheck as they say.'

~

Gerry and his father sat with the door closed in the small office Gerry realised was entirely his brother's domain. They waited in silence as the solicitor's secretary put them on hold. Gerry Senior had taken the news badly. Shocked wasn't the word for it. The dread of having to tell Pauline sat between them like the proverbial elephant in the room. Martin Mulcahy was matter of fact.

'They're holding Donal pending an initial hearing,' he said. 'I'll do my best to get bail, but ignoring that summons to appear in court wasn't his smartest move.'

That was the trouble with Donal. He couldn't just man up and admit he was wrong. It had been the same all down the years from when they were boys fighting over who scored the most goals in football. When they were older it was about money. Who bought the bigger house, the more expensive toys for the kids, had the more expensive holidays with their now ex-wives. It was always Donal, whether or not he had to invent the numbers. It had never bothered Gerry unduly. He took his brother in his stride, ignoring the machismo, but this was different. Donal's fiddling with the facts could cost them their livelihood. For Christ's sake, this was supposed to be their parents' ticket to retirement. And where was his brother now? Holed up in a police cell, leaving Gerry to steer the ship out of disaster.

When they'd sold the bakery, Gerry had thought about buying a little catering business himself, but Donal had got in there before him and persuaded his dad they should all go into the pub. At the time Gerry had acquiesced, thinking that being in business together would be a safer bet. He'd accepted the same wages as the other staff, paid his way in the flat, believing in Donal's promise of sharing the spoils when the pub established itself. The Stables was stowed out every lunchtime and at least four out of seven nights a week. To an outsider, the place was a goldmine. Taking the stairs three at a time, he went to the flat, packed an overnight bag and made a couple of phone calls.

'Aidan, old bean, you've done bar work before?'

Great, he had Aidan on board. His dad was already downstairs managing the place. No response from Ellen. He wouldn't let that put him off. Between Aidan and Gerry Senior, the Stables would be in safe hands. If he'd ever needed a night off, this was it. He'd be in West Cork before closing time.

Chapter Twenty-eight

Setting the kettle on a plate of the cast-iron range, Ellen wished she'd taken her laptop. A good Skype session with Louise or Tracey would have restored her. She wondered if Granny O'Shea had ever been lonely with so many of her family and friends living nearby. All the photographs smiled at Ellen from the magnolia walls. It was a bit like asking someone how they were and getting 'fine thanks' in response. They told you nothing really. And yet she fancied she saw in her grandmother a contented look. It irked her to wonder if she herself would ever be content again.

In the parlour, she stoked the fire and set the guard across the hearth. Tomorrow she would wash her clothes and hang them to dry there as her grandmother would have done in days gone by. That was about as far as she managed to plan. The kettle whistled on the range and she went and took the biggest mug she could find from the dresser. Armed with steaming tea, she gathered up her bag and climbed the staircase that seemed narrower than when she was a child.

Her dad was right about her relations looking after the place. Ellen knew they would have done the same for her grandmother who, like the house, would have been allowed to keep her dignity. The bed had been made up in one of the spare rooms, thanks to Eamon's wife, Orla. Even the bookshelves were freshly dusted, still bearing their yellowed copies of Catherine Cookson and Barbara Cartland novels. Ellen took one now and opened it. *March 1977 To Mrs O'Shea, Happy Mother's Day, Love Maureen.* At the sight of her mother's handwriting, Ellen caught her breath. She would have been little more than a toddler at the time, her parents in their early thirties and Granny in her fifties.

In her mind she could hear laughter coming from the kitchen and the clattering of her cousins' feet as they chased each other up and down the stairs, the front door banging behind them as they were thrown out to play; and the sound of her grandmother's voice breaking into a *sean nós* song, that haunting traditional unaccompanied singing that would calm the cousins when they came back in and threw themselves in tired heaps around the kitchen table.

⌐

Wrapped up in bed, Ellen bookmarked *Feathers in the Fire* and switched off the rosy-glass bedside lamp as her mother would have done hundreds of times before. They'd had such good times here. Not half the scolding she and Aidan got at home. Perhaps this was where her mother could relax, away from the expectations of the priests and the city neighbours, or maybe she just eased off on being the boss here in deference to her mother-in-law. Ellen could dwell on her poor relationship with her mother and agonise over missed opportunities at reconciliation, but what good would it do her? Better to look forward than back as Nick had always said. Anyway, her energy was best spent on being a good mother to Louise. She wondered how her baby girl was faring on her travels and how it would be to have her here, as the groan of the wind and the swell of the sea lulled her to sleep.

—

Crookhaven wasn't exactly a happening place on a cold weeknight in February. The road was eerily quiet as Gerry pulled over. Turning on the inside light, he took a look at Aidan's directions. The hand-drawn map reminded him of Ellen's letter with the picture of her house on Ocean Road. The déjà vu sent a rush of adrenaline through his veins. He knew he was close.

He turned the car onto the boreen and then eased it along the overgrown driveway. The stone-cut house stood before him, half lit in the headlights, its tired front door and weathered windows reminding him of the property advertisements that said 'has potential'. There was something lonely about the house, standing there between the sea and acres of farmland.

It was a wild night. The wind was gusting up to what must have been forty knots and the forecast low had brought the rain in with it. There was no response to his gentle knocking. No sign of life, but he knew Ellen must be inside. Trying the doorknob, he was surprised to find the house open. He let himself in to the hallway.

'Are you there, Ellen?' He wasn't sure why he was whispering as he moved along the darkened passageway, looking in at the empty parlour where embers glowed in the fireplace. At least it was warm for her, he thought. In the kitchen, the light was on but there was no sign of her here either. What a place. He took in the cast-iron range with pots and utensils hanging from an ancient wooden rack someone had built into the alcove. The long table and mismatched chairs looked like they could tell the O'Shea family history. The Formica press reminded him of one they'd had at home when he was a small boy before his mother got the built-in kitchen. Looking around, he was at a bit of a loss. He'd driven for hours and had promised to be back on deck at the Stables in the morning. Leaving his shoes at the bottom of the stairs, he decided to go up.

Four rooms opened off the dimly lit landing. The first had a massive double bed against a wall peeling with layers of wallpaper fashionable in a different century. A floorboard creaked under him and he thought he heard a heavy sigh from the room furthest along. As he stood outside its half-open door, Gerry saw Ellen sleeping on her side, facing away from him just as he'd seen her in Ocean Road when he'd wanted nothing more than to spoon in beside her. But he'd resisted the impulse. Tonight, he had no such misgivings. The woman he had loved since his teens, the only woman he could honestly say he had really loved, had come a long way to be with him. Still in jeans and shirt, he slid under the blankets and put an arm around Ellen's waist.

Strands of fine blonde hair fell across his face as she began to turn toward him.

'Mmm . . .' she moaned sleepily.

He waited for her to register his presence, smiling to himself as he imagined her joy to find him beside her once again.

'Ahhh!'

Gerry covered his head with his hands against the sound that threatened to burst his ear drums and the thrashing of Ellen's arms as she spun round to face him.

'It's me, Ellen, Gerry . . .'

She sat up and drew herself as far away from his body as she could, blankets dragged up to her chest. In the low light from the landing, he saw the terrified expression.

'Gerry Clancy, of all the audacity!' she shouted. 'Did you think you could just come in here and . . .'

He eased himself away toward the headboard, hands raised like a disarmed cowboy.

'I'm so sorry. I tried ringing, but to be honest, my luck with ringing you has been abysmal.'

She listened, a thumbnail between her teeth, blankets still firmly in her grip.

'I know you saw me with a woman . . .' He paused, resting an arm on his bent knee. 'It was stupid of me, but I honestly thought you'd given up on me.' He wanted to say it wouldn't have been the first time she'd rejected him, but that would have sounded self-pitying. 'I'm sorry, Ellen. Please believe me when I tell you you're the only one I want to share my life with.'

Ellen's frown softened, but she still didn't say anything.

'Say something. I'm dying here.'

She sat up a little straighter and pulled her legs away from him under the covers.

'If I meant that much to you, why did you even consider being with someone else?'

He bent his head. It was a fair question.

'A weak moment?' he began. 'I suppose I was flattered that someone fancied me. Thought life would get away from me if I didn't put myself out there.'

'And what about the woman?'

'I haven't slept with her.' He was embarrassed to have to go into the details, but they were details she deserved to know. 'Much to her disappointment, I'm sure.' He braved a cheeky grin and watched as Ellen released the blanket, plumped up the pillows and leaned back, resting her head in her hand.

'So where do we go from here?'

It was all the encouragement he needed. He shifted down the bed and laid in symmetry beside her, taking in the way her hair fell over the collarbones he'd loved to trace with his fingers. Moving in closer, he reached out and began a slow exploration of her frame. She lay there, letting him touch her until his fingers reached her hardened nipples and she pulled him closer into the hot deep kisses he'd dreamed about.

Afterwards, lying in each other's arms in the comfort of the cosy bedroom, a peaceful silence fell between them as they let what had happened settle like a fresh fall of snow.

—

'Are you trying to get me closed down?' Donal was roaring like a lion when he arrived at the Stables the next morning, bloodshot eyes blazing as he stomped into the lounge where Gerry was setting up for the day's trade, having reluctantly left Ellen in a satisfied slumber at five a.m. He gripped the tea towel he had slung over his shoulder and stood waiting for the rant to finish.

'Why did you have to call Dad, you lousy squealer? And Aidan O'Shea. What the fuck does he know about running a pub?'

It was obvious Donal had only half heard, or more likely half listened to, the reason why he'd taken a night off. Gerry couldn't help a wry smile. Gratitude had never been Donal's strong point.

'What's so funny? Huh?'

It occurred to Gerry that his brother's bullying skills might serve him well if he were sent to jail, but under the present circumstances they were utterly misplaced. It was about time he was told a few home truths. Gerry threw down the tea towel and walked toward the bar where Donal was pouring himself a 'cure'.

'If it weren't for me, you'd have been closed down a long time ago,' Gerry began. 'I've slaved in here since you opened, never took a penny over and above the lousy wages you pay.'

'What are you talking about? Haven't you a roof over your head?'

'You know damn well what I'm talking about, Donal. That share in the profits, remember?'

Donal looked a little sheepish now. 'Ah Jesus, Gerry. This is no time to be looking for profits and I in the shit with the taxman.'

'For God's sake, Donal. We both know you only have yourself to blame. I've worked my balls off to help make this place a success and all you do is treat me like a lackey, and now you're throwing this "poor me" crap in my face.'

Given a choice, Gerry would have jumped in his car right that minute, headed back to West Cork and never worked a single night in the Stables again. He wished he were Noely or Paul, no blood ties, no obligation. But this was his only brother. And besides, their mother and father wouldn't cope with a major falling-out. 'Blood is thicker than water,' Gerry Senior had always told them. If it weren't for his parents, Gerry would sooner settle for water.

Martin Mulcahy's call rescued Donal from the candid conversation. When he returned from the office, his face was ashen. Gerry thought he might keel over if he weren't holding on to the bar.

'The bank could foreclose on us. I'll have to sell off the assets to pay the fine, and God only knows what that wanker, Martin Mulcahy, will charge in fees.' Donal sat at the bar with his head in his hands. Gerry stood like a stunned mullet, trying to take it all in. The business was basically falling down around their ears and he hadn't had an inkling. He drew a hand through his hair, not knowing whether to feel disgust or pity for his brother.

'How long have we got?'

'A month,' said Donal. When he looked up, Gerry could see moist patches under his red eyes. 'Life's a bitch.'

'I'll do what I can to get you through it, Donal, but I want to make one thing crystal clear.' He paused to make sure he had his brother's full attention. 'I'm doing this for Mam and Dad. How you ever got to a point where you thought it was okay to throw away their money on racehorses, I don't know. You need professional help, man, because I'm done with bailing you out.'

Donal sneered and took a mouthful of the stiff drink. Before walking away, Gerry turned to him. 'And by the way, I'll be taking a few days off as of today.'

The other staff began to trickle in. Gerry took to his tasks with a quiet determination. Once the lunchtime rush was over, he left the Stables. A taste of his own medicine mightn't do his brother any harm.

Ellen was taking a long soak in the bath when she heard his voice.

'In here,' she called and immediately lowered her shoulders under a heap of psychedelic bubbles in a fit of modesty. It had been dark when Gerry had made love to her through the night. Perhaps the sight of her naked forty-two-year-old body wouldn't be so appealing in the cold light of day. He came into the bathroom and took a long look at her.

'I didn't expect to see you so soon,' she said, cursing the bubbles as they subsided, leaving only a thin film of soap to cover her.

He unbuttoned his shirt and cast it aside.

'I knew you'd be pining for me,' he said with a wink. 'And besides, I couldn't keep away if you paid me.'

He undid his jeans and let them fall to the floorboards. She felt a quiver in her belly as she tried to keep looking into his eyes.

'You're beautiful,' he told her as he plunged in.

Later, as they lay lolling in the lukewarm water, Gerry told Ellen about the Stables.

'What are you going to do?' she asked him.

'Well, I've been thinking about that as I was driving up and down the road . . . and . . . well, what I do next really depends on you.'

Ellen hadn't dared to think about the future, any future. The past year had been such a struggle that at times she'd had enough to do with finding the will to live. But this was an opportunity she couldn't let go. The prospect of a future shared with Gerry Clancy was a gift that had to be held on to with both hands.

'Do you want me in your life?' she asked him.

'More than anything,' he said. 'But only if that's what you want too. I know you've had it hard . . .'

'I want it,' she said, tears welling in her eyes.

He held her close and kissed the top of her head. 'I will always love you,' he told her.

They spent the next two lazy days walking the desolate beaches and deserted coves of West Cork as though they were the only two people in the world.

On the last evening, as they lazed again in the bathtub, Ellen asked, 'So where exactly do you think you'll be loving me forever?'

He took her hands in his own.

'Are you desperate to get back to Australia?'

It wasn't the reaction she'd been expecting. She'd come here to show Gerry she was serious about him, but putting her Australian life on hold hadn't been on her agenda. The prospect of living in Ireland again had been fantasy, something she'd always toyed with when circumstances overwhelmed her. God knows, when Louise was born she had a terrible bout of homesickness she could hardly stand. She remembered how she'd cradle the parcels with baby presents before opening them, savouring the sight of the Irish stamps, even smelling the brown paper packaging thinking they smelled of home. When Nick died, she felt again that overwhelming sadness for all those special Irish parts of her she'd left behind: her dad, her brother, Gerry, the many friends she'd loved. It would be a twisted irony indeed if, after helping her to reconnect with her Australian life, Gerry was asking her to abandon it. But Gerry had loved Australia, said he'd wished he'd moved out as a young man. Had she read too much into that because it suited her? Not wanting to throw cold water over his enthusiasm for their future together before it had even begun, she spoke carefully.

'What would we do here?'

She waited as he hesitated.

'This might sound a bit mad, but what about doing something with this place?' He looked around the room with its mouldy walls like someone would regard a much-loved face, accepting blemishes and wrinkles as part of the package. 'Who owns it now?'

Her mind was in overdrive. Do up her grandmother's house? For what? A bed and breakfast, a holiday rental? Surely to God he didn't mean for them to move in. She'd heard of people who divided their time between Australia and Europe, and there were those ping-pong poms, as they called them, who couldn't decide where to live. No, this long-term stuff was threatening to overwhelm her. Small practical steps were what was needed. She looked at Gerry, trying desperately not to show the fear in her eyes.

'Eamon would know the ins and outs. Let's talk to him first.'

Later as they curled up on the couch in the parlour in pyjamas and woolly jumpers, Ellen wondered what Lizzie O'Shea would make of it all. Would her grandmother be willing her on as she had done on many a simpler project in years gone by, like helping with difficult words in a story book or knitting a sweater for a teddy bear? Or would she wag her finger and gently chastise her, like when she stood too close to the open fire, *'Bi curamach, a leanbh.'* Be careful, child.

Chapter Twenty-nine

Louise thought she could hear a distant beeping as she stirred from sleep in her room in Athens. *I'm on holiday*, she thought and let her head and shoulders sink a little deeper into the pillows with their sweet smell of Greek laundry powder. Eyes still closed, her brain registered the noise coming from her phone at the other end of the room. Someone was trying to call.

'Lou, wake up, it's your mum.'

The excitement in Toby's voice made her jump out of bed. She shook her head as she saw Toby sitting on the armchair, chatting to her mother like a long-lost pal. She couldn't help smiling. It wasn't every mother that would invite their daughter's boyfriend on a pilgrimage overseas, especially a boy she hardly knew. Toby handed her the phone and left the room to give them privacy.

'How's Ireland, Mum?'

'Hello, love,' said Ellen. 'I have so much news. I don't know where to start. But first, I want to hear how you two are doing.'

Louise filled her in on what they'd done in Santorini after her mother had left and how the Athens lap of their trip was panning out. They'd jumped at the offer to stay with Dimitri's brother and sister-in-law who ran a small guesthouse in Plaka.

'We're right at the bottom of the Acropolis hill, Mum.' She had so many stories to share about the ancient site, the smell of handmade leather shoes she loved, the strawberries and souvlakis, Toby's brush with a pickpocket, but the tales of her travels could wait. Right now, she was desperate to know how things were going in Cork.

'So what about Gerry?' she asked, willing herself to sound neutral.

She knew by the sound of her voice, her mother was happy. But when she explained Gerry's idea about turning her grandmother's house into a bed and breakfast, she thought she detected a trace of discomfort.

'That's a great idea, Mum. But isn't it all a bit rash?'

'There's nothing set in stone, sweetheart,' her mother was saying. 'I'm just considering the possibility. I wanted to know what you thought.'

Louise stifled a cry and took a tissue from the small dressing table.

'It's okay, Mum. You've got to do what's right for you.'

When they said their goodbyes, Louise felt strangely alone in the world. She climbed back into bed and drew the covers up around her. When Toby came in, she was in tears.

'What's up, Lou?'

She didn't want to sound melodramatic and tell him she felt like an orphan. Neither could she keep the problem to herself. She'd tried that once before and almost lost him.

'It's Mum,' she began. 'She and Gerry are thinking of making a go of it in Ireland.'

He held her closer, but if he was surprised he didn't say anything.

'I just can't imagine her living so far away. After all we've been through . . .'

Toby wrapped the blankets round them and let her sob.

'I'm here for you, Lou,' he said softly.

Lying in his arms, Louise hoped she would never take this boy for granted. If her dad's death had taught her anything, it was that you never knew how long you had with those you loved.

—

Ellen felt uneasy as she rang off. What if Louise was right and this was all a bit rash? Was she seriously considering living on the other side of the world when she and Louise had just gotten back on an even keel? She told herself again they were only exploring their options and put her reservations to the back of her mind. There was a lot to do. She'd already spoken to her father who'd confirmed what Eamon and

Orla had told them. Granny O'Shea had left the farmhouse to her four children. Now that only two were still living, it was the property of her father and Nancy, his sister who'd lived in America for most of her adult life.

Bill O'Shea had been a little taken aback when Ellen phoned, but after a few questions and thoughtful pauses, he gave her plans his blessing. He was happy for her to turn the house into a business, but would retain joint ownership with Nancy as long as she was agreeable to the project. In a lengthy trans-Atlantic conversation, Ellen managed to win over her aunt who enthused at the prospect of the old house being brought back to life. She even promised to seriously consider a trip home to check on progress. Buoyed up by their enthusiasm, Ellen headed to Cork for her father's surprise birthday party with just a hint of dread about meeting Frances Brady again.

They were under strict instructions to be inside the function room at the Nautilus Hotel by seven-thirty sharp. Ellen was grateful to be flanked by Aidan and Gerry as they walked in at twenty past to an already crowded room. As a gaggle of Frances Brady lookalikes began herding guests into a huddle on the dance floor, Ellen felt as though she were having an out-of-body experience. Here were herself and her brother, capable adults, like a pair of hangers-on at their own father's seventieth birthday.

'Shh, shh . . .' The Brady bunch were in a flap, signalling with fingers to lips and hands waving in a patting down motion in an effort to ready the crowd for the arrival of the guest of honour. Hugs and handshakes would have to wait as Ellen took her place among the throng, managing mere half-smiles and the raising of eyebrows in recognition of those long-lost cousins and can't-put-a-name-to-the-face acquaintances in attendance.

A mobile phone call cued Bill's arrival in the building. Someone killed the lights and everyone began a muffled countdown.

'Five, four, three, two, one . . .'

There was an awkward pause before the doors opened.

'Happy Birthday!' The cheer went up, the lights came back on and a suitably surprised Bill O'Shea was led into the room by none other than the neighbour from hell. Ellen resisted the impulse to roll her eyes and clapped and cheered obediently. Her dad was already swamped by Frances's sisters when she joined the queue of well-wishers.

They took a seat at a table of relations she hadn't seen since her mother's funeral.

'I'd introduce you to more people,' she told Gerry, 'but I don't recognise half of them.'

It was mostly the younger ones she had trouble with. She knew they must be the children of Eamon and other cousins, but they looked nothing like the baby pictures her grandmother, God rest her, had sent with letters to Australia. Apart from Bridget, whom Ellen had met at the shop in Crookhaven, she was relying on physical features and mannerisms to make out who was related to whom.

She was grateful when Auntie Betty came to the rescue. The ageing teacher did her best to help Ellen join the pieces of the family jigsaw despite the loud background music.

'It's great to see them all,' said Ellen, doubtful she'd be able to remember all the names and relationships.

'You wouldn't be saying that if you were seeing them every day of the week,' her aunt replied, a knowing smile crinkling the lines about her eyes.

'Ah now,' said Ellen, 'I'm sure they're a good bunch.'

'Same as you'd get anywhere, I suppose,' Betty went on. 'No better, no worse.' She took a large gulp from her wineglass and eyed the dance floor where Bill and Frances looked resplendent as they twirled to an old-time waltz.

'What do you make of that?' Betty asked without taking her eyes off the couple.

Ellen wasn't at all sure what to say. 'Well, I suppose Frances makes him happy,' she offered.

'Happy, my eye,' Betty scoffed. 'I'd say she's a gold digger.'

Ellen couldn't help laughing at the remark. 'Auntie Betty, you're a tonic,' she said.

''Tis queer laughing,' said Betty. 'Take it from me. I might be getting on, but I know your father, and if what he put up with from Maureen, God rest her soul, is anything to go by, he'll be under the thumb with this new one an' all.'

Ellen watched Frances grip her father's back with hot-pink nails and tried to imagine living near them. Her dad might be more supportive of her if he thought he could help in a practical way with the project and Frances, well, she would just have to get used to the idea.

'A little bird tells me you might be moving back,' said her aunt. 'Are things so bad in Port Lincoln?'

'No. Things are pretty good,' said Ellen. 'I had a tough time when Nick died, but I'm back on track. Went back to work and all that.' She looked across at Gerry who was deep in conversation with Aidan. 'I have Gerry to thank for that,' she told her aunt. 'Do you remember him?'

'Oh I remember that fella as a teenager, all right. Made for an interesting time in the classroom,' Betty laughed. 'Mad about you, he was. Never recovered from that broken heart you gave him . . . obviously.' She knocked back the last of her drink before speaking again. 'Doesn't mean you have to give up everything for him now though.'

Give up everything. Only Betty and Aidan knew what that meant. Only they had walked with her around Port Lincoln, slept in the house on Ocean Road, lived a little of her Australian life. Yes, she had missed out on all these people's lives, but at the end of the day, she had made a life of her own. And Louise was at the centre of that life. What if Betty was right? Was it foolish to contemplate giving it all up to be with Gerry?

Aidan and Gerry had stopped talking and were getting out of their seats.

'Come on, Auntie Betty,' said Aidan. 'I'll take you for a twirl.'

'Are you dancing?' asked Gerry.

Ellen blushed as she took Gerry's hand and let him lead her to the dance floor. God, this felt like déjà vu. Her skin tingled at the feel of his firm hold around her waist and the smell of Kouros on his stubbly chin. For a moment she was a teenager again, holding onto a younger, leaner Gerry Clancy, grateful for the slow dances.

The music faded and they slowed to a stop. Ellen didn't want it to end. Gerry held her in his arms a little longer and whispered, 'I love you.' She was in no doubt he meant it. But that was the trouble. She'd come all this way to find out if he loved her. It was supposed to be the holy grail, the very thing that would sustain her, give her a reason for living. But when it came to the crunch, this love meant finding a way to be together. Did that mean leaving her daughter, her career, her friends behind in Australia? Or throwing away this chance of happiness? No matter which way she turned, the stakes were high.

The Stables was still heaving when Gerry let them in the side gate and took Ellen round to the back entrance. They slipped past the empty kegs in the small hallway and disappeared upstairs before anyone could spot Gerry and con him into helping out. The flat was quiet, but the smell told him Donal had been up here recently. The dishes piled beside the kitchen sink confirmed his suspicions.

As they brushed their teeth side by side in the bathroom, Gerry said, 'I could get used to this.'

Ellen didn't respond. She'd been quiet on the way home, but he'd put it down to the party and the drive from West Cork. In the bedroom, she undressed quickly and got into bed.

'You okay?'

He stripped down to his boxers, but she didn't look at him. Instead she lay on her side, facing the other way. Spooning in beside her, he stroked her hair from her face and bent to trace the contours of her neck and shoulders with his lips. But she drew away from him and sat upright against the headboard.

'I'm sorry, Gerry. I'm not sure I can do this.'

'It's okay,' said Gerry. 'We can just sleep.'

'I don't mean that,' said Ellen, pressing a hand into her eyes and sniffing hard. 'I don't think I can stay.'

He was trying to work out exactly what she meant as she went on.

'It's something Betty said. It's all happening too fast. I didn't expect you to show up on my doorstep. I didn't expect to fall in love with you again after all these years.' She was crying now.

'It's okay,' he soothed, reaching out to touch a knee she'd drawn to her chest. He wanted to say it would all be fine, but he'd learned enough about women to know he just needed to listen.

'I miss Nick,' she sobbed. 'I miss Louise. What kind of a mother am I? Thinking I can just leave her in Australia and take up where we left off twenty years ago?'

Slowly, he sat up beside her and took her hand.

'I'm sorry, Ellen. I didn't think I'd fall in love with you either, but the truth is, I never really stopped loving you in all those years we were living separate lives.'

She wiped away tears with the back of her hand.

'I should never have asked you to stay,' he said. 'I got ahead of myself, with the old farmhouse and everything. I suppose I was being selfish, wanting a future if this place goes to the wall.' He looked around his brother's spare bedroom that had been the closest thing to home since his marriage ended.

'You could come to Australia,' she said.

It was a prospect he'd quietly considered. There were plenty of people emigrating to find work and a better life. Kieran loved it and had hinted he might even stay. And then there was Louise. He would love the opportunity to get to know her better if she'd let him. Living in Ireland wouldn't give him much hope of that. Stephanie was even talking about travelling like her brother. The saying about old dogs and new tricks came to mind, but he didn't want to sound flippant.

'That would be huge for me,' he said aloud.

'I know,' said Ellen, 'but nothing's impossible. You taught me that.'

They lay back against the pillows, legs entwined, quiet in their thoughts.

Gerry's phone buzzed on the bedside table. Looking at the screen, he groaned. 'It's home.'

'With all that's happening, you'd better answer it,' she told him.

He moved off the bed and checked the screen.

'Mam, are you all right?'

'Oh Gerry, your father just told me what Donal's done.'

He gestured to Ellen to wait as he listened to his distraught mother.

'Jesus, Gerry we had no idea. Had you any notion of how bad the gambling was after getting?'

'No, Mam. Unfortunately, he kept it well hidden.'

'I'll talk to you about how you got on in West Cork another time. I'm distracted from this tax business. I can't even think straight. Here, let me put Dad on to you.'

'Night, Mam.' He doubted his mother would sleep a wink.

Gerry Senior sounded exhausted.

'She knows me too well, son. I had to tell her.'

It was the kind of conversation he'd never wish to have with his parents. They'd worked all their lives to provide for their children. It should have been their turn to be looked after.

'While you were away, I sat down with Martin Mulcahy,' his dad began. 'Donal was doing all sorts of dodgy deals, paying people in cash, avoiding employer tax . . .'

'Jesus, Dad, I wish I'd been more on top of it.'

'You and me both, son. But now we're all under the spotlight. There'll be court proceedings. Martin only got him out on bail because of my good name, but that mightn't carry weight for long. They've tightened up the tax laws. All business partners are liable. Ignorance is no longer a defence. All three of us could be looking at jail time.'

His dad had every right to speculate as to what might happen, but Gerry needed the facts.

'How much are we talking about, Dad?'

'I'm not sure, son, but they'll go after us for the winnings on the horses an' all. God knows how much he's won and lost over the years.'

Gerry had to think on his feet. He could certainly handle the running of the Stables, but for the books he'd need help.

'I'd understand if you wanted to get out, son,' his dad was saying. 'We'll have to sell anyway if the bank forecloses on us when they get wind of the mess we're in.'

'I'll run the place, Dad. We'll take advice from accountants, lawyers, whatever it takes. If we lose the Stables there'll be nothing for your retirement.'

'Oh, son, I'm sure you had your own plans . . .'

'No, Dad. I'll see it through, whatever the outcome.'

As he sat down on the edge of the bed, Ellen put her arms around his chest and rested her head on his back. She held him as he let the tears out. *Just when you thought things were looking up, Gerryo.*

Chapter Thirty

In the days that followed, Ellen returned to her grand-mother's house in West Cork, this time with her father and brother.

'I'm proud of you both,' her dad told them as they sat round the kitchen table, late into the evening, sipping on mugs of steaming tea and enjoying the warmth from the range. Ellen and Aidan eyed one another, the rare compliment surprising them both.

'No, I am,' Bill went on. 'I know your mother was the type of person you could never please, God knows I didn't measure up, but the pair of you have done well for yourselves.'

'Thanks, Dad.'

As silence fell between them, Ellen's mind was like a roller coaster, but this time alone with her father and brother might be her only opportunity to ask the question she'd been longing to voice for twenty years.

'What about Nick and Louise, Dad?'

Her dad looked down at the table and worried at the well-worn wood with his fingertips.

'I could say your mother was angry with you,' he began, 'or that we'd only wanted what was best for you ... but I blame myself.' He tried to smile, but she could see the watering of his grey eyes. 'I should have tried harder to talk her round, made her visit you.'

She reached out a hand and calmed his moving fingers.

'Your Nick was a lovely bloke,' he went on, grasping her hand. 'I remember, after your mother's funeral when you'd all gone back, thinking how I'd like to have spent more time with him.'

'It's not too late to get to know Louise, Dad.'

He turned and smiled at her, the tears pooling in his eyes. 'I'd like that.'

Across the table, Aidan shifted in his seat. 'I'll take you over when I get a few contracts paid in, Dad.'

'Thanks, son. We could go, just the two of us.'

'Just the two of us,' Aidan echoed.

When their eyes met, he and Ellen stifled a laugh.

'It's good you have Mrs Brady for company and all that, Dad,' he explained, 'but it's still a bit weird for us.'

'I know what you mean, son. She's not your mother. But she's a good person all the same.'

Ellen knew Aidan shared her doubts, but they let the matter rest.

'And what of your plans for this place?' her dad asked, sounding grateful to have moved on from the topic of family shortcomings. 'I know you've decided to go back, Ellen, but Gerry's idea wasn't so daft. It would be nice to do something with the place as a family. God knows, we've left it idle for long enough. Yourself and Louise, and you, Aidan, would always have a place to come to . . . like a second home.'

'It would take a lot of cash to renovate,' said Aidan. 'I'm not sure I'm in a position to put anything into it right now with building the business and everything.'

'Well, I'm not going to be around forever,' said Bill, 'and I do have some funds I'd like to leave you both.' He looked from one to the other. 'What if I plunged that into the renovations while I'm still healthy enough to be part of it?'

Ellen and Aidan locked eyes, realising this meant they came before Frances Brady in their father's list of priorities.

'If you're sure, Dad,' said Aidan. 'I could do most of the labour for nothing.'

'What if we rent it out as a holiday home when none of us are using it?' said Ellen. 'It'll pay for itself.'

'That's inspired, Ellen,' said Bill. 'We could come to some arrangement with Eamon and Orla to look after bookings and all that.'

'Just one other thing.' As she leaned her elbows on the table, she felt the heat rise in her cheeks. 'Would you both be willing to let Gerry be part of the project?'

Aidan grinned, but waited for their father to answer.

'My dear girl, if you want Gerry involved, we're happy to have him on board.' He turned to Aidan. 'Aren't we, boy?'

It wasn't much, but it was something, a connection, the lifeline she would need when she was on the other side of the world without him.

⌐

'You got everything?' Gerry asked as they drove out of town. Part of him wished she'd forgotten something important like her passport and they'd have to turn around, making her miss her flight and give her time to rethink this whole departure. But she'd had all week to mull over their future. It was only right she put Louise first, but he couldn't help feeling it was all a bit ironic that the best thing to come out of their relationship was the very thing keeping them apart. He also knew he should just man up and follow her. They made it look so easy in movies. But his own hands were tied. If he didn't keep the Stables afloat, who would? It wasn't just his future, but the future of his parents he needed to secure. The odds were well and truly stacked against him, but the optimist in him made him believe it could be for the best. Maybe it was all just too soon, and Ellen could do with more time to heal from her tragic loss.

⌐

The girl at the check-in desk chatted brightly while her perfectly manicured fingertips tapped at her computer.

'Were you over on holidays?' she asked, smiling at Ellen without moving her eyes from the screen.

'Yes, I'm on my way home.'

'How long are you over there?'

'Twenty years.'

'Did you never get the urge to come back?'

'I did, but you know yourself . . .'

The girl turned to tie labels on her luggage. 'Home is where the heart is, I suppose.'

Ellen's heart felt like it might be split in two right now. She thanked the girl and turned to find Gerry. He cut a lonely figure, standing with hands in his jeans pockets, looking dejected.

'Cheer up! It might never happen,' she said.

'It already has.'

'Well, you know where I live.' She didn't want to sound flippant, but what else could she say? They'd been over and over the reasons why she had to go back and he had to stay.

He took both her hands in his and looked into her eyes.

'I should have followed you twenty years ago.'

'It's not too late,' said Ellen.

He wrapped his arms around her and kissed her hair. With her head buried in his shoulder, she could feel him squeeze her tight, but she didn't complain. It only made her feel his pain in having to let her go. They both knew this hurt like hell.

'One day we'll get the timing right,' he whispered.

───

As the plane taxied along the runway, Ellen closed her eyes and thought about what lay ahead. On the other side of the world, her Baby Lou would soon be joining her for a few days in Adelaide to share and reflect on the highs and lows of their journeys. Then it would be on to Port Lincoln where the Chrysler sat awaiting her return. She could almost hear Tracey's Ford hurtling along the dirt track, its driver eager to hear her stories. Tyson might be feeding the chooks or stroking Spots in the paddock. Ellen hoped she wouldn't always be alone in the house, but for now it was enough to be going home.

Epilogue

Tyson had been right about taking advantage of the fine Easter weather to give the house a facelift. Ellen had hardly held a paintbrush in her life, but that was all before she'd been brave enough to step up and do more of these practical jobs for herself. Nick would be laughing if he could see her now in his old overalls, hair spattered with paint. The girl who couldn't change a light bulb. Well, if she was to wait around for a man in her life, the house might crumble down around her. She shouted down to where Tracey was standing with one hand on the ladder, the other on her hip, 'I hope you've got a good hold on this.'

'Yes, darl,' said Tracey, not looking up.

Ellen would have preferred if her friend was holding on to the ladder for dear life instead of looking around her. This was no time to be taking in the view. She took a deep breath and climbed down to move the ladder a few metres along before climbing back up with her paint pot and starting again.

'You guys going okay?' she called to where Tyson and Louise were working from the other end of the house.

'Just fine, Mrs C,' Tyson answered. 'Me 'n' Lou make a great team, don't we, Lou?'

Louise high-fived him before reloading her roller and generously coating another section of cladding. Ellen let her shoulders relax. What could be better than having her good friends here and her beautiful daughter home for the holidays? As the paint dried in the autumn sunshine, she could see the difference their hard work would make. She tried to ignore the fact that Tracey was on her phone and concentrated instead on the job at hand and the sound of Tyson whistling with the birds in the quiet afternoon. When her arms started to ache, she suggested they take a break, but none of them wanted to stop.

'Where's your stamina?' Tracey teased.

'It's all right for you,' said Ellen, 'catching up on your newsfeed . . .'

'Sh . . .' Tracey held up a hand.

Ellen lifted her head and listened. All she could hear was a car thundering up Ocean Road. From the top of the ladder, she could make out a jeep. She turned back to her work.

'That'll be that lad I told you about,' she said to Tracey. 'Said he'd drop off the supplies for the new fence I'm—'

'I think you'll need to get down off there, darl,' Tracey interrupted.

'Oh for God's sake, I just got back up here. Let him wait a minute.'

As she stroked her brush under the eaves, she heard the car turn into the driveway. Just this section and she'd get down, pay the young man for his fence posts and take a well-earned break. Leaning into the furthest spot she could reach, she heard the car door open and the crunch of the gravel as the driver stepped out.

'Just a sec,' she called down over her shoulder.

It took a moment for her to register the silence. Resting the pot on the top of the ladder, she turned to look down. Gerry Clancy was standing beside the car looking up at her, with the most beautiful bouquet of flowers in his hands. Her breath caught at the sight of the smile and the twinkly blue eyes she loved. She shot a look to Louise and Tyson. It was hard to know who had the biggest grin. She wanted to ask if they were all in on this, but she couldn't speak.

She wasn't sure how she managed to get down. For all she knew, she might have flown down from the ladder and floated off her front steps, but she would never forget how Gerry lifted her off her feet and held her in the warmest hug.

'I couldn't stay away,' he said, setting her down gently. As he took her face in his hands and kissed her, Tyson, Louise and Tracey let out a cheer. When they drew apart, she couldn't help beaming. She held his hand and pulled him toward the house.

'I don't know how long you can stay,' she told him, 'but I hope you'll feel at home on Ocean Road.'

Acknowledgements

I could never understand why publishers and editors occupied the top spot in acknowledgements pages and worried that my mother would be mortified to be relegated to the end. After surviving the process of publication, however, I (and my mother) completely understand.

My heartfelt thanks and admiration to Rebecca Saunders, publisher at Hachette Australia, for seeing the potential in my manuscript and, like a good coach, pushing and supporting me to make it better than I could have believed. To all the team at Hachette, you are amazingly talented and I am in awe of what you have done to put my story out there. Samantha Sainsbury, you are a fantastic editor. I am so grateful for your insights. Julia Stiles, you pushed me just that tad extra which drove me mad, but I'm sure will make all the difference. Irina Dunn, thank you for believing in my book and endorsing me. To Eyre Writers, each of you deserves to share in the success of this book; when I joined you I thought I'd be making the tea, but your passion for the written word was infectious and you all played a part in mentoring and inspiring me. In particular, I wish to thank Diane Hester for blazing the trail and sharing the insights of her journey with such generosity. Kathy Blacker, Suzannah Windsor Freeman and Carol LeFevre for teaching me to edit. Bruce Greene for telling me my writing was like something you'd pick up in an airport. I hope that happens. To my lovely beta readers and friends, Kathryn Doudle, Alison Gassner, Norma McNeil, Sara Garforth, Claire Leslie and Paula Weeks. Joe McElwee, for your rapid response to my queries on tax evasion despite being just out of hospital. Marie McMillan and her friends for help with Sydney. Eleni Leslie, for your insightful answers to my 'Greek' questions and Dayna Dennison for sharing memories of Santorini and Athens. Romance Writers of Australia and the South Australia Writers Centre for keeping this social animal in the loop. Devonport Writers Workshop and the Tasmanian Writers Centre for keeping me connected in Tasmania.

To my sister, Mercedes, for your steadfast support and encouragement and to my nephews for cheering me on from afar. To my mother, yes the aforementioned, for being my number one fan and honest critic. To Paul O' for your letters and humour. All the friends I hold dear, far and near, thanks for being there. My daughters for keeping me sane and my son, for keeping the volume down, sometimes. And finally, to my husband, Mike, thank you for the voyage thus far.

BOOKS with HEART
Stories that make you feel

Books with Heart is an online place to chat about the authors
and the books that have captured your heart . . .
and to find new ones to do the same.

Join the conversation:
(f) /BooksWithHeartANZ • (v) @BooksWithHeart

· ·
Discover new books for **FREE** every month
· ·

Search: Books with Heart

Search: Books with Heart sampler

Passion. Shared.
get the whole story at **hachette.com.au**